Horn of the Kraken
by: Stephen B. Pearl

Published by Pendelhaven 2015, 2016

Pendelhaven
121 2^{ieme} Bourbonniere
Lachute, Quebec, Canada
J8H 3W7
www.fateofthenorns.com
www.pendelhaven.com

Based on the Fate of the Norns world created by Andrew Valkauskas

Cover artwork by Natasa Ilincic

Map artwork by Soni Alcorn-Hender

Editing: Hepzibah Nanna,
Joy Hughes-Pearl

ISBN 978-0-9940240-5-3

Published in Canada
Printed in the USA

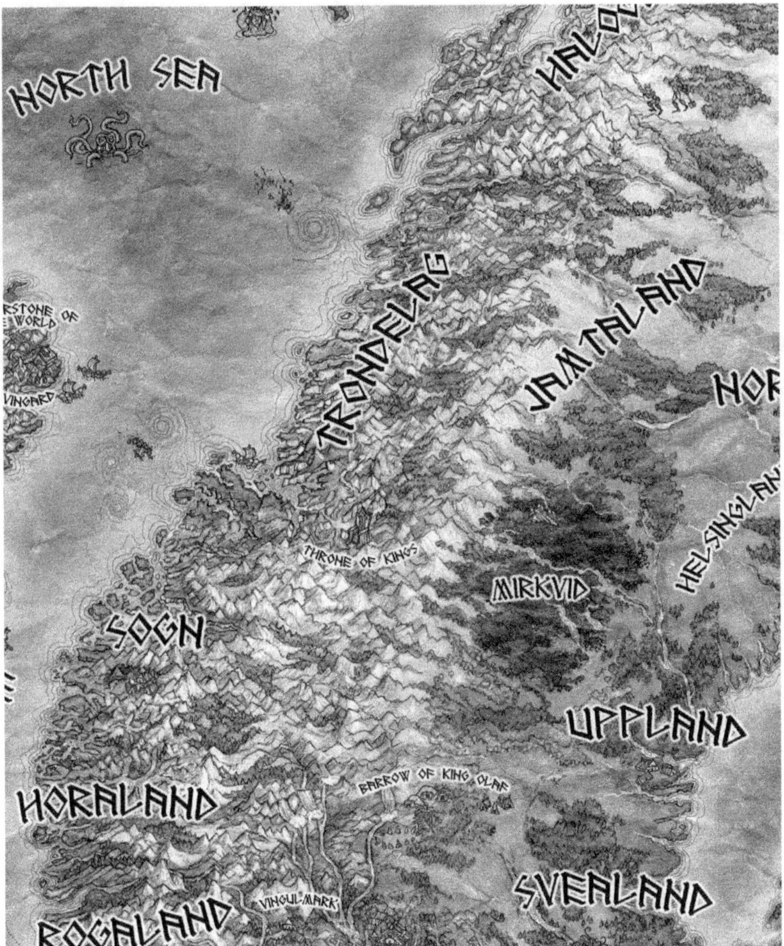
NORTH SEA
TRONDELAG
JAMTALAND
THRONE OF KINGS
MIRKVID
SOGN
UPPLAND
HORALAND
BARROW OF KING OLAF
SVEALAND
VINGUL MARK
ROGALAND

CHAPTER 1

A GATHERING STORM

There was a war horn's cry, like Heimdall sounding the Gjallarhorn on the last day. Eternal night shrouded the ice-covered slope down to the harbour where the dragon-prowed, raiding boats ground onto the frosty shore to disgorge their cargo of hungry, desperate men in patched and broken mail and leather.

The warriors of Orkney massed behind a palisade of logs and stone overlooking the harbour. Their armour was less ragged than that of the men below, and while all were thin, the Orkney men were not as starved as their foes.

Urd floated above the impending battle. Scattered flakes of snow passed through her translucent form as she looked on dispassionately. The bitter cold did not even cause her breath to mist, despite the fact she wore only a light dress and summer cloak. Her golden hair was pulled into braids, which revealed delicate ears and the Norn's countenance was that of a lovely maid. Her skin was unflawed.

A wolf's howl, so fierce that it sent a shudder through even the most stalwart heart, split the air.

The war horn on the battlements sounded again. This time, it was met by an answering roar of voices raised as one. The raiders charged. Flights of arrows darkened the sky, falling on the attackers but men with nothing to lose thought little of death. Thus the survivors came on across the ice field, with its litter of tree stumps, as their comrades fell, with only the vague promise of Hakon's White God's heaven for comfort.

The gate on the palisade was thrown open and the warriors loyal to Erik Bloodaxe charged onto the ice.

\#

It was an Axe Age, a Sword Age, where shields were cloven.
Brother fought brother, with no quarter or mercy.

\#

The armies met. Sword and axe were bloodied, shields rent and the ice grew dark under a river of red.

Fjorn faced his foe, a hulking man who seemed to tower into the dark sky. The invader swung his axe. Fjorn leapt aside while bringing his sword across his enemy's stomach. The mail turned the strike. The invader caught Fjorn's blade and, with an experienced twist, sent it flying through the air. Fjorn scrambled for the dagger on his belt as he stepped away. He tripped over a tree stump, falling backward onto the ice. Howling, the invader swung from the side hooking Fjorn's shield and tearing it from his grasp. Smiling through broken, rotted teeth, the larger man raised his axe for the final blow.

"Do you wish to live?" The voice was like music.

Fjorn glanced around. Everything seemed frozen in time. Above the Rainbow Bridge, those shimmering bands of light that graced the northern sky, was still. Unbelieving Fjorn blinked. Lord Odin's warrior women, Gunn and Rota, their long tresses flowing behind them, mounted on magnificent steeds carried men from the field towards the still lights above.

"Do you wish to live? I will ask but three times."

Fjorn shifted his gaze to see a beautiful, young woman dressed for summer. She floated to his side. If he looked hard, he could see the stilled battle through her. "Am I dead?"

"That has yet to be known. I have need of a servitor who bears the blood of Frey. You will serve as well as any. Will you pledge your service to me and live, or go to Hel an untried boy with no sword in your hand? Do you wish to live?"

Fjorn gazed at the beautiful spirit. "I do."

"Ready yourself for a voyage. You shall be summoned." Drifting upwards, Urd noted where the mail on the man attacking Fjorn had been broken and patched with leather thong. Floating above the battle she paused by an arrow frozen in its flight and released a breath, little more than a sigh. The arrow quivered shifting less than a hair's breadth to the side.

Fjorn watched the beautiful spirit float away. Time restarted. The invader roared holding his axe over his head, then a look of shock filled his face and he toppled. Pushing with all his might Fjorn crawled out from under his attacker's corpse and looked down to see a feathered shaft protruding through a hole in the man's mail shirt.

Shaking his head, Fjorn collected his sword and shield and rejoined the defence.

#

Sigurlina trudged through the dark and cold, a heavy burden of wood on her back and a cargo more precious than gold in her hands. The forest around her was dead. Trees towered; stark skeletons against the vermilion light that tainted the horizon from Muspelheim's flames. She could barely see her own tracks in the snow in front of her.

"You're going the wrong way. Let me in and I'll show you," spoke a voice in her ear that she tried to ignore.

"Don't listen to him. He doesn't want to help you. Why don't you stop and rest, dear. I could keep you warm; if you'd let me enter you," spoke a woman's voice.

"Be silent, shades. I am not fool enough to listen to you."

"Over here, a fat buck ready for the taking. I was a hunter, I could get him for you," called yet another voice.

Sigurlina stepped into a clearing before a snow-covered mound. A spot of light spilled out staining the snow with dancing red waves.

"She will die soon, and then she won't be able to protect you. You'll let us in, and then you can wander the darkness," snarled the female voice.

Sigurlina trudged to the opening in the mound and stooped to enter. Inside, the chamber widened into a long passage defined by large, stone slabs roughly-chiselled flat. Side chambers were sealed off with walls of smaller stones. A fire burnt in the middle of a clear space at the front of the passage with a tripod over the flames. Wood was piled at the back of the passage. A mound of poorly-tanned hides filled the space between the fire and the wood.

The transparent form of a muscular man in his middle years, dressed in mail and girthed with a sword, stood by the mound of hides.

"I am sorry, my little cat, but no. I welcome you here because you are my granddaughter. I held you on my knee when you were in swaddling, and now you are close to death. Sigurlina is too far both in kinship and in her time of mortal life for me to extend my courtesy. This is a house for the dead. The living do not belong here."

"I'm standing right here, great, great grandfather," said Sigurlina

"So you are, distant daughter of my line," replied the shade.

Ignoring the spirit, Sigurlina held up the two trout in her hand and moved beside the pile of hides. "I was able to break a hole in the ice and retrieve my line."

"That is wonderful, dear." A hand, that was age spotted skin stretched tight over bone, emerged from the hides and stroked Sigurlina's cheek.

Sigurlina closed her eyes and smiled.

A wolf's howl pierced the eternal night and even the dead warrior trembled in fear.

"Gram howls, Gram howls. The Sword Age is begun." A crazy-haired, old woman, in dirty clothing, flew through the rocks baring a side chamber.

"We are all Seithkona here. We all know the Hel hound's call." The aged figure from the hides spoke in a frail voice.

The crazy-haired shade dove towards Sigurlina. The girl's body jerked and her features sneered. "Then we all know there is no hope. The Sword Age will give way to the Wolf Age and none will be spared," spoke the shade's voice through Sigurlina's lips.

"Silence, Katla, and get out of my descendant! I will not see my mortal line end while Odin still stands, and I yet rule in this house," snapped the warrior shade.

Sigurlina collapsed to her hands and knees while the shade of Katla manifested beside her.

"Useless, weak thing! No control. If you had the courage to follow Laufey, she'd teach you control, and then no spirit could treat you thus."

"Be silent, Katla. You're just jealous because I chose Freya. She's at least able to keep her man," snapped Sigurlina's grandmother who fell into a fit of coughing.

Sigurlina roused herself and moved to comfort the old woman who waved her away.

"Prepare the fish, and be sure to make offering to our hosts," instructed the aged voice from the piled hides.

The task of preparing the fish steadied Sigurlina's nerves. Spirits crowded about the flames jabbering at her. Many she could invite in or push away, but not the powerful ones. Her grandmother had saved her dozens of times from spirits that entered and wouldn't leave, and Sigurlina was afraid of what would happen without the old woman. She made sure to put the bones and fish heads in the fire to carry them to the otherworld. This stilled the shades for a moment while they all vied for their share of the offering, like hungry wolves tearing at a kill.

When the food was ready she scooped it into their wooden bowl and moved to her grandmother's side.

Milky eyes opened on a withered face. "You eat it, dear. I do not need it."

"Grandmother."

An aged hand rose silencing the protest. "This will be my last night in mortal flesh."

"I--." Sigurlina felt her throat close on her words.

The aged face smiled gently. "I should have passed when the Axe Age began, would have, but after the bastard Hakon slaughtered your mother someone had to teach you the way of Seith magic."

Sigurlina felt her thoughts drawn back. She had been but twelve when Hakon's crusaders came to their village calling for all to bend knee to their White God. They had accepted hospitality, but in the dead of night, they betrayed their hosts. Half the men were dead, throats slit in their sleep, before the alarm was raised. The crusaders, swords dripping blood, herded the men into the town's common. The crusaders were so arrogant, they thought nothing of the woman. With a cry, the shield maids fell upon the invaders, armed and ready. The town's men escaped in the confusion and ran to armour themselves as their wives, mothers and daughters held the foe at bay.

Sigurlina hung her head as she remembered seeing her own mother, a Seithkona of great power, standing in their doorway warping the spirits to bring the invaders down. Then, a feathered shaft struck her and she fell. Her father, now armed, had rushed to his wife's side, and held her as she breathed her last.

"Run, flee." It was the first time Sigurlina had heard a spirit's voice. She looked up and saw her mother floating before her, but she could see the hut's wall through her.

"Mother, teach her." The spirit smiled at Sigurlina. "My little

Seithkona."

"I will," agreed her grandmother, then her mother was gone.

"We must get to the docks," snapped her father as he picked up his beloved and lay her on their bed. He kissed her a final time. Taking a brand from the fire, he thrust it into the straw mattress.

"A fitting pyre," said her Grandmother.

"They won't despoil her in death," her father grunted.

They raced from cover to cover, her father striking down the enemies they couldn't avoid, while her grandmother cast shroud spells, turning the crusader's eyes away from them.

At the dock her father joined the warriors who held back the crusaders while the village folk boarded the ships. Blood flowed and Sigurlina watched from her ship as Valkyries carried the fallen away.

She heard her father's voice commanding, "Cast off. Cast off." Crying she tried to run to him, but aged hands with an iron grip held her back. Three crusaders rushed her father who held the dock. He parried a blow and his notched sword broke. The crusaders bore her father down. The last she saw of him was his transparent form mounting a Valkyrie's horse. After that, it had been an arduous journey to Finnmark, the land of her grandmother, where the only shelter or generosity they could find was with the dead.

Sigurlina shook all over. "You can't die. I can't control the spirits. I'm not strong enough. I still need to learn."

"You must listen." Her grandmother's voice bared no objection.

Sigurlina nodded.

The old woman seemed to sink into the hides and her voice was a whisper. "When I am gone, you alone can avenge our family. Hakon must not be permitted to slaughter and force his ways on our people. Swear to me that you will avenge us."

"I swear." Sigurlina's voice was tear chocked.

"Good. When I am gone, you must make a pyre. Burn my body and keep the flames going for three days. Use the motion of the stars to keep your time. When that is done, sift the ashes and you will find all you need."

Sigurlina hugged the old woman then released her and devoured the fish. For the first time in days the gnawing in her belly stilled. Exhausted, she slept by the fire.

"Sigurlina. Wake up, dear."

Sigurlina opened her eyes and stared at her mother. Only it wasn't her mother. The eyes were different. They were blue and her mother's had been green and the jaw was more square.

"Grandmother?"

"Always so vain, Freya lover," snarled Katla's shade.

"Be quiet, you old bat," replied grandmother's shade. She turned to Sigurlina. "Remember."

Sigurlina sat up and shivered. The fire had burnt down to coals. She moved to add more wood.

"Let it die," commanded the shade of the warrior.

"Great, great, grandfather, Jarl Ingvarr..." Sigurlina looked into the shade's hollow eyes and pale, corpse-like face then fell silent.

"This is a house for the dead. You are not welcome here."

"Or you could let me take your form and stay," breathed Katla's voice.

"Leave," commanded Ingvarr.

"I'll gather my things and set the pyre then--."

"I SAID LEAVE!" bellowed Ingvarr and dust fell from the ceiling.

Sigurlina faced her ancestor and her heart quailed, then her eyes fell to the still pile of hides on the floor and something hard gripped her. "No."

"NO? THIS IS MY HOUSE. I RULE HERE," bellowed Ingvarr. More dust fell.

"I am Seithkona, shade. I will take what is mine, and do what I have promised before I depart. This may be your house, but I am Seithkona!"

Ingvarr backed away his features taking on the appearance of the vital man he'd been in life. He smiled and nodded. "Very well, daughter of my line."

Sigurlina swallowed in a dry mouth. Never before had a powerful spirit showed her deference. Taking an armload of wood from her store, she built up the fire before starting the arduous process of building the pyre in the clearing before the barrow. Hours later, she pulled away the layers of hides from around her grandmother's body. The shades had been oddly silent as she worked. When her grandmother's corpse was revealed, it was a wizened, desiccated shell. Nothing of the vital force that had played such a role in her life remained.

Sigurlina picked up the corpse, bore it outside, and laid it on the piled wood. The shades from the barrow appeared forming a ring around the body.

"No one should do this alone," explained Ingvarr, standing beside her.

She nodded then went back to the barrow, piling her meagre possessions outside the entrance. Using a stick to push flaming coals from her fire into the empty cauldron she carried them out to the set wood.

"May Freya watch over you. Goodbye, grandmother." Tipping the cauldron, she dropped the coals onto the dry wood. The flame took and roared up. She stood, surrounded by the dead, in service to the dead, for a long time.

The first sleep passed in fitful dreams of the sea. She stood on a raiding ship, the wind whipping her cloak back from her body. A man, maybe a year or two older than her, stood beside her. He was handsome with dark-blond hair, grey eyes and a muscular, broad-shouldered form. She took his hand and watched as the sea rose up in a towering wall of water. She awoke to an odd feeling, finding herself standing beside her body that writhed on the ground as two shades tried to occupy it.

"Get out, by Freya, get out." She dove back into her physical form, displacing the spirits.

"Laufey would teach you so they wouldn't dare try that." Katla whispered in Sigurlina's ear.

"Be silent, hag," muttered Sigurlina.

"Make me. But I think you have larger problems." The mad-looking spectre gestured to the edge of the clearing where the dimming fire revealed yellow eyes staring at the mortal. After building up the fire, Sigurlina moved to the stone that had sealed the barrow, located to one side of the entrance. It had been nearly three years, the entire Axe Age, since her grandmother had called on the spirits to pull it aside. Sigurlina placed her hands on the stone and focused as her grandmother had taught her.

"You won't do it. You are too weak," taunted Katla.

Sigurlina ignored the shade and called the spirits. For a moment nothing happened, then the stone rocked. She pushed harder and it rolled. Moments later the barrow was closed.

"Sleep well ancestors, until Heimdall sounds his horn." Moving back to the fire, she watched the flames.

The second night she dreamt of crusaders. All around her, flame reflected off their helms as ships burned and docks crumbled into ash. Tentacles writhed up from the water, striking anyone who drew near them. A sword drove towards her. She jerked awake to see her form using a long stick to pull apart the coals of the fire.

"Stop!" she cried and dove into her body. It felt like falling flat onto water. She had to push to dislodge the spirit. When she was safely inside herself she built up the flames. The shaggy, gray forms that prowled the clearing's edge retreated.

"You're lucky it wasn't me," spoke Katla.

"I thought you were in your barrow."

"That would be boring if I couldn't get out. Why struggle? The wolf will howl, the Aesir will die, and Surt will burn it all."

"Then I will die a child of the Aesir. There are worse things than Surt's fire. They killed my mother and my father. If such as they take the nine realms, I would beg for Surt's flames."

"I will take your vengeance for you. Let me in and I will make them suffer in your name."

For a moment, Sigurlina felt tempted. An end to the struggle, but then she took a deep breath and steeled herself. "Go. I command thee, return to your barrow."

"Look who's getting above herself, little girl. Pushed a rock and now you think you're a Seithkona. In my day..."

Sigurlina ignored the shade, but others clustered nigh each demanding or cajoling.

"Bring me vengeance." / "Where is my child?" / "Join us." / "Give us an offering."

Before her grandmother had commanded the spirits to silence; now, they threatened to overwhelm Sigurlina. Still she fed the flames and eventually sleep took her.

"Do you wish to live?" The voice was soft.

Sigurlina opened her eyes. A pair of wolves hung in mid-air to either side of her, as if pouncing for her throat. She leapt to her feet and moved away.

"You shouldn't meddle," snapped Katla.

"Norns do not meddle, old shade. We are the spirit of what must be, will be, and, when we are lucky, may be. Be silent, I am not speaking to you." Urd turned her full attention to Sigurlina. "I will only ask thrice. Do you wish to live?"

Sigurlina pinched herself. "What do I have to do?"

"Get thee to the town of Ekenas on the coast; a ship will meet you there. You will know it when you see it. I will say this much. My goals and your vengeance are aligned. More will be revealed in time. I ask a final time. Do you wish to live?"

"Yes."

The wolves continued their leap, but without their target to still their momentum, they slammed into each other. Sigurlina took a heavy piece of fire wood and slammed it into the closest wolf, driving it into the fire. The wolf leapt clear, its mangy coat smouldering, and bolted towards the woods. The remaining wolf, a starving, stunted thing, snarled at her.

Sigurlina focused her will and commanded, "Drive him into the fire."

Lesser shades clustered around the wolf that trembled then leapt into the flames. It howled in agony but Sigurlina held it there until it died. Using a stick, she pulled it from the fire.

"That wasn't anything. In my day..."

Sigurlina ignored Katla as she gutted the wolf. Spiting the heart she cooked it over the diminishing flames as she started another fire away from the pyre to dress the rest of the meat.

When the pyre was reduced to ash and warm coals, Sigurlina sifted through the remains.

"You shouldn't do that. It's disrespectful. You are a very evil girl." Katla harangued Sigurlina, who continued sifting through the coals. Other shades appeared until there was a clamour of voices. Sigurlina ignored them. Her hand came across something hard and round about the size of the end of her thumb. She pulled it out. It was a purple stone.

"You should put that back." There was panic in Katla's voice.

Sigurlina kept searching, finding another stone, then a third.

"Put them back. Put them back, they aren't for you," howled the shades that had clustered nigh.

Sigurlina held the stones. They hummed with a power that mingled with, and seemed to complement, her own.

"Silence," she commanded. The shades fell silent. "Return to your graves and barrows until I have need of you." She spoke the words as her grandmother had taught her. All but a single shade departed. Sigurlina stared into a face, which looked like her mother's.

"Grandmother, did you do that?"

"No, dear. You did. All the stones do is help you focus what is inside you. You'd need them not if I'd had more time to train you in life, but this will do until you catch up to yourself."

"You're staying."

"I'll drop by. It's time for you to have adventures of your own. And dear."

"Yes?"

"You should turn that wolf meat you're drying before it burns."

Sigurlina looked at the drying meat. When she turned back her grandmother was gone.

Sitting by her fire she ate the wolf heart, and then packed the rest of the barely dried meat. Later she shouldered her pack and choosing a long, straight, hawthorn staff started for the coast.

#

"Where in the nine realms are we? You told me we weren't near land," snarled a tall, burly man wrapped in dirty furs and a thick, woollen cloak. Despite his height, he was still a head shorter than the man beside him.

Audun stared out past the dragon prow of the ship watching for icebergs in the eternal night of Fimbulwinter. "I swear by Aegir, we're not."

"Then what are those lights? We're supposed to be in the middle of nowhere, so unless polar bears have started building fires; there has to be land nearby. If we run aground, Jarl Erik will feed us to the crabs with his own hands. Now, you're supposed to be a map maker, so you tell me the course I need to set."

Audun sighed. "Oski, the closest land should be Norveig, and it's half a day's hard sailing away. Maybe the seas have changed."

"Right." Oski rolled his eyes. "More of your Ragnarok gibberish. Check your maps. I've heard tell about places where boiling rock wells up and makes new land. Way things are nowadays, I'll not cry false to that. Go, I'll keep the ice watch."

"These are dark times." Audun moved amidships to his trunk. Men lay on the deck by the oar stations, huddled in blankets looking more like poorly-stowed cargo than people in the dim light cast by the torches on the gunwale. The oars had been shipped and the square sail held taught in a following breeze. The centre of the deck was crowded with crates. Audun opened the chest containing his maps and extracted one of the shaved sheepskins. Unrolling it revealed a detailed drawing of the Norveig coast labelled in his clean, runic script.

The wind carried the sound of a horn, but it was muted with an odd quality. A minute later Oski appeared.

"Sorry about not trusting your map, Audun. Lights must be on another ship. They should have sounded sooner. Some captains just don't keep their eyes open. I'll be glad to make harbour on Shetland. Markland is too far to sail for salt cod and dried roots by anybody's count."

Audun nodded and rolled up his map. The ship pitched as if running aground.

"Freya's tits! What did we hit?" Oski raced forward but before he got three paces a crewman towards the rear of the ship screamed in terror.

"It's..." Audun stared at a huge, sinuous tentacle with cup-shaped bits lining one side that waved up from the side of the ship and swept the deck. The tentacle slammed into a crew man and wrapped around his waist before pulling him into the water.

"A kraken!" bellowed a voice from the ship's bow followed by a scream. Audun turned in time to see another tentacle pull one of his shipmates into the sea.

"This can't be. Kraken never hunt in pairs." Audun stood frozen with shock.

The tentacles had returned and were now joined by a third set amidships.

"Fight now, think later," bellowed Oski.

Audun drew his battle axe and raced to land a flurry of blows on a tentacle that had grabbed another crewman. The tentacle was driven back. There was a cry from the tiller and the helm's man vanished into the icy waves. The ship keeled hard over and water poured onto the deck. Audun was knocked off his feet. There was a resounding crack and the ship tipped up. Ropes snapped and cargo slid across the deck slamming into the crew, sending more of them into the frigid waters.

Two kraken, which were each the size of a war horse, pulled their squid-like bodies onto the deck. A third remained in the water making a horrible, discordant, chirping sound.

Audun felt his mind bubble with rage. He struggled to rise from the broken rope and smashed cargo boxes that entangled him. His crewmates fell on the kraken, seemingly with no thought to their own survival, and were thrown one by one into the sea or onto the frozen shore of the iceberg the beasts had driven them onto.

The strange horn sounded again. The kraken shuddered then fell back into the water dragging whatever hapless sailors they had gripped with them.

Audun felt his mind clear and worked his way free of the ropes and debris. Standing, he looked around. The ship was perched on an iceberg; over half of the vessel was out of the water. The sail was sodden and already beginning to freeze in the frigid air. On the water another ship drew up to the stern of his vessel. The new ship tied off to their stern and men armed in chain with cap helms leapt aboard. Audun felt hope stir until the newcomers reached a seaman lying on the deck. They beheaded the seaman without even placing a weapon in his hand.

Audun scanned the deck for his battle axe but couldn't see it. Before he could do more he found himself surrounded by five crusaders with blades drawn.

"Northman. Treasure where?" The smallest of the men spoke with a foreign accent so thick Audun could barely understand the words. The man had a scar that marked the length of his jaw.

"You're standing on it."

"You kiss!" the crusader held up the White God's cross.

Audun readied himself for death. "No."

The blow came from behind. Audun awoke, tied hand and foot, on the ice with a pain in his head.

"They're all awake now, captain," spoke a man with a Wessex accent.

A muscular man stepped into view. "This is your lucky day. You can join with King Hakon the Good and the White God and be saved. Just tell us where you left the treasure. We know that brother killer, Erik Bloodaxe, has been squirreling it away. Tell us where the treasure is. We'll bring our priest and he'll do you proper. Then, we'll all go back to Wessex.

"Freeze in Niflheim," spat Oski. A crusader walked up sword in hand and thrust down. Audun heard his friend scream, there was a gurgling sound, then nothing.

"It's his own fault, he made us do that. Now where is the gold?"

The enemy captain gestured to a dark-haired man of maybe twenty who lay bound on the ice. A crusader raised his blade.

The dark haired prisoner sobbed, "Please. I don't know where they put it, but he's the map maker." He gestured towards Audun with his chin.

"A map maker." The captain smiled and moved to Audun, pulling his head up by his hair. "Will you accept the White God's mercy? Where is the treasure?"

"You're standing on it," Audun glared into the captain's eyes.

"Kill the rest. We only need this one."

There was the sound of a throat being cleared and the captain turned to look at the crusader with the scar on his jaw. He had removed his helm, revealing black hair and a swarthy completion. "We... Priest bless, redemption."

The captain rolled his eyes. "If you say so, shepherd." He turned to the bound men. "You can join the White God or join the fish, but do it quickly."

A black robed man stepped into Audun's field of view. He went to the man who'd pointed out the map maker, spoke some words, dipped his thumb into a silver cup, and rubbed it over the seaman's forehead. Two crusaders hoisted the seaman up and marched him away. The black-robed man moved to the next seaman. One sailor tried to bite the White

God's godi. A crusader slit the sailor's throat. Of the six crewmen who'd survived the attack, three boarded the enemy vessel.

The black robed godi knelt by Audun. "This is all unnecessary, give up your heathen ways. Join the one, true, only and right way."

"May you freeze in Niflheim!" Audun braced for the killing blow.

The crusader with the scar said something in a foreign tongue and Audun found himself hoisted up and held so that he was looking at the enemy captain.

"So you won't join us. No matter. Where is the treasure? You must know. Why else bring a map maker than to record where it was hidden."

"I told you, you're standing on it."

The blow sent Audun to lie on the ice.

"Think we're fools. We've looked. Only thing you've aboard is food. You'll answer my questions." The captain grinned evilly then spoke to the crusaders in the foreign tongue. "Is unus est quoque fervens caput capitis. Frigus is quod ligamen is sursum in vinco."

Two crusaders tore Audun's tunic from his body. The shock of cold stole his breath as the crusaders slit the ropes on his legs than shifted the ties on his wrists so that they were bound tight over his head.

"Join us. Hakon the Good can be most generous to his friends, if they accept the right path," tempted the black robed godi.

Audun spat in the godi's face.

"Right. We'll see what a night or two in the rough will do to your heathen tongue. String him up," ordered the enemy captain.

The two crusaders dragged Audun to the mast of his stranded vessel. Looping a rope through the bindings on his wrists, they suspended him an arm's length above the deck.

#

I know myself hanging on the wind cold tree.

#

"I'll leave the priest and some men to keep you company. If you come to your senses, call them. The priest is an obliging type. He'll invite anyone into the fold. God's warriors, well, they'd be wanting the gold to send back to the church. They do so enjoy their indulgences. I'd think long and hard about where that treasure is, map maker. I'll be back in three days to pick up my men. If you aren't frozen by then, we'll talk again." The enemy captain took a step. The one he'd called shepherd grabbed his arm stopping him.

The shepherd spoke in a babble of sound. "Nos non licentia meus men hic glacio."

"We know the way it's drifting and in this murk if they set a fire we'll spot it from six hours away. I won't waste your men, but we have other ships to sink with your horn and we don't want them kraken attacking the iceberg until we know where they hid the treasure, now do we?" The enemy captain continued towards his ship with the shepherd falling reluctantly into step beside him.

When the ship cast off, the three crusaders left behind built a fire in the iced ship's cooking brazier using wood from the shipping crates and feasted on the salt fish and other foods that had been the cargo. As the evening wore on they found the mead kegs. Soon one was breached. The black robed priest held up his hands in admonishment. Audun watched as the crusaders passed over several silver skatt. The priest nodded and sat by the fire as the other men drank.

The cold bit into Audun. The fire looked so inviting, but it was too far away to comfort him. He closed his eyes and tried to think. Time became a blur until two crusaders lurched up along the deck both leaning on spears and laughing. Audun ignored them until a spear slammed into the mast behind him. Another spear followed grazing his side.

#

Wounded by the spear, consecrated to Odin.
I consecrated to myself.

#

The black robed priest appeared and shouted at the crusaders in their foreign tongue. The two men laughed and lurched back towards the fire.

"They didn't mean to hit you. It was like the game of braids. You see, we are not so different."

Audun turned his head away and the White God's godi left.

Audun felt the cold wind bite him. His body shook and his teeth chattered. The enemies down the deck huddled close to the fire, eating and drinking. He focused eyes, nearly frosted shut, on the blue-black tattoos that covered his arms. Runes ran the length of his forearms and several lines of them bound his chest. He focused on them, thinking of new combinations, contemplating their meanings until sleep took him.

Time became meaningless pain. Each day the priest would ask where the gold was and demand he forsake the Aesir. Each day he would reply with silence.

Audun hung on the mast, his mind lost between sleep and waking, his body half frozen, hunger gnawing at his belly. A wolf's howl, more terrifying than anything he'd ever heard, split the night.

"Garm howls. Garm howls," he muttered, half delirious, but no one heard.

#

They offered me neither bread nor wine. So, I bent down in search.

#

"Do you wish to live?" The voice was comforting.

Audun forced his head up. It was almost more than he could do. His breath caught in his throat. In the distance the fire was frozen in place as were his tormentors. Around him the air felt warm and there was a scent like apple blossom. Urd stared at him. She was the most beautiful thing he had ever seen. He knew he should look away, but the Norn was simply too beautiful. He knew that if his days ended at that moment he would be content so long as she was his final vision.

She smiled as if guessing his thoughts. "Do you wish to live? I can ask but thrice."

"May I serve you?" His voice was its normal timber, not the ice harsh rasp of the last few days.

Urd looked pleased. "That is the purpose, and you must live to do so. Thus I ask a final time, do you wish to live."

"Yes."

"You will be called and know the calling." Urd drifted to the back of the mast and lightly brushed her hand against it. A piece of ice dribbled away revealing a shard of a broken sword blade left during a battle years before.

The fire flickered on the deck. Audun mustered his last strength and felt along the mast. There was something sharp. He began working the bonds on his wrists against it.

All the crusaders were passed out, deep into their cups, when Audun's bindings snapped. It seemed like he fell forever. As he fell, mist clouded his vision and burning runes filled the air. He grasped for them, drawing them to himself. The tattoos on his arms and chest glowed.

#

I recognized the Runes; wailing I grasped them.
Until I sank down from the tree.

#

Audun measured his length on the deck.

Fingers trembling he traced the runes tattooed on his arm.

The runic power came alive; the world glowed and his skin tingled. All thoughts of cold were banished as the archetypal forces flowed through him. Slowly he stood. The frost bite on his fingers was gone. Cautiously he wiped the frost from his eye lashes. His foes still slept.

He crept towards the fire. All the weapons, except those of the crusaders', had been stolen by the other ship's crew. Again he traced the runes on his arm, this time choosing a new pattern, shaping the forces of the world tree itself into a long, slender blade of glowing, blue energy. Audun leapt and the first crusader died on the ground, the Rune blade through his heart. The second fell; his head separated from his neck as he scrambled to stand. The third died; the rune blade through his eye. Audun, spattered in blood, with blood still geysering from the decapitated copse behind him, faced the godi.

The godi froze for a second, then leapt off the deck to the iceberg and ran.

Audun huddled by the fire, letting its warmth penetrate his body before turning to the crusaders' corpses. Taking their cloaks, he wrapped himself against the cold. One crusader carried his battle axe.

"It isn't stealing if it belongs to me. As for the cloaks, I hope you will forgive me, but my clothes seem to be missing."

After warming himself by the fire, while devouring half a salt herring and two tankards of mead, Audun searched the ship, finding his sea chest with his replacement clothing. Turning to the corpses he wondered at them. They had all been brown skinned with brown eyes, like the Picts, but taller. Shrugging, he called over the deck.

"Godi, I know not your ways, but I will swear by Mjolnir to give you safe passage if you have Angel of Death duties to perform for your White God."

There was no reply. Sighing, he shook his head. "I don't think they like pyres, and I may need the wood later." Grabbing the first corpse he dragged it from the broken ship. Minutes later, the three bodies were laid in a row on the iceberg with a sword secured in each of their hands using the ties from their boots. The decapitated head was set carefully in its proper place.

Reverently, Audun pulled off the corpses' boots. Using a dagger, he trimmed their toenails to the quick before putting the boots back on.

"No reason to hasten Naglfar's completion." Standing Audun looked over the bodies then spoke. "Lord Odin, they are not yours, but I know not their words. Please show them the way to where they may best serve." Audun bowed his head then went back to the fire and slept.

He awoke to a snuffling sound and opened his eyes. A huge, white bear stood at the edge of the fire's light. The bear's nostrils flared and it rose to its hind legs and roared.

Audun's fingers tightened on the haft of his axe, although, he knew it would do him little good.

"I'm not going to hurt you. Would you like some fish?" he asked. Slowly, he moved to the barrel of salt cod by the fire and pulled out half a fish. With a heave, he threw it to the bear. The bear dropped to all fours, sniffed the fish, licked it, took a tentative bite, and then released a grumbling growl. Two fluffy cubs appeared out of the darkness and began tearing into the fish.

The mother bear looked at Audun.

Audun pulled another fish from the barrel and tossed it to the mother who devoured it. Minutes later another barrel of fish was opened and the mother and cubs basked in the warmth of Audun's fire as they nibbled contentedly at the last of their meal.

"What should I call you," Audun spoke to the bear that regarded him benignly.

"Lady White. Yes, I think Lady White suits you."

The mother bear made a gruffing sound. The cubs began to wrestle on the deck tumbling back and forth.

"And you can be Tumbler and Leaper," Audun spoke to the cubs.

The mother bear put her head down and went to sleep.

The stars had moved on in the sky when Audun saw the torches of a ship coming through the eternal night of Fimbulwinter. He huddled behind a crate and loosened the battle axe on his belt.

Lady White rose from beside the fire, moved to the stern and released a tremendous roar.

"God's teeth, it a polar bear," the voice came faint but clear over the waves.

"Don't even bother docking. She'll have eaten the lot of them. Hakon's going to have my nuts for this." The enemy captain's voice was resolved as the ship moved away from the iceberg.

Audun made it a point to remember that voice. Hakon and that captain owed him, and he would collect.

Lady White roared again and returned to the fire's warmth. Audun built up the fire and opened another barrel of fish.

#

"Dorrund, aren't you the naughty one?" Ragna ran her fingers across the broad, naked chest of one of the two men that stood in the smithy with her. The forge was banked and the cat-sized forge beast was curled up beside it. The beast's dragon-like form expanded and contracted as it breathed and its stubby wings trembled as it dreamed its fiery dreams. The smithy and the attached living area was the warmest place Ragna had been in months.

"You bring that out in a man," said Ginnarr, as he rolled out an extra blanket on the platform that flanked three sides of the living area of the shelter. The back of the platform was stacked with disused woman's gear, like a loom, with a half finished piece of cloth on it, and a querm, its round stones ready to turn grain into flower with a woman's touch.

The two men were of a kind, both stocky and short by Norse standards, with huge arms. Sparks had left a pattern of tiny burns on their faces and chests. The most telling difference between them was that one was bald and the other had long, black hair pulled into a braid that fell down his back.

Ragna continued to tease Dorrund. Taking the end of his braid and tracing it over the nipples on his massive pecs with one hand, while she undid the tie for his leggings with the other. The leggings dropped around his ankles.

Ginnarr's powerful hands closed on Ragna's slender arms. He pulled her to him back first. Her slender, petite form conformed to his with the top of her head barely reaching his chin. Her large, brown eyes focused on a necklace lying on a cloth by the forge. She reached behind her and undid the tie for Ginnarr's leggings, dropping them around his ankles.

"That's a girl. This will be fine." Ginnarr bent to nibble on her shoulder, as Dorrund moved to kiss her.

Ragna licked her full lips and kissed the end of Dorrund's bulbous nose while pulling away from Ginnarr. She stepped back and picked up the necklace.

"This is so beautiful."

"It's our finest work, as promised," said Dorrund.

"Well, I guess the only question I have is which one of you wants to put it to, I mean, on me first?" She struck a pose that thrust out her bosom and made her simple, blue dress shape to the body beneath.

"First?" breathed one of the smiths.

"I wouldn't want you to fight over it." Ragna's pixyish features pulled into a seductive pout.

"I'll go first," said Dorrund.

"Fasten this for me. The clasp is always so tight the first time." Ragna turned her back and held the necklace to her throat.

Dorrund raced to fasten the necklace. His arms were just reaching around her when Ginnarr pulled him away.

"By Dvalin, I'll go first. I smelted the gold," said Ginnarr.

"I'll have her first. I pulled the cursed wire," Dorrund growled.

"You're brothers, you shouldn't argue over me. You've shared so much. Living together, working together. It's like you have nothing all your own." Ragna spoke in a voice like poisoned honey.

"You. You're always taking. I'll go bloody first," screamed Ginnarr.

"Me taking? It wasn't me that stole the deed to the shop when Papa died."

"I'm the eldest."

"I'm the better smith."

"You take that back."

"By Sindri, you know it's true.

"It isn't."

"Is so!"

"If you weren't my brother!"

"Don't let that stop you!"

Ragna had almost reached the door with the necklace when a wolf's howl split the air sending a bone chilling bolt down everyone's spine. They all froze. Then two sets of eyes turned to her.

"Where do you think you're going?" the brothers demanded in unison.

"Oh Svartalfheim!" Ragna barely dodged the brothers' first rush because they tripped over the leggings about their ankles. She danced away, but found herself trapped in the living area of the hut with the brothers between her and the door.

The brothers hauled up their leggings each holding them up one handed.

"Thought you could cheat us," snapped Dorrund.

"She's a real Ratatosk," agreed Ginnarr.

"Well come here little squirrel. We'll give you some nuts." Dorrund dove towards her.

Everything froze, as the smith was in mid-lunge.

"Do you wish to live?"

Ragna glanced around for the source of the voice and watched Urd float through the hut's wall.

Ragna felt her jaw drop. For once, she was at a loss for words. She tried to look away but couldn't. The Norn glowed with an unearthly light and there was a scent like baking bread. Ragna could faintly hear a harp playing. Weak at the knees, Ragna sat on the sleeping platform that surrounded the living section of the hut.

"Do you wish to live? I can ask only thrice."

"Who? They won't kill me, they'll just..." Ragna shuddered.

"With the punishment for raping a free woman, how could they let you go? I ask a final time. Do you wish to live?"

Ragna stared at the brothers for a split second then replied, "Yes."

"Look for she who walks in the shadows and dines with the dead. Your paths are intertwined."

Urd floated through the hut lightly touching the draw string on each brother's leggings then stroking the back of the forge beast. Ragna gained her feet and moved to the side of Dorrund's dive.

Time started. Dorrund lunged past Ragna as Ginnarr moved to block the door. The forge beast awoke and leapt off the forge getting under Dorrund's feet. The smith whipped around, letting go of his leggings and throwing his arm out to catch himself. The leggings dropped around his ankles entangling him. He stumbled headfirst into the forge's stone side.

Ginnarr pulled the cord on his leggings to tie them up and it snapped, one end disappearing into the track. The leggings dropped; he bent to pick them up again. Seeing her chance, Ragna leapt, stepping on Ginnarr's head and half sliding down his back, landing behind him facing the door. She drove her buttocks into his; causing the unbalanced smith to stumble forward measuring his length on the floor. By now, Dorrund was scrambling to his feet; clutching his leggings with one hand and rubbing his head with the other.

Ragna jerked open one side of the smithy's double door and sprinted onto the street. Lanterns burning over the Tradesmen's signs of the shops that flanked the dirt passage lessoned the gloom. Frozen garbage from the shops littered the street.

Ragna paused to get her bearings then sprinted down the lane.

"Get her," yelled the brothers, as they burst through the smithy's door jamming against each other, finally clearing the exit at the cost to Ginnarr of scraped skin.

Dorrund stumbled into the street, slipped on a patch of ice, and flipped into the air. He seemed to float for a second, then fell flat onto his back. His hand jerked, tearing the tie cord on his leggings.

Ragna leapt atop a cart that partially blocked the lane and, using it to reach a roof, pulled herself onto the frozen thatch.

"There she is," the smiths called in unison, as they hoisted up their leggings.

Dorrund charged after her, hit a slick ice patch and dropped like a tree, his face finding evidence of a horse's passing that had not yet fully frozen.

"Ginnarr, Dorrund, what's all this ruckus about? And where's your clothing? You'll catch your death like that," snapped an elderly woman, who leaned out of a cooper's shop.

"It was a thief. She took our property without paying." Dorrund scraped horse dung off his face.

"And just how was she paying? You being naked, I wonder?" said the woman.

Ginnarr looked at the open doors where his neighbours stood listening to every word. Sweat accumulated on his barren brow despite the cold. "We... err. We were working the forge."

"That's right, the forge. And it was hot," confirmed Dorrund.

"And I'm sure there are places you'd rather not have sparks landing, so maybe you could use some sense. Get back inside 'fore that lizard of yours burns your shop and takes the street with it." The woman in the cooper's shop rolled her eyes.

"Right, Brynhild. Can't have that now," said Ginnarr as he managed to hoist his leggings up and hold them at his waist.

"No, mustn't have that." Dorrund copied his brother. They walked back to the smithy with wounded dignity and closed the door.

Ragna chuckled as she slid down behind the peak of the roof trying to keep the frozen thatch from mangling her dress. She leapt into the next lane over from the smithy, hugged herself against the cold, and fingered the necklace that she still held as she vanished into the maze of streets that made up the town of Ekenas.

After a short walk, she reached the docks where she approached a tall, slender sailor supervising the loading of a dragon ship.

"Sigurd," she called.

The sailor turned to her "Do you have it?"

Ragna held out the necklace. "The brothers aren't too happy."

"Forget them. After the way they cheated me on those axe heads, this is justice." He took the necklace, then reached to the top of a nearby crate and pulled down a wool bundle. "Wear it in good health.

Ragna took the bundle, which proved to be a thick cloak and a hood. She donned it immediately, slowly she stopped shivering.

"Did you hear the wolf howl?" Ragna moved to stand outside Sigurd's reach.

"I heard. Me papa would have said it was Garm was singing at the gates of Niflheim. Not that it could be much colder there than here."

"What do you think it was?"

"I don't know. I follow the White God." The sailor held up the wooden cross he wore on a thong about his neck. Ragna noticed that the symbol of a fish had been carved into the long bar of the cross. "Would you like to hear about him?"

Ragna sighed. "There was a monk in my father's hall. He told me all the stories and taught me some of the tongue that the White God's godi like to use. Back then, I'd dance with the druids and listen to all sorts of godi. I didn't see why one should push out the others. Then, the crusaders came." Ragna hung her head and her voice became small.

The seaman shook his head sadly. "Not all folk are bad in anything, girl. It's one thing to be a fisher of souls, it's another to hunt them down and take them at sword point. I have no truck with the second way. Here." He held out a small cloth bag.

Ragna moved closer just long enough to snatch it from his hand. She opened it to find a loaf of journey bread.

"Cook made a little extra. Look after yourself. Watch out for Dorrund and Ginnarr."

"I will."

With a nod, Sigurd returned his attention to loading the ship. Ragna bit into the hard bread, hunger making it the finest thing she had ever eaten.

#

The huge, red wolf loped through the snow with the white, furry body of an immature snow serpent held in its mouth and draped over its back. The wind blew through the dead trees as snow fell from a sky where clouds blocked even the faint light of the stars.

A wolf howl split the night and Vidurr added his voice to Garm's in exaltation. The day of reckoning was near. The thought made him shudder with blood lust. The smell of ash interrupted his thoughts. He sniffed the air. Blood!

His wolf form stretching and driving forward in a graceful, ground eating sprint, he followed a track pounded into the snow by the feet and paws of his pack. As he neared the coast the air warmed. Coming to the edge of the steep-sided valley that sheltered his village from the winds he stopped and stared. Below lay a burnt out ruin. The neat circle of huts flanking the great hall was nothing but scorched timbers and ash. Nothing moved below.

He threw his head back and howled in dismay. From the top of the valley there was an answering howl, but it sounded strange. He dropped the snow serpent's corpse, then, teeth bared in a snarl, ran towards the holy grove from whence the howl came. He slowed just before he stepped into the clearing. The clouds parted allowing the dim, twilight illumination of the stars to reflect off the snow. The grove was maybe fifteen strides across by as deep, flanked on all sides by winter killed trees.

Vidurr stared into the clearing, howled then shuddered. A moment later, a powerfully built man with wind-roughened features and a mane of red hair stood in the wolf's place. He was clad in a heavy, fur cloak with the hide side of the furs turned out and a simple tunic and leggings. A long sword rested in a shoulder scabbard. He drew the blade and cautiously entered the sacred grove. The statue of Surt on the eastern end of the clearing had been smashed and a crusaders' cross erected in its place. Vidurr felt a howl of rage building in his throat then his voice was stolen.

Huddled naked in the snow before where the statue of Surt had once stood was a powerfully built man with gray hair that fell down his back in a tangle.

Vidurr felt his heart scream, but nothing passed his lips. The man's hands and feet had been cut off and as Vidurr watched, a face he had known since the cradle turned to him to reveal gouged out eyes and a mouth that lolled from the removal of the tongue.

"FATHER!" Vidurr raced to the old man's side. Ripping off his cloak he wrapped the ruined form in it. He felt the handless arms embrace him. He looked through the blur of tears to the crusaders' cross where Surt's statue should have stood. Gently, he laid his father, wrapped tight in the heavy, fur cloak, to one side and with a strength born of furry gripped the cross and tore it from the ground. Finding the head of the shattered statue he set it in its proper place then returned to the old man.

"I took the cross down, and I'll find the rest of the statue."

The old man sighed and nodded. He was a godi of Surt, and Vidurr knew he'd want the grove set to rights.

"I swear to you by Surt, they will pay. I will not let you suffer the straw death. I promise." Tears choked out Vidurr's voice.

For a long time he held the ruined man; keeping him warm with his cloak and body. Then he pulled himself away and built a fire. When it burnt well, lending warmth to the grove, he arranged his father as comfortably as the wounds and frostbite allowed and followed the trail to the decimated village.

A line of stone cairns, each marked with a cross, occupied what had years before been a farmer's field. Vidurr, his blood seething, walked to each cairn, toppling the cross, and unearthing the body below.

"Feed the crows, vermin," he spat on each corpse. One had been buried with a broad sword laid on his chest. Vidurr took the blade. "Such as you can go to Hel unarmed."

Next he searched the town finding nothing save scorched bones. "Asdis, did they take you? Have they taken our cub? Oh my bitch, are you these bones?" He ran his fingers through the ashes that had been his hut then howled to the darkness.

Collecting the snow serpent he returned to the grove. Pulling a small pot from his pack he made a broth that he brought to his father, who dozed in the fur cloak.

The old man refused to drink shaking his head and waving his handless arms.

"You need some strength for the voyage to Muspelheim." Vidurr said in a tear chocked voice.

The old man tried to speak with a tongue-less mouth and waved his stump, the fire reddened end a contrast to his pale skin.

"I swore I would not let you suffer the straw death. I have one of the enemy's swords. You will die in combat; as you deserve. Father, in this, trust me."

The old man quieted and drank the broth.

Later Vidurr collected the stones that made up the statue of

Surt and piled them back on the altar rock telling his father what he was doing. The broken statue was hardly recognisable. Vidurr prayed that Surt would accept his effort and true devotion. Next he dragged a log between his fire and the altar stone. Using his hatchet he carved a crude seat in the log.

Taking his father from the fur cloak he sat the old man in the seat. Using thong Vidurr secured the crusader's sword to the stump of the old man's arm.

"Keep a place by the lake of fire for me. I will see you in Muspelheim, father. I... I love you. Now just like when I was little. TOP LEFT"

Vidurr swung his long sword at a quarter speed after announcing the blow. Memories flooded back of his childhood when his father had first taught him to use a blade. The hours of drills until the blocks, parries and attacks became a thing of instinct. Hours learning from the old wolf, first with wood then blunted steel. Finally, he received his first, true blade from the hands now cruelly taken.

The old man, awkward from the lack of his hands, brought the sword up in a clumsy block. A smile spread across the aged features. He threw his head back and howled. Vidurr howled with him, and then called out.

"Bottom right."

The slow blow was intercepted.

"Attack thrust." Vidurr stepped back from the clumsy, blind attempt to strike him.

"TOP LEFT." Vidurr bellowed because if he didn't yell tears would steal his voice. The slow blow was blocked.

He swung his sword at full speed without announcing the blow. Blinded and crippled as he was, the old godi seemed to sense the blow coming and brought his blade up, but too late. The blow struck home, severing head from body. The head flew to one side and blood shot into the air falling on the broken statue of Surt.

Vidurr watched until the blood stopped, and then collected the severed head. There was a smile on the lips.

"Valkyries of Surt; Svafnir, godi of Surt, veteran of many battles comes to you blade in hand; fresh from combat. Take him to Glassisvellir, the lake of fire, that he may fight on." Using a stick sharpened on both ends he mounted his father's head on his body then left to gather wood. Hours later he laid the body on its pyre, kissed his father's cold forehead a final time, and set the wood alight. The flames roared up. Transforming himself into a wolf, he howled, warning all that Svafnir's strong arm and mighty blade were come to Muspelheim.

Vidurr slept in wolf form by the pyre until the coals were cooling then transformed back into his human shape. Looking down the valley he saw a longship. A cross stood out on its deck and armoured foreigners were disembarking.

"They must have seen the light of your pyre, father. Thank you for bringing them here. Now is the time for revenge."

Drawing his blade, Vidurr strode down the steep trail which led to the burnt out village. He emerged onto the snow-clad fields that surrounded the site. The men from the boat called and drawing weapons raced towards him. Vidurr howled in defiance, brandishing his blade. Everything froze.

"Do you wish to live?"

Vidurr gazed at Urd and felt fire course through him. Fate had brought him to this. Fate was his foe as much as the bloody handed assassins who stood frozen in time. His vision clouded red. This was a world beyond all he knew, yet he would greet it with rage.

"I care not!" he roared.

Urd floated closer her face growing darker, a cold fire seemed to kindle behind her eyes and her hair became the colour of midnight. "Then I will alter my bargain. Do you want vengeance?"

"I will have vengeance. I will send them to Niflheim, where cowards belong. No being worthy of a blade would condemn a hero to the straw death as these tried to do."

"You would kill three, maybe four. Is that enough for you? Serve me and you may have rivers of crusaders' blood. Blood enough to dampen the fires of Muspelheim itself."

Vidurr stared at the men who stood frozen in their approach. "Rivers of their blood?"

"All your sword and teeth can drink and more."

"I will serve thee." Vidurr raised his sword in salute.

"Become the wolf and run up the trail to Surt's grove. Wait there and I will grant you your first portion of vengeance. You will know when your service begins."

Vidurr transformed into the huge, red wolf and ran up the path to the sacred grove.

Urd floated up along the valley's side over the snow-clad slopes to their top. With a warm breath she dislodged a few pieces of ice that slid down the incline dislodging others then she was gone.

Vidurr reached the sacred grove and turned. There was a roaring sound as the snow on the valley sides released all at once and thundered down, catching his pursuers. The tide of snow tore down the valley as crusaders' raced towards their ship only to be engulfed in the snow's smothering embrace. The snow slammed into the ship in the harbour driving it into the frigid surf and snapping its timbers as the ice and snow formed a shallow, sloping shelf in the sea. Then it was done. All was silence.

Vidurr returned to human form, built up the fire and began cooking snake meat. His vengeance was only just begun.

CHAPTER 2

COMMON CAUSE

Fjorn stepped back from his latest kill, his sword smeared with gore. The battle had shifted away from him. He took a moment to scan his surroundings. His breath caught in his throat when he saw the grizzled, bearded form of Kjorn lying on the icy ground amongst a pile of their enemies.

"Please Odin, no!" Fjorn rushed to the old sailor's side. There was a deep gash running the width of his belly. Closing his eyes Fjorn reached for the dregs of his power and sang. "Youth to the gods, golden apples of grace. Idun's power, heal mortals of faith."

Sparkling lights enveloped Kjorn and the old sailor's wounds began to close. His eyes fluttered open and he smiled. "Nicely done, boy. They'll make a skald of you yet."

"Better a skald than a karl. " Fjorn stood and returned to surveying the battle. The invaders were being held to a line on the ice field before the town. The enemy reserves, who had hung back by the ships until now, were moving up fresh and ready for the fight. The war horn on the palisade sounded thrice. Long, Long, Short.

Fjorn watched the steep slope over the harbour as it exploded like a snow flurry. Dozens of armoured men threw off the wool blankets that had hidden them against the snow and swept down on the invaders' rear. The new force split. Half turned to the dragon ships where they were beached, pushing through the light guard that remained there, taking the ships. The rest fell upon the rear of the invaders' main force.

Fjorn felt Kjorn standing beside him.

"We should get back into it," said the old sailor.

"Are you up to it?"

"I'm feeling a lot more me self, thanks to you. I thought I'd be drinking mead with the all father for a while there."

"Let's--."

There was another three long blasts from the horn on the battlements.

"Reinforcements? Where did my father find reinforcements? Is he sending out the shield maids?"

"Don't look like maids to me. Least ways, if they are, it's enough to put you off the idea of wrenching ever again." Kjorn shook his head. "Could have come in through the landward gate and mustered behind the wall."

Fjorn's eyes tracked to the village gate which had been thrown open. A hundred men, who were almost giants, armoured in mail, stepped onto the battlefield and rushed to join the defence.

"Come on lad. We can't let them have all the fun." Kjorn raced to where the fray was thickest. In minutes the invaders were trounced. Fjorn stayed to help with the wounded, so the feast was well underway by the time he entered the great hall, with its thatched roof and solid walls. The great hall was lit by the central fire and torches in sconces nailed into the support pillars.

Fjorn looked to his father's seat at the end of the hall, but his father wasn't in it. A robust warrior with dark hair just beginning to gray lounged in the chair; a drinking horn in one hand and a haunch of meat in the other. A golden-haired woman, who was taller than most men, with a regal demeanour sat to the warrior's left. She moved with a dancer's grace and her face was worthy of song. Fjorn couldn't help but let his eyes linger on her. When he pulled his gaze away he noted that several huge men in chain flanked her along the table's length. Fjorn's father, Karl Gildnar, sat to the warrior's right, looking nervous. The household guards stretched out on that side of the table.

"Lord Fjorn." The voice was soft and seductive.

Fjorn turned to look into a pair of lovely, blue eyes on a beautiful face framed with golden hair in braids. He smiled. "Well hello, Eir. You look lovely today."

"Thank you, my lord. Your father has given me leave to keep your company. Why don't you find us a private place? I'll gather a feast that we can share and bring it to you?"

Fjorn eyed the woman. She was maybe five years older than him, curved in all the right places. Beyond that, he knew she was kind. When his mother had passed at the start of Fimbulwinter Eir had been his comfort. He had been hers for the taking ever since. "That sounds...

Why the change of heart? I..." Fjorn thought for a moment. "Did my father order you to do this?"

"I." Eir looked at the dirt floor. "I am but a thrall; I must obey."

Fjorn lifted the woman's face with his finger so she looked into his eyes. "There is that which I will not command or have commanded for me. I've told you that before, Eir. Only by your will will we lie together. Why does my father want me out of the hall so desperately?"

At that moment the warrior in Fjorn's father's seat stood up. "A song. We need a song to celebrate. Is there not a skald to be had in this village?" The warrior turned to Geldnir beside him. "I've heard tell your son has a voice passing fair. Bring him out. I would see the boy."

"Jarl Erik, I think he is still helping with the wounded. He often stays after the battle to do so."

Erik Bloodaxe regarded his bondsman. "As he should, but send for him, man. Surly the wounded have been seen to. I would know the heirs to my karls' seats."

Fjorn stepped forward. "If it pleases you, Jarl Erik. I am fresh come from my duty to the wounded."

Fjorn felt the eyes of the beautiful woman beside Erik drill into him; as if she would strip the flesh from his bones to find the secrets beneath.

"Come forward, lad." Erik beckoned with his mead horn. Fjorn stepped forward, watching the blood drain from his father's face.

Erik smiled. It was a smile that instilled loyalty; that spoke to a man who would give you as much as he took. "So, have you a song in you for your jarl?"

Fjorn cleared his throat. "If it pleases you. I am sung hoarse from the wounded. Might I slack my thirst first?"

"A skald indeed, first at the mead cup." Erik laughed. "Come boy, drink a jarl's portion." Erik held out the drinking horn. Fjorn walked up and took the cup, draining a good portion of the watery mead it contained before passing it back.

"You can drink at least, now the song." Erik regarded the young skald with shrewd eyes.

Fjorn closed his eyes sifting through the songs he knew; measuring each against his jarl's apparent mood, then he began to sing.

"In time before time when the sun was new.
When the moon was silver in Midgard's skies.
Frey, hostage prince to the piece of gods.
Walk through worlds of space and time.
Frey, he espied a mortal maid
and honoured her with a lusty babe.
From Vanir's blood, a line was born.
To with heroes and jarls this world adorned.
Ages came and ages went, but Frey's blood was not content.
From Harold Jarl was Norveig forged.
Northmen united on many shores.
And so we stand as Northmen proud.
Our courage and glory to sing aloud.
With Erik Bloodaxe to show the way.
We'll honour great Odin and Frey each day.

Fjorn's voice trailed off. The room was silent then Erik began to laugh. The sound grew slowly, but soon the jarl was roaring, tears streaming from his eyes. All gathered joined in. After draining his horn and catching his breath Erik eyed Fjorn.

"You have some wits about you, boy." He held out his horn for a refill keeping one finger held straight. He quaffed from the refilled horn then beckoned Fjorn close and passed him the horn. Fjorn took a long drink and had to fight to keep himself from coughing as the mead burnt its way to his stomach.

"Geldnir, I like your lad. He knows there is a time to bend knee, but from what I heard about the battle today, he doesn't live on them." Erik eyed Fjorn. "You have a familiar look, boy. Who was his mother?" Erik turned to look at Geldnir.

"My wife, she was Loftveig, a karl's daughter from the Ivar line. She was fostering here as part of a peace bond during your father's reign."

Erik looked contemplative. "Bring him, it's time to speak."

"Sire, I... The mead has been flowing freely. Perhaps," began Geldnir.

"Now we will plan. We will not do until the mead has turned to piss. Come, boy. I would hear the words of a man of courage in battle and discretion in the counsel hall." Erik rose, as did the woman beside him. A guardsman helped Geldnir to his feet and passed him a cane.

Fjorn fell in at the back of the processional, thinking that his father looked scared. They moved into a room walled off from the great hall with a large table in its centre. Candles burned around the edge of the table. A guardsman brought a chair for Geldnir, but the rest stood. The table was nearly filled with a map of Midgard. Fjorn was amazed to see it even included the coast around Markland and Vinland far to the west.

Erik sipped then passed the horn he held to Fjorn, the expansive nature of the great hall falling from him like a cloak.

"Finish that for me. Don't ever tell anyone," ordered the jarl.

"Yes, my Jarl." Fjorn drained the horn knowing he was likely to regret it.

"Geldnir, part of why I'm here is my father always said you were the best man he'd ever sailed with. We have a problem."

Geldnir examined the map. "The missing ships?"

Erik nodded. "I don't know what my bastard half brother is doing, but I can barely move cargo. Getting to Orkney was a risk, but when my spies told me about the coming assault on your seat, I decided it was warranted." Erik grinned. "The royal guard was getting restless sitting around Alvaldsnes. To be honest, the capital was beginning to weigh on me. Bureaucrats everywhere. If I had to listen to one more pasty-faced weasel go on about tax rates, I'd have picked a fight with Bergelmir himself. Being frozen by a frost giant would have been preferable."

"Husband." The tall, beautiful woman sighed. "We need to talk about the lost ships."

"With all due respect, Queen Gunnhild, the seas are more treacherous since Fimbulwinter began," said Geldnir.

"Not like this, fair karl." Gunnhild's voice was like honey. Fjorn felt his eyes riveted to her. "Hardly any of our ships are getting through. We sent vessels to gather food from the far reaches of Midgard, and still our people go hungry. I have consulted the oracles. They are unclear. But one thing is certain. All signs point to Hakon and some foul magic from outer Midgard. I have never encountered its kind."

"Relax Gunnhild, no one knows everything." Erik stroked her shoulder.

"But a royal must appear to. We must resolve this before we begin the tour of the karls."

"Why not simply delay your tour until we can deal with this?" asked Geldnir

"The loyalty of the karls is in question. I have to be at Islandia for Yule. If Hakon can sink my ship, the whole of Norveig will fall to squabbling. If I delay the voyage, I show fear. The karls will split, each declaring themselves a jarl, and Hakon can pick them off one by one."

"I need to rally the karls. I need to get my food shipments into the towns, but a good third of the ships I send out vanish, crews and all. Most captains are afraid to leave harbour, and I can't blame them. Half of them think that Jormungand itself is prowling the waves, and with the sun and moon eaten they might be right. What can I do?" Erik stared at the map.

Fjorn felt hot and his brain was full of fizzle and pop. The mead had been exceptionally strong. Discretion seemed a far off thing.

"Hakon can't chase two rabbits." He'd spoken before he realised it.

"Fjorn! Please forgive the boy, Your Majesty," pleaded Geldnir.

Erik held up his hand. "What do you mean, boy?"

Fjorn tried to get the map to stop wobbling in front of him and swallowed the saliva pooling in his mouth. "You have some time before you have to leave for Islandia. Send out ships to as many towns as you can with a message about when and where you intend to visit. Let the crew of each ship think that you're going to be visiting the town they go to on Yule. Only tell the captain the real date for your visit, and they are only to tell the karl of that area. Then when you go to Islandia you don't stop at the Faroe Islands, like everybody does, you just pass them by."

"And what will that do?" Gunnhild's fingers drummed together as she eyed Fjorn.

"Have you ever known a sailor that can keep a secret? One night getting into the mead cups and Hakon's spies will be telling him you're going to be all over Midgard on Yule. Just like Odin and the hunt."

Erik smiled indulgently. "And where am I supposed to get ships to do this?"

"They don't have to be big ships. There are ten that could carry the message in the harbour right now. The men who attacked were Hakon's, pledged to the White God, and they don't do funeral ships. Just get my father's pet monk to dribble some water on the bodies and toss them in a snow bank. From what I hear the water dribbling is all they want, or expect." Fjorn smiled and slid down the wall to sit on the floor.

"You have a godi of the White God here?" Erik eyed Geldnir suspiciously.

"He has no love of Hakon or the crusaders, my Jarl. He was running from the crusaders because he dared say that men should choose their own way and that forcing a man to pledge to a god at the point of a sword was no pledge at all. When his leaders in outer Midgard heard he was saying such things they ordered Hakon to have him killed. He escaped and found his way to me. He has some knowledge in healing and, more important, can speak and read the language of his church. As long as his earthly loyalties are to me, I give him shelter and let his spirit go where it will. His version of the White God sounds much like Baldur. I think the ones like him may have just gotten the name wrong."

"As long as he is loyal to you. Now about this plan?" Erik eyed Fjorn who lay on the floor breathing deeply.

"It might work. Whatever Hakon is up to, he obviously can't do it everywhere at once. This plan won't stop the sinking's, but it could get you to Islandia and give us time to learn what is really going on." Geldnir stared at the map. "With the ten ships we captured we can make a start. You'd have to inform the karls when you intend to join them anyway, and rumour is faster than Sleipnir. We can have the ships stocked and fitted in hours."

"We need to send a vessel to Finnmark anyway, my love. I need ingredients for my castings, and it is the only place to get them. It need not be a large ship, but it must make port at Alvaldsnes before the night of the dead. I think the karl's son should captain it. It was his plan after all. He looks right ready for a man's task." Gunnhild stroked her husband's arm, and if there was a cunning gleam in her eyes, it didn't reach her face.

"He isn't much of a sailor, and it will be a dangerous journey," commented Geldnir.

"How is a young man to grow if he always hides behind his father's shield?" There was a harsh edge behind the honey of Gunnhild's voice.

"She has a point, Geldnir. This is a fair plan, and I hope Hakon chases his own tail straight into his new master's Hell with it."

"But, my Queen. My son knows nothing of the items you would have him obtain for you." Geldnir sounded desperate.

"That is easily dealt with. I will send a list. If your son cannot read, then send someone who can. Transporting a few things from Finnmark shouldn't prove too difficult for a karl's son." There was a note in the queen's voice that was almost venomous.

Fjorn didn't quite remember how he got there, but he awoke lying in a corner of the conference room with a head that felt like it had been used as a striking post. He crept from the chamber. A lone man sat by the central fire. People slept all around the great hall, some in pairs or even in threes. Fjorn moved to the figure by the flames, recognising too late to back away that it was Erik Bloodaxe.

"You're awake," Erik smiled.

"Yes, sire. I am sorry--."

Erik cut him off with a dismissive wave. "That was ice mead three times frozen. It's surprising you didn't empty your guts. Sit. Your father has arranged for you to take ship. You will be captaining a vessel bound for Finnmark."

"I, yes, Your Majesty. I..."

"Yes."

"Why? I'm barely a seaman, and to make me captain? Frankly, to put me on a boat at all. I get seasick. My father knows this. Why is he sending me?"

Erik took a swig from his horn and smiled. "He's afraid, and with good reason."

"If he wants to protect me, sending me to sea with what is happening seems strange."

"There are dangers greater than the sea, boy. Let me tell you a story. You have probably already heard it.

"Not long ago an ambitious man wanted to inherit, so he invited all of his brothers, and there were many, to a meeting. Somehow, the hall they were in caught fire and all the brothers died." Erik took a swig of mead and stared into his horn. "Some people blamed the ambitious man."

Fjorn swallowed noticeably. He'd heard the rumours about how Erik had cemented his hold on the thrown.

"Now let me tell you another story. It starts the same, but as the brothers met one of them was rude and crafted strife between those that needed to be friends. Eventually, the brothers threw the one brother out; making fun of the fact that his mother had been a thrall.

"It was a foolish thing to do. Maybe if they'd told him he was being expelled because he was a loud-mouth ass, things would have been different. Maybe he'd been berated because of his mother's station all his life, and it made him angry. Maybe, something broke in the brother. He was young. In any case, when everyone was asleep that young brother pushed a cart up against the hall's door and threw burning brands into the thatch. Only the brother who was hosting survived. The young brother ran away." Erik drained his horn and held it out.

Spotting a keg well away from the fire, Fjorn refilled the horn and passed it to his jarl. "Which story is true?"

"It all depends which brother you like more." Erik released a mirthless chuckle. "In the ages to come, it will all depend on who wins the war, I guess. Truth changes, boy. We choose our own truths. Look at my father, Jarl Harald Fairhair. Jarl Harald, the Great Jarl. Jarl Harald, man whore!" Erik took a long swallow. "I loved my father, but I watched my mother die a little with each bastard born."

"What does this have to do with my father sending me away?"

Erik took a long pull on his horn draining it. "Good night, boy. We may never meet this side of the rainbow bridge again, but know you have made a jarl smile." Standing, Erik Bloodaxe weaved his way to the private chamber reserved for his sleeping.

"There you are." Geldnir whispered as he walked towards Fjorn. "Father."

"Come along. Your ship is provisioned and it just needs its captain."

"I don't want to--."

"You're going! I've already packed your sea chest and Kjorn has stowed it for you." Geldnir put his cane arm around Fjorn's shoulder and stepped forward with his good leg, forcing Fjorn to move or dump him on the ground. Fjorn moved towards the door.

"But why make me captain. I--."

"Because you are a karl's son and of an age where it would be unseemly if you were not, at least for a boat of this size. Don't worry, I'm sending Kjorn. Just listen to him and use some sense. You have a supply of that, so long as there's no bosoms involved."

"Father, the jarl."

Geldnir let go of Fjorn so they could exit the great hall. Outside, the karl walked using his cane on the icy ground.

"You are my son. Your mother was a karl's daughter, and that is all you--."

Fjorn remembered the words of the Norn. "I'm of the line of Frey. You... You are my father, but you are not my sire. Are you?"

Geldnir froze and seemed to shrink in on himself. He spoke in a whisper. "Harald Fairhair was a great man. Loyal friend, brilliant in war, generous in peace, and a complete ass when it came to women. I told him to stay away from your mother, but he didn't listen. It could have meant war with Hibernia, threatened all he was striving to build. The use of my leg wasn't the only thing that back-stabbing Saxon cost me. I married your mother, claimed you as my own."

"I am your son." Fjorn spoke softly but with a certainty that could hold back the seas.

Geldnir smiled and hugged his son. "After your mother died of that fever, I thought it would never come up. Harald and his cursed jaw line, Jarl Erik recognised you. I need to get you away from him for your own protection." They continued towards the captured longships.

"I don't think I have to fear him." Fjorn looked back at the longhouse. "He seemed sad."

"He's see too much combat, son. You'll understand one day if you live long enough, but he isn't the only one to worry about. Gunnhild is a woman with a crown on her head who means to keep both. Hakon has proven a problem and she's not one to repeat mistakes."

"What should I do?"

"You've made a start. Make yourself too valuable. You need to be more than a karl's son, or a karl. You need to be a hero. Also, try to stay away from Jarl Erik and his wife. Out of sight, out of mind, and you don't want them thinking about you, and grow a proper beard, hide that jaw line." With this father and son reach the boarding plank of a small longship.

"May Odin walk with you and Aegir calm your seas." Geldnir hugged his son, slapping him hard on the back.

"Stay well, Father." Fjorn returned the hug then mounted the kravi.

Kjorn yelled orders to the ten-man crew as Fjorn stared through the murk at the only father he'd ever known.

Two hours later Fjorn leaned over the gunwale emptying his guts. The kravi pitched back and forth driven by a strong wind.

"That's a lad. Should be easier now that you've emptied out that special mead the jarl was tossing back. How he stays upright is a wonder." There was respect in Kjorn's voice.

Fjorn thought back to how 'generous' Erik had been with his mead horn and understood some of his sovereign's prodigious reputation for holding drink. "What's our course?"

"First to Kristiansand in Vestfold, then Soder in Gotaland, then Ekenas in Finnmark. A few other stops to sleep and take on fresh water, but those are the important ones. We've a bit of shopping to do for the queen in Ekenas. She wrote down the things we are to get."

"Where's the list?" Fjorn stepped away from the railing as Kjorn pulled a roll of hide from his belt-pouch and passed it to him.

Fjorn scanned the document. "I don't know what half of these things are. We'll have to find a Seithkona when we reach Finnmark to serve as a guide."

Kjorn went pale. "I'm not that taken with witch women."

Fjorn smiled. "People are people. You don't bite the hand giving you gold. We'll find someone who stays bought. The queen says we must complete the voyage and have her purchases in Alvaldsnes before the end of Haust-Manudr or we will be considered outlaw. Have you ever seen the capital?"

"I have, back when there was still sun and moon. It's a sight. Rivers flowed everywhere and bridges connected the buildings, but the most amazing thing was the castle. You'd think you were looking at a bastion in Asgard's wall. Stone cut smooth as ice; at least the height of five tall men lain end to end. Doors hewn from whole trees; stacked one on the next and bound with iron. Armies could break against it like the tide on the shore." The old sailor's eyes became far away.

"I'm glad I'll get to see it. I--." Fjorn's eyes widened. "Excuse me." Fjorn dove for the gunwale and vomited over the side.

Later he took his turn at the tiller and the ice watch before forcing down some dry journey bread and a tankard of weak mead. He then wrapped himself in his blanket on the deck and slept. He awoke to Kjorn shaking him.

"What?" demanded Fjorn.

"Light to starboard. I sounded the horn, but there wasn't any answer," said Kjorn.

"Show me." Fjorn stood and moved with his vassal to the ship's side.

"There."

Fjorn gazed at a spot of light on a hulking darkness that blocked the light of Muspelheim from the horizon. "It's too big to be a ship. Is it an iceberg?"

"Could be, but what about the light?"

"Take us closer."

"Is that wise? It could be a trap. We have a mission for the jarl, and the queen has us on a tight schedule." Kjorn sounded concerned.

Fjorn knew with a certainty that he had to go to that light. "It could be a shipwreck. We have a few days leeway. Cut our course."

Kjorn looked at his young captain and shook his head. "Can we at least arm ourselves?"

"Of course. And tell the helmsman to be ready to steer away."

Nearly an hour passed before they drew close enough to make out the vessel driven up on the iceberg. The light came from a fire burning in a brazier on its deck.

"See Kjorn. That could be a nice bit of skatt in both our purses if the cargo's intact." Fjorn slapped the older man on his shoulder.

"What I want to know is, what could drive a ship that far up on the ice?" Kjorn loosened his sword in its sheath.

"Storm?" suggested Fjorn.

"Too clean, the ship looks intact and--. FREYA'S TITS! It's a frost giant and a bloody polar bear!"

Fjorn and Kjorn stood open mouthed as a huge figure, dressed in a long cloak that barely reached the top of his thighs, with the hulking form of a polar bear beside him, threw wood on the fire and waved at them.

A voice reached them faintly across the water. "Over here. Hey, over here."

Fjorn looked from the unlikely pair to Kjorn.

The old sailor shook his head. "Don't ask me."

A moment later two cubs walked up to the polar bear. The man moved to a barrel on the deck and threw half a salt fish to the cubs.

"Prepare to board," Fjorn yelled out for lack of another clear action.

Minutes later they were tied off to the stern of the ship marooned on the iceberg. The boarding plank bridged the gap between the ships. Fjorn walked the plank jumping down onto the deck of the larger vessel.

"Welcome. Come aboard." The huge man approached with the bear at his side.

"I, umm. Is she yours?" Fjorn looked at the mound of white fur and muscle nervously.

The man glanced at the bear and smiled broadly. "Lady White, she's my friend. Opening his cloak he produced half a salt cod and tossed it back on the deck. With a gruffing sound Lady White followed the fish.

"I'm Audun. I was the navigator for this ship. Crusaders attacked." A shadow crossed Audun's features.

Fjorn followed the big man's gaze to a dark stained section on the ice below. "There were three crusaders there. I fear that Lady White may have added them to her food hoard while I was sleeping. In any case, I'm the only one left," finished Audun.

"Well, Audun Bear's Friend, I am Captain Fjorn. It's a good thing we saw your fire. Any foe of the crusaders is welcome among us. Who did you sail for?"

Audun stepped back his hand straying to something hidden by his cloak. "This is a ship of Jarl Erik Bloodaxe."

"As are we. What was your cargo?"

"A cargo more precious than gold." Audun gestured over the deck. "Food. Food enough for a village for a month, though those thieving crusaders took a good portion. Still in all, it's a rich cargo in these dark times."

Fjorn nodded. "We won't be able to fit it all, but we'll take what we can." He waved his men aboard. "Fill our ship, all we can safely carry." Gesturing Kjorn to the side he spoke softly. "Check this ship. Jarl Erik needs ships and if the hull is intact maybe we can get this one back in the water."

"And who's going to crew it," demanded Kjorn.

"I've checked the hull, it's intact. Five men could get her to a port in Jutland. Part of the cargo could hire on crew to take her to Alvaldsnes."

"We weren't speaking to you," snapped Kjorn.

"Still, we should have been. Why Jutland?" Fjorn turned to face Audun.

The big man shrugged. "The current is pulling that way and the wind will cooperate. It's easy sailing, and it's close."

"Why not go to Alvaldsnes direct?" challenged Kjorn.

"You'd have to fight the sea current. A ship this size; that would take more than a five man crew, even with a good wind, and you won't get them this time of year."

"You are a navigator?" Fjorn stroked the beginnings of a beard on his chin.

"Finest there is. I've sailed all the way to Vinland and back.

"If we can do it; we should do it. Audun, we could use a good navigator, so I'd like you to stay with us."

"My lord," objected Kjorn.

"My decision is made. Audun, stow your sea chest and charts aboard my ship."

The big navigator left to get his things and Fjorn turned to Kjorn. "Maybe he is what he says he is, maybe he isn't. But I'd rather keep my eyes on him until I'm sure."

Kjorn nodded. "There's something to be said for that."

"Good. When you pick five crewmen to man the salvage, make sure Bifindi and Forni are among them."

"Bifindi can't be trusted around mead on watch or off, I understand him, but why Forni?"

"Forni listens too much. He's always there when people talk. It makes me wonder who he passes things on to. Didn't you notice how my father made sure he had the watch while the jarl was visiting. Kept him out of ear shot. I'm not saying anything certain, but if my father thought it best not to trust him, I'll follow his lead."

"Right you are. So, how are we going to shift this ship?"

Hours later, a fire roared on the ice above the stranded vessel sending streams of water against the hull. Several piles of salt fish on the ice and the lack of oars in the larger ship suggested where the wood for the flames had come from. Lady White and her cubs watched curiously from a distance while the humans tied long ropes from the little ship to the large one. The little ship rode low in the water from cargo. The large ship was nearly empty and heavy chests covered the ice around it. Audun had insisted on painting rune's to shield the hull from harm along the ship's length.

"Now pull," yelled Fjorn.

Twelve oars bit into the sea. The smaller vessel sped away then jerked to a halt when it reached the end of the ropes.

"Back oar." Fjorn watched behind him as they pulled up behind the stranded craft.

"Pull!" he yelled. This time when the line jerked taught the larger vessel slid on the water slicked ice, pulling halfway into the sea.

"Back oar." Fjorn had sweat on his brow and felt the strain in his arms. "One more time. Pull!"

The crew pulled, the line played out as they gained momentum, then the line jerked taut and the ship slid into the water.

Transferring the crew and rigging the reserve sail on the large ship took minutes. Fjorn sailed away leaving the five crew men to reload the cargo from the iceberg. Lady White, content with her piles of fish, continued to watch benignly. Audun waved to her and she stood on her hind legs releasing a roar.

"Bear Friend indeed. What drove your ship up there?" asked Fjorn.

"Kraken."

All who heard shuddered.

"Worse, I think Hakon has a way to control the beasts."

"That's nonsense," interrupted Kjorn. "No one can control kraken. May-as-well try to control Jormungand itself."

"Believe me or not. I know what I saw." Audun moved to his oar station, wrapped himself in the too short crusaders' cloaks and settled himself to sleep.

They made their first port without further incident and traded some of the food they'd rescued for the service of two replacement sailors the local karl recommended.

As Fjorn suspected, after one night in the great hall with a barrel of mead taken from their cargo and liberally shared, not only was the rumour that Erik Bloodaxe would be there for Yule firmly planted, but he and his men were favoured guests of the karl, invited to return any time.

The next morning they took ship and followed the coast of Vestfold towards Rahrike.

Audun jerked out of a doze. The last notes of a terrifyingly familiar horn call were fading. He leapt to his feet and raced to Fjorn at the tiller.

"We have to move, now!" he snapped.

"And good morning to you."

"You don't understand. That horn, it's what calls the kraken."

Fjorn sighed. "Audun, nobody can command kraken. They're just animals, big scary animals but still--."

"You have to believe me. Is there another ship nearby?"

"Hold us steady." Fjorn passed Audun the tiller oar and stood up scanning the horizon. In the seaward middle-distance he saw a light like torches. "It looks like a ship."

"Please, you have to listen to me. Even if I am mad, we're on the start of the Volga Trade Route. These waters are favoured by pirates."

Fjorn looked at the vessel in the distance, stroking his stubbly beard as he thought. "I'd rather not run into anyone. All right, Navigator.

Show me how good you really are. Plot a course to some place we can hole up if those lights are unfriendly. I'll wake the crew."

Audun scanned the stars and horizon, then smelt the wind, "Set them to the oars. We might make a harbour in Rahrike I know of before they catch us." Holding the tiller with one hand Audun drew his battle axe and began tracing runes on the blade with his finger.

Minutes later, the longship sped through the water, eight men pulling on the oars and Audun manning the tiller.

"This is foolish. The giant has a nightmare and we have to row despite a fair wind," griped Kjorn.

"That ship I saw in the distance is coming closer. Maybe it's nothing, maybe it's something. But I'll not risk nine men against a full, longship's crew." Fjorn looked over the stern to where the lights from the other ship had grown in the darkness despite their haste. He was just about to look away when a tentacle snaked over the stern towards Audun.

"LOOK OUT!" Fjorn's voice carried through the night.

Audun threw himself to the deck as a kraken pulled itself half over the stern. Its tentacles flailed.

"Have at ye, spawn of Jormungand." Audun swung with his battle axe releasing the power he'd placed within it with in an explosive blast that drove the kraken off the stern.

"Draw blades," snapped Fjorn. A tentacle came up over midships threatening to topple the boat. He dove at the tentacle slashing it. Another tentacle waved over the stern trying to grab Audun who released the tiller oar and fended it off with his battle axe. The Kavi swerved to seaward.

"Keep us on course." Fjorn began to sing as he slashed at another tentacle.

"The Shields of Asgard are shields of might.
"Turn the wrath of giants to flight.
"Shields to hold a warrior's might.
"The Shields of Asgard are shields of might."

A shimmering dome covered Audun, holding the tentacles at

bay as he steered towards the shore line.

Kjorn hacked at a tentacle that sought to grip the tiller oar, loping the tip off. The other tentacles waved wildly as the crew drove at them with steel, leaving deep wounds. A tentacle lashed out grabbing a sailor around the neck and jerking him into the sea.

Fjorn swung his sword and stepped back. His legs came up against a barrel of salt cod they'd breached for snacking. Inspiration struck. Scooping out a handful of salt he threw it into one of the wounds on the kraken. The tentacle convulsed and vanished into the sea. "SALT ITS WOUNDS."

Kjorn followed his young captain's example. The tentacles retreated into the sea giving the crew a moment's respite.

"Stand ready, it will be back." Fjorn and the men watched the railing. A tentacle appeared, the end was hacked off and salt thrown on the open wound.

Minutes passed with only brief appearances of the tentacles.

"FREYA'S TITS! Look." Kjorn pointed over the stern.

A kraken, without wounds, crested the surface. The kraken they'd been fighting fell in beside it and the two sped towards the small ship.

Audun looked for the telltale light that would guide him into a safe harbour. When he'd nearly lost hope, he saw a flame well back from the coast. It had to be the right place. "Drop sail and man the oars," he bellowed.

"Get to it. Kjorn and I will hold the beasts back," ordered Fjorn.

The crew obeyed and the Kavi turned on side to the wind and headed into a v-shaped channel between cliffs of jagged rock.

The kraken closed the distance behind them. The rock channel narrowed and broke the wind. The men rowed for all they were worth. A tentacle reached over the stern of the boat. Fjorn slammed his blade down on it. Kjorn tossed salt into the wound. The bow of the Kavi grated on something and it shuddered to a halt. The kraken seized the boat and threw it forward over a long, shallow slope of ice. The crew dropped their oars and grabbed their weapons. The kraken pulled themselves up onto the ice, with their tentacles lashing.

Fjorn tried to strike one of the beasts. The water around him roared up creating a shield that deflected his blow. The kraken's tentacle swept towards him. At the last second, a red-haired man pounced onto the beast driving his long sword deep into the bulbous central body.

The beast thrashed its tentacles. Audun drove through the tentacles and buried his battle axe deep in the creature's body. Both men wrest their weapons free and the kraken slid towards deeper water.

Fjorn turned his attention to the other kraken, slashing off a tentacle. There was the distant sound of a muted horn. Both kraken shuddered then slid back into deep water and were gone.

"So, do you still say no one can control kraken?" Audun glared at Kjorn.

Fjorn turned to the red-haired man. "Thank you, I am Captain Fjorn. Do you have a fire we could warm ourselves by while we dry out? We have food to share."

#

Vidurr eyed the wet, dripping humans with disgust. Several wore the hammer of the Aesir assassin as pendants around their necks. He'd almost not come to their aid but it had felt like he had no choice. They were the first ship by since the Norn had recruited him, and he needed to get on with his vengeance.

"Village is gone, crusaders. Fire's in the grove." Vidurr started across the snow up the valley.

"Secure the ship and be quick. We need to dry off." All worked to hall the ship further up the ice then, taking supplies from the stores, they followed Vidurr's tracks.

Audun moved up to Fjorn's side and began to speak. "I should warn you. This village, well... they followed Surt."

Fjorn held his breath for a long count of seconds before speaking. "Surt, well. Right now the gods can do what they like. We need a fire before we freeze to death, and our friend there has one. Besides, did you hear his voice when he spoke about crusaders?"

"Just be careful."

They climbed the trail to the sacred grove. The broken statue was pieced together and stood in its proper place. A huge, red wolf prowled around the fire and snarled at the sailors as they approached.

Fjorn and his crew all clutched their weapons. Audun motioned for them to stand back and walked into the clearing, speaking as he approached. "Very nice, friend. I visited your village before. Svafnir displayed his skill for me. He was a great man, and an impressive wolf. I'm Audun. Please, it is easier to speak as men."

The wolf seemed to consider, howled and Vidurr stood by the fire. "Are you an Aesir lover?"

"I follow Odin, but I judge no man by his god. Please, we are cold and wet."

Vidurr snorted but gestured towards his fire.

CHAPTER 3

GIRL'S A RAVEN

Sigurlina stood shivering just inside the entrance to a great hall that had been turned into an inn. The first few feet of the hall had been divided by a wall with a door in it. A bald man, with a red beard and arms that were thicker than her neck, blocked the doorway. The entry area was warmer than outside, but not by much.

"It's two hundred skatt for a place in the common and a meal," repeated the man.

"I only need a place to sleep, I won't eat anything," pleaded Sigurlina.

"Well, that's different. That will be two hundred skatt, and you can choose not to eat." The big man sneered at her. Or you can try your luck with the braids. Two days food and shelter for an hour's work. The man gestured towards a thick board with a hole cut in its centre.

Sigurlina could see the shade of a wasted-looking, young woman beside the board. Half her black braids were hacked short, the others stood out as if pinned away from her head.

"Don't do it. Find another way," pleaded the shade.

Sigurlina looked longingly into the inn. A fire burnt in the central pit with a cauldron of something that smelt like mutton stew over it. An old woman in tattered clothing ladled the stew into bowls that the various guests brought to her. On a table to one side there was bread, carefully portioned.

"Please, I'll freeze. I only just got into town. I don't have anyplace to go."

"If you aren't going to pay, or work the braids, leave," the big man snarled at Sigurlina.

Sigurlina stared through the door longingly. Support pillars threw up long shadows against the wall of the private chambers on the far end of the room. Someone screamed and the man in the door turned his back to watch two women fall to the ground wrestling and cursing. He still blocked the door. The wall cast a shadow beside her.

"Grandmother, please don't let me make a mess of this."

Focusing her skill Sigurlina stepped into the shadow by the door and out of the one cast by a support pillar. She shuddered and felt dizzy; tipping to lean against the pillar. A man lurched by, obviously into his cups. Sigurlina focused her will on him. The man collapsed, much to the amusement of those around him.

"That was good. He's the one that got me," said the shade who'd been by the braiding board.

"I'm glad it was him then." Sigurlina revelled in the warmth from the fire.

"I'm Munin, like Odin's raven. My father always said I was his memory of my mother. She died giving me life." The shade stared at the floor.

"I'm sorry. I'm called Sigurlina," she whispered, afraid that people would see her talking to herself.

"You can get some food now. Brunn, the one at the door, he's half blind. He'll not recognise you now that you're inside."

"I shouldn't. I just needed to get warm. If I ate, it would really be stealing."

The shade rolled her eyes. "I'll let you have the meal I was entitled to. I stood there for almost an hour with people throwing axes and knives at my hair before that drunken fool missed."

Sigurlina considered, but the smell coming from the cauldron was too enticing. Setting her staff to one side she fished her bowl and spoon out of her pack and walked up to the cauldron. The old woman ladled a helping into her bowl saying. "Don't forget your bread dearry. One piece to a customer."

"And half of it sawdust, you old bat," added Munin.

#

Ragna watched the young woman in a ragged, too small, dress and tattered, thin cloak step out of the shadows at the back of the hall's common. The young woman leaned against the pillar and gestured at Ragna's meal ticket, who had gone to buy more mead. The man collapsed, apparently passed out from drink.

The ragged, young woman seemed to speak with herself then went to get food. Intrigued Ragna moved quietly closer to her.

#

"Then my father died and I didn't have any skatt. Our farm is nothing but ice and snow. I was starving, so I agreed to play the Game of Braids and that was the life of Munin. Named for a memory; now just a memory." Munin's shade chattered on to Sigurlina as the girl found an open space on the platform surrounding the hall's dirt floor. Taking a wooden plate from her pack Sigurlina put half a spoon of stew on the plate and a few crumbs of bread.

"Oh thank you, that is so nice. No one here ever makes an offering, and it's not as if you have to give much to a shade, and we really appreciate it."

Sigurlina half listened as Munin nattered on. "Do you know anything about ships that come in?" she finally interrupted.

"Who are you talking to?" asked a woman so small she could be mistaken for a child except for her shapely form.

"Me? I... well." Sigurlina stuttered.

"I'm Ragna. Neat trick stepping out of the shadows." Ragna dropped her tone. "Is that a Seith thing?"

"I ahh." Sigurlina knew the fear her kind could instil in some, and the violence that fear could lead to.

Ragna stood silently watching Sigurlina.

"Don't trust her, she's trouble. In here with a different man every night, them buying her food and drinks," warned Munin.

"I'm not going to make trouble for you. I thought you'd like to talk to someone other than yourself." Ragna sat down straight through Munin. "Do you feel a chill?"

"I... err... You just sat where Munin was. I mean..." Sigurlina trailed off.

"The girl that played the braids last week. Tell her I'm sorry. So, you are a Seith?" Ragna whispered the last.

"I..." Sigurlina bit her lip. "Yes."

"You, how'd you get in here?" Brunn loomed over the two women.

"Sorry, I guess he isn't as blind as I thought," said Munin, who stood behind the big man.

Ragna leapt to her feet her head barely reaching the middle of Brunn's chest. "Brummy, now don't be like that." She pouted up at him and toyed with the front of his tunic. "This is my friend. Jolnir paid Fjola for her before he passed out. He thought the three of us could play in one of the private rooms."

The big man looked suspicious. Ragna's free had vanished between them and his face went red.

"Fine," his voice was high. He cleared his throat. "Fine, as long as she's paid up." Turning, he walked back to the door.

"That will do. A real Seithkona. Can you see any spirits around me?" Ragna returned her attention to Sigurlina.

"I... only Munin. I'm sorry, were you hoping for someone?"

Ragna sighed. "It was silly. He's probably in Valhalla. So, where are you from, and what brings you to Ekenas?"

The women talked then curled up on the platform surrounding the fire to sleep. The hall was noisy, but exhaustion coupled with the warm air and full belly drove Sigurlina into unconsciousness. She awoke to the sound of raised voices.

"Where is it? Where's the necklace?"

Sigurlina opened her eyes to see a short, powerfully-built, bald man holding Ragna by the arms and shaking her.

"Where is it? Thought we'd give up did you? It will be a long time before we forget your thieving. Tell me where it is, or by Davlin, I'll shake the life right out of you."

"I don't have it." Ragna's voice was harsh and she looked dishevelled as if she'd been caught sleeping.

"That's Ginnarr. He and his brother run a smithy across town. I tried to get work there since they don't have a woman in the house, but I didn't want to do the kind of woman's work they wanted me to do," remarked Munin. "I guess she'll be company at least."

Sigurlina quietly donned her pack, picked up her staff, wiped the sleep from her eyes and took a deep breath. Mentally she opened a passage into the essence of the nine realms. She could feel the spirit of the smith being pulled towards the vortex and at the same time felt the dregs of her exhaustion fall away.

Ginnarr released one of Ragna's arms and rubbed the back of his neck glancing around nervously. "I... What are you all looking at? She stole from me!"

"You could just take the loss like a man. It was your brother who wanted to fight. I just wanted to know who was first. He's the one who thought he was better than you." Ragna eased her arm out of Ginnarr's grip.

"I...You'll still pay up?" Ginnarr stared at the diminutive trickster.

"Well, you did scare me; the two of you fighting like that." Ragna pouted. Just then Dorrund burst into the hall. "You found the little thief, good!" He stomped towards Ragna.

"Time to go." Sigurlina grabbed Ragna's arm. Ragna snatched her cloak off the platform and they both bolted behind a support pillar. All the shadows in the hall seemed to deepen and darken, creating pools of blackness where vision was useless.

"You let her get away!" snapped Dorrund as he dove into the shadow Sigurlina had pulled Ragna into. The women emerged on the far side of the pillar and raced over the blanket shrouded forms on the platform to the next shadow.

"She said she'd--," began Ginnarr.

"She lied! Get her." Dorrund ran after the women stepping on guests who were rudely woken. A fist flew out catching the smith between the legs as he straddled a recumbent form.

"I paid good skatt for a warm place to sleep and a bite that wasn't ship's fare, and you woke me up, you bugger!"

Dorrund collapsed to his knees clutching himself as a vaguely human-shaped mound of muscle threw off its blankets and stood towering over him.

Ginnarr threw himself on his brother's attacker causing him to trip over another man on the platform. The next man rose aiming a punch at the sailor.

"We better go." Ragna whispered into Sigurlina's ear as they emerged from another pool of shadow. The inn was fast degrading into pandemonium as others joined the fray. Ragna led the way towards the door pausing only to snatch a half-eaten bowl of stew and a money pouch that someone had carelessly left in their path. The brawl was in full swing and Brunn was cracking heads in an effort to restore order when they slipped into the cold darkness of Ekenas' streets.

"Bergelmir freeze it. That was the last inn in town where I was welcome. Let's see what we got." Ragna passed the bowl to Sigurlina. "Help yourself." She opened the purse. "A piece of journey bread and seven skatt. Not worth the trouble." Pulling out the journey bread she tied the purse to her belt.

"You stole that," breathed Sigurlina.

"I told you she was no good," Munin chimed in.

"You can leave the inn?" breathed Sigurlina.

"Who are you talking to? We better keep moving. Get away from the brothers stupid." Ragna led the way down the street and Sigurlina fell in beside her.

"I was talking to Munin. She's still with us."

"I like you. I never had a reason to leave the inn before, but you're fun. Her, well at least she isn't boring." Munin stared at Ragna.

"I don't think it's good for you to be away from the place that, well, from the inn. You need something to link onto so you don't become a Haugbui."

"Talking to the ghost again? Hair cut girl, I'm not judging, but you might like to ship your oars when Siggy is with the living. People will think it's strange her talking to herself."

"Siggy?" Sigurlina sounded confused.

"Sure. We need to leave this town. I've got a reputation, and with Dorrund and Ginnarr chasing me, I need to put some sea miles between me and them. Have you ever been to Alvaldsnes? A couple of smart women could do all right there. Land a government official, or maybe one of the jarl's guardsmen. What do you say?"

"I don't know about the capital, but I need to go to the docks," agreed Sigurlina.

"Siggy, this could be the start of something beautiful. So, can you get spirits to tell you things, like where they hid their skatt? I mean, they don't have any use for it, and..."

Ragna led the way through the maze of Ekenas' streets eventually coming to the docks.

"No ships. Well, that's bad luck." Ragna stated when they could clearly see the three long piers thrusting out into the dark, icy sea.

"There are lots of ships." Sigurlina pointed at the six small craft flanking one of the piers.

"Those are just the local fishermen. They'll not take you further than a village or two up the coast, and they all smell like codfish. Most of them love their wives, so it's not worth trying." Ragna felt like someone was watching her and glanced around. "We need to go."

"Where?" Sigurlina sniffed the air. "There's a storm coming."

"You can smell weather. Is that a Seith thing?" Ragna eyed her companion.

"When you live in a barrow mound for three years you pick some things up. We're going to need shelter."

"What part of, I need to get out of town, didn't you understand?" Ragna rolled her eyes.

"I know a place," offered Munin.

"Where?" asked Sigurlina.

"It's my old farm. It's only a few miles away. If we put on a fire you could last out a storm, and I have some clothes and things there that you might like. Your dress is awfully tight. When I first saw you I thought you were like her." Munin glowered at Ragna.

"Munin knows a place we can wait out the storm. Maybe when it's over a ship will have come in."

Ragna glanced around nervously. "I guess it's better than waiting for idiot one and idiot two to find me." Sighing, she led the way to the gate in the palisade that guarded the town's landward side. They exited Ekenas onto a well trodden trail but soon turned up a side path that was little more than a series of prints made by snowshoes. This path sloped steeply up and the air seemed to grow colder with every step. Dead trees closed in and snow started drifting down.

"It's colder than Niflheim. We should go back to town," grumbled Ragna.

Sigurlina hugged herself, shivered and answered through chattering teeth, "You're the one who had to leave town."

"I didn't say I wanted to freeze. I can't see where to walk. Are you sure that ghost of yours isn't just trying to get us killed to keep her company."

"She's mean!" Munin came back along the trail oblivious to the snow.

"I can maybe help with the light." Sigurlina dropped to one knee, set her staff aside, shucked her pack, and opened the bag extracting a candle lantern with a tallow candle and a tinder box. Digging a depression in the snow to break the wind, she laid a metal plate in the bottom and piled some dried pine twigs on the plate. A few seconds working with flint and steel and the tinder caught. She lit her candle from the small flame and took a moment to warm her freezing fingers near the fire.

"Wonderful, we have a hearth, now what about a house."

"I could probably build us a shelter to get us through the storm."

"It's just a little farther. Trust me," pleaded Munin.

"We should go just a little farther. I can always kindle a fire from the candle." Sigurlina shouldered her pack and picked up her lantern.

"Just a little farther, just a little farther, and freezing our nips off all the way," griped Ragna.

A hundred strides later the path opened onto a large barren of hard-packed snow. There was a dark mound in the middle of the field. Clouds blocked the light of the stars leaving only the distant flames of Muspelheim and the candle lantern for vision.

"That's home," squealed Munin. "Come this way." She strode off through the thickening snow fall.

"We should gather firewood while we're close to the trees," suggested Sigurlina.

"I wish there was a big, strong woodsman to help," grumbled Ragna.

"I found it, and it's full." Munin shot out of a snow drift right in front of Sigurlina who stumbled back and fell onto her butt.

"Don't do that," Sigurlina's voice had a harsh timber.

Munin backed away an axe wound appearing on her forehead. "I'm sorry," she pleaded.

Sigurlina stood clutching her tattered, too small cloak about her. "Forgiven. What did you find?"

The axe wound vanished. "You'll like it. Over here." Munin led the way a little into the woods then pointed down.

A raven, with its foot caught in a wire snare, stared up at Sigurlina its black eyes clouded and its body shivering.

"Did I do good? Did I?" pleaded the ghost.

"Yes." Sigurlina bent and picked up the bird carefully loosening the snare on its foot.

"My father set the snares before... Well before. Now, you can eat and maybe make an offering and--."

"What you got there?" Ragna walked up carrying a bundle of sticks.

"The answer to a problem." Sigurlina tried to smile, but it felt like the cold was eating her alive. Bracing herself she took off her cloak and wrapped the large bird in it.

"Looks like the problem's dinner and what to have." Ragna licked her lips.

"I have wolf meat in my pack. We should get to the cottage."

"What else is a bird good for?" demanded Ragna as they trudged across the barren field. Reaching the cottage they found that snow had drifted in to bury everything but the door and the peak of the thatched roof. Sigurlina cradled the bird and tried to stay out of the bitter wind as Ragna checked that the building was safe. In minutes, they were both inside the cottage. It was a single room with a raised platform around a central fire pit. The light from the candle lantern showed the tools of daily life. Ragna closed the door while Sigurlina laid the bird on the raised platform and collapsed shivering.

"There are blankets in the chest near the wall," advised Munin.

"B b b blankets," stuttered Sigurlina through chattering teeth, as she pointed to a wooden chest.

Ragna opened the chest and wrapped the younger woman in a heavy wool blanket. She then turned to the fire pit.

"The snow is falling harder and we didn't bring enough wood." Ragna complained as she set the kindling.

"There's a wood store under the sleeping platform. I left because there was no food, not because I was lazy," snapped Munin.

"Under ppp platform wood," Sigurlina passed on.

"You can take or use whatever you want. I thought it would be nice to come home, that maybe my papa would be... but he isn't. I hope he went some place nice." Munin seemed to shimmer and fade and grow pale. Blood seemed to ooze from her forehead and her braids waved wildly.

Sigurlina felt exhaustion claw at her as she shivered in the blankets. "Ragna, m m m make the f f fire q q quick."

"What do you think I'm doing? What's the hurry?" demanded Ragna.

"Munin is about t t to t t turn into a Haugbui unless s s she is f f f fixed to m m Midgard by a n n new b b b body." Sigurlina forced herself to stand, clutching the blanket around herself and moved to the half-frozen raven. She stroked its head with a trembling hand. "It w w won't be so b b bad. You were going to f f freeze anyway." Remembering back to when she was a little girl and her mother had shown her the spell, Sigurlina forced herself to stop shivering. "Munin, will you serve me? Will you live again and know the joys and pains of flesh, embracing a new form and destiny?"

"A Haugbui! Odin's beard, what have you gotten us into?" snapped Ragna as she set wood for a fire.

"It's so cold. I'm hungry. I want to..." hissed Munin.

"She who was Munin in life. Will you pledge to me and escape the shadow realm between realms?" Sigurlina fought to keep her voice steady despite her teeth trying to chatter.

"Is ghost girl going to try and eat us?" Ragna lit a taper from the candle and thrust it into the kindling at the base of her set wood.

"Answer me," snapped Sigurlina.

"I will." Munin now looked like a transparent corpse with glowing red eyes.

The dry kindling caught and flared up sending a wavering light through the cottage.

"Two I now make one. Spirits joined, minds conjoined. Fuel from a fire smothered, kindled in a new hearth. Be one and now be mine!"

The shadows inside the hut swallowed the light from the fire. Regna shuddered as the temperature seemed to drop and a sound like the wailing of mourners hovered on the edge of hearing.

"Squawk." The raven stood up on the platform. The light from the fire drove back the shadows, and warmth crept back into the room.

Sigurlina lay on the platform shivering and teeth chattering. The raven hopped to her side and gently began grooming her hair with its beak.

"Maybe making friends with a witch woman wasn't such a good idea," whispered Ragna.

"Yura bitch," squawked the Raven.

"I never," Ragna glared at the bird.

"That's a lie." Sigurlina heard Munin's voice in her mind as she plummeted into unconsciousness.

As the fire chased the worst of the cold from the cottage, Ragna inspected her surroundings. In the corner she found an iron tripod with a cauldron hanging from it. Minutes passed as she pulled it over the fire then taking a pail she also found, opened the door. Arctic winds blasted in bearing a burden of snow. She scooped up a bucket of snow and put it in the cauldron. Five more buckets and the cauldron was full and she closed the door. The raven watched her the entire time.

"Hot water for drinking, and, I don't know about you, but I could use a wash."

"Use a wash, use a wash," croaked the raven nodding its head.

The snow in the cauldron melted and Ragna banked the fire. Sigurlina lay like death under her blanket. Her skin was still icy to the touch.

Taking another blanket from the chest Ragna spread it over Sigurlina and crawled in beside her. Minutes later she fell asleep to the howling of the wind.

Sigurlina woke to find Ragna pressed tight against her. The storm still howled outside, but the banked fire lent the cottage a pleasant warmth. Rising she felt an ach in her bones.

"Munin," she whispered.

The raven opened a beady, black eye and Munin's voice commented in her mind. "I'm a bird."

Sigurlina shrugged. "It's better than dead, isn't it?"

The raven regarded her speculatively. "You warmed up?"

"For now."

"Look in the chests."

Sigurlina moved to a large, wooden chest and opened it revealing a dress, old boots and a belt. Lifting these out revealed a heavy cloak.

"That's my third best dress. I wore the first and carried the second when I left, and my papa's cloak. You won't have to freeze anymore."

Sigurlina clutched the garments to herself overwhelmed by a sense of gratitude to the shade that was now her familiar.

"Can I have some meat?" asked the voice in Sigurlina's mind.

Opening her pack Sigurlina pulled out a long strip of the semi-dried wolf meat and passed it to the raven who gobbled it.

"Are you going to give all our food to that black chicken?" Ragna asked from her covers.

"Munin is my familiar, and she..." Sigurlina looked at the raven, which comically tried to look under itself and tipped over rolling onto its back.

Ragna rolled her eyes and shook her head.

"I meant to do that." Munin commented in Sigurlina's thoughts. "I'm pretty sure it's still she. How do you tell with ravens?"

"We'll go with she until someone says differently." Sigurlina fished another piece of wolf meat out of her bag and gave it to Munin. "Munin needs to eat too, and she's given me a new dress."

"Not like she could stop you taking it." Ragna sat up. "So, do humans get to eat too?"

"We should make a stew. The broth will help us keep warm," Sigurlina glanced into the cauldron. Most of the water was gone leaving it maybe a quarter full.

"So get cooking, I'm hungry," grumbled Ragna.

"Yura bitch," commented the raven for all to hear.

The women passed the time by eating the wolf stew then heating water for washing. Sigurlina donned the new clothes, finding that they mostly fit.

"You look good," commented Ragna as Sigurlina tried to see herself in the water warming in the cauldron.

"I... I haven't had a new dress in three years. I just kept letting out the old one and patching it with bits of an old blanket we found. Do I really look nice?"

Ragna smiled. "At least, with some room to breathe, you don't look like a twelve-summers-old boy anymore."

Sigurlina ran her hand down her slender, athletic form with its subtle curves. "I... I don't feel like a twelve-summers-old boy anymore either." She pulled a lock of her long hair, loose after washing, forward. It was the colour of barley honey.

"Sit down. I'll braid it for you." Ragna patted the platform beside her.

"Thanks."

"Keep yura braids. Keep yura braids," cackled the raven.

"Don't worry, Munin, I intend to." Sigurlina sat in front of Ragna.

They slept again and when they awoke the storm was done. Taking snow shoes that were too large for her from a hook on the wall, Sigurlina opened the cottage door. Snow had drifted waist-high in front of it.

"I can't get through that. It's as tall as I am," Ragna griped.

Munin swept out of the cottage cawing and flew over the snow fields.

"Good riddance. Now, how am I supposed to get back to town?" Ragna glowered at the fast vanishing bird.

"Put on the skies we found." Using the bucket, Sigurlina began scooping out a ramp into the snow that she could climb. The feel of the new thick cloak around her was as heady as mead.

"One problem. Town girl, remember? I don't know how to ski." Ragna threw her hood up so her face was lost in shadow.

Sigurlina sighed. "Put them on. I'll use the snow shoes and pull you."

Sigurlina completed her ramp. Using her old dress twisted around itself as a rope she started across the field using her staff for balance and towing Ragna.

"This isn't so bad," said Ragna.

Sigurlina grit her teeth and decided not to comment as she trudged forward. Munin circled in the air, then landed on Sigurlina's shoulder and spoke into her mind. "The snow looks shallower once you reach the trees and there's a ship pulling into the harbour. If you hurry, you should reach the docks about the same time they do."

They trudged to the town's gate where they slipped in behind a trapper entering with a load of pelts. They reached the docks just as a small longship was finishing tying up.

Sigurlina scanned the crew. A huge man, clad in a too short crusader's cloak, was securing the bowline. A burly man with weathered features sat in the stern scowling at everything. The third man; Sigurlina's breath caught. It was the face from her dream.

"It looks like they're in with the crusaders. We better not get involved." Ragna grasped Sigurlina's shoulder when she didn't respond. "Are you listening? I don't think--."

"Munin, fly over and listen to what they are saying." Sigurlina couldn't take her eyes off the man from her dreams. He had a light beard growing in over a chiselled jaw, noble features and a powerful bearing for one so young.

Munin flew over and landed on the gunwale of the boat.

\#

"I still think we should have gone straight to Alvaldsnes once you believed me about the kraken," grumbled Audun.

"You don't want to be disappointing a queen," countered Kjorn. "Especially a witch-woman queen. Any other order I'd have said telling the king was more important, but who knows what magic her majesty is cooking up. For all our sakes, it's best to get her the ingredients and be done with it."

"That and the jarl is no more likely to believe our story than we were to believe yours. The idea that someone could summon kraken takes a lot of getting use to. I need time to think about how I'm going to convince him, and that would be harder with the queen speaking against us because we failed in our assigned task. We need to find someone who knows enough about Seith to get us the ingredients then get back to the capital. That storm cost us time we didn't have." Fjorn rubbed the back of his neck as if easing stiff muscles. "Kjorn, you and the men take a keg of mead, a crate of dried meat and five of those dried apples and find us food and lodging. Make sure there is a private room for me. For the price of those apples we could buy half this town. Audun, you're with me."

Munin launched herself from the ship's gunwale and flew back to land on Sigurlina's shoulder. "They need a Seithkona to buy things for the queen, and then they're going to Alvaldsnes."

"We should go." Ragna tugged on Sigurlina's cloak.

"They're going to Alvaldsnes and they need a Seithkona to help them shop. This couldn't be better." Sigurlina stared at her diminutive friend.

"Really, Alvaldsnes? Small boat for that, but if it gets me away from here. That sure is a big one in the crusader's cloak. I wonder if everything is proportional."

Sigurlina wrinkled her brow. "His hands and feet look about right for his size. What else?" The mocking smile on Ragna's lips stilled her words and brought a blush to her cheeks.

"So, go talk to them. You're the Seith." Ragna pushed her friend towards the pier and fell into step behind her.

"How do you go about finding a witch woman?" asked Fjorn.

"You could try asking nicely," Sigurlina stepped onto the pier.

CHAPTER 4

DEAD MAN'S BLADE

Fjorn turned his gaze on the two women and felt his world narrow. The one with the raven on her shoulder and the staff in one hand was tall, thin and elegant with strongly sculpted features and hair the colour of barley honey. He cleared his throat as his natural instinct took over. "Hello, and who might you be?"

Sigurlina looked at the way the handsome stranger eyed her. A blush rose to her cheeks and her stomach did flip flops. "I... I'm Sigurlina, and..." She paused for a long moment then said in a rush. "I'm a Seithkona. I mean, I know about... I... well."

An elbow to the ribs saved Sigurlina from the need to speak as Ragna pushed forward. "What my friend means is she can help you find what you need, if the price is right?" She threw her hood back and smiled up at the men.

"This seems too convenient," cautioned Kjorn. "We need a witch woman and one just happens to be waiting at the docks."

"My raven saw your ship coming in and we came to meet it." Sigurlina's voice was small and it looked like she was trying to hide behind Ragna's tiny form.

"That's right. My friend is one of the best. She listened to the breezes in Yggdrasil's branches and knew that you'd need her here and now. What more proof do you need that she's a powerful practitioner of the arts? I'll tell you, you won't find better anywhere in Midgard."

"We just need someone to do some shopping, and we're in a hurry," blurted Audun.

"Then, why waste time looking for what you already have? What do you need?" Ragna smiled broadly.

"We have a list." Fjorn held out the shaved hide the queen had given them.

Sigurlina blushed and looked at the dock. "I can't read," her voice was small.

"Who can? An unnecessary skill for a Seithkona. Magic isn't reading." Ragna grinned up at the men.

"Allow me." Audun stepped forward and took the parchment.

"A barrel of Yddrasil's bloody gems."

"That's Ash berries." Sigurlina grunted as Ragna elbowed her in the ribs.

"That was just a demonstration. To show our good faith. Keep reading."

"A box of corpse skin, two cases of Hel's flowers, a crate of Invaldi's compassion."

Sigurlina nodded. "I can get all of those."

"Why don't you prove yourself by getting that much for us?" said Fjorn.

"It will be difficult and expensive," blurted Ragna.

"Ragna, enough." Sigurlina looked at her friend. "To get you what you're asking I want passage for the two of us."

Munin squeaked.

"I'm sorry, the three of us, to Alvaldsnes. That includes shelter, food and everything."

"And a thousand skatt," blurted Ragna.

"I don't know," began Fjorn.

"For what you've said so far you can forget the skatt." Sigurlina petted her Raven's head and stared at the men.

"Siggy, we need to talk," began Ragna.

"Deal," said Fjorn.

"Swear by Mjolnir," added Ragna.

"I swear by Mjolnir and by my blood," Fjorn smiled. "Now, my lovely, young enchantress, how long will you need to obtain the test items?"

Sigurlina blushed crimson. "Come with me and bring your purse." She started walking towards a building on the landward end of the pier.

Ragna ran to Sigurlina's side. "Do you mind telling me what you're doing? I had them. They would have paid good skatt."

"They're taking us to Alvaldsnes. I don't want them mad with us. What kind of trip would that be? Besides, this is just a test. There's still the rest of the list. So shush."

Sigurlina led the way into a spice shop and waited while Fjorn and Audun picked up heavy looking boxes from the ship and followed her in. They entered to find a small, burly man standing behind a counter. Barrels, some open, some not, covered the floor.

The man's eyes tracked up Audun's form. "Aegir! What did they feed you? Sorry. What do you need?"

Fjorn and Audun set down the crates they were carrying.

"A barrel of Ash berries, a box of white birch bark, two cases of stewing lichens and a crate of dried, reindeer testicles," answered Sigurlina.

"You're in luck. We have a special on reindeer testicles today. Thirteen skatt off the regular price when you buy a case or more. Will that be all?" The storekeeper began collecting the items.

"No, I'll need some other items if you have them." Fjorn read aloud from his list.

The shopkeep scurried happily around the floor collecting items. "I'm fresh out of Snow Serpent hides, but I'm sure if you go to Svafnir's furs he'll have some. I don't deal directly with trappers. Will this be skatt or barter?"

"How much in skatt?" Fjorn drummed his fingers on the top of the crate he'd carried in.

The shop keep puckered his lips. "All told three thousand and that's me giving you a break on the reindeer testicles mind."

"And if we barter?" Fjorn smiled and opened the crate he'd carried in. "Salt walrus meat from the land of the Skraelings across the Great Sea."

The shopkeep walked up and examined the case. "Looks like reindeer to me."

Fjorn's voice went cold. "Are you calling Fjorn, son of Karl Geldnir of Orkney a liar?"

The shopkeep looked into the younger man's face and swallowed hard. "No, my lord. Just making an observation."

Fjorn smiled and warmth crept back into his voice. "Very well. I will agree, it does look like reindeer, but it is walrus."

The shopkeeper nodded. "I'll trade even for three cases."

"Done. I'll tell my man to let your people take another case when you deliver our order. We're on the far right pier."

"Very good, sir." The shopkeep opened the second crate and took out a haunch of salt meat inspecting it."

"For reindeer testicles we sailed a week." Fjorn shook his head.

"It could have been worse." Sigurlina smiled at him.

"How?" asked Fjorn, grinning for no reason.

"I could have let Ragna do all the talking."

"Oh, thank you very much, I'm sure." Ragna looked up from examining a jewelled dagger hung on the wall.

"Now will you trust me with the rest of your list?" Sigurlina faced Fjorn as he picked up his packages.

"There was only one more item I didn't recognise. Karl Hovi's dagger."

There was a thump as the shopkeeper dropped a haunch of salt meat.

"Freya protect us!" Sigurlina went pale and made the sign against evil.

"Who and what now?" Ragna exploited the shopkeeper's inattention to snatch a handful of dried nuts out of a barrel and put them in her pouch.

"Get out!" ordered the shopkeeper. "I'll deliver your order, but I don't serve dead men in my store. Get out!"

They exited into the street.

"What did I say?" Fjorn stared at Sigurlina.

"It's a story my grandmother told me, but I won't speak of it in the dark and cold." Sigurlina hugged herself despite her new, warm cloak.

Fjorn read her features and saw real fear.

"She's right. There are tales that should only be told in places of light and warmth." Audun towered over his companions, but in the eternal night, he seemed more a bastion of strength than an imposing threat.

"Let us go to the inn. You can buy a lady a drink and a bite," Ragna leaned into the big man.

"Very well. Your story, in exchange for a hot meal and a warm place to sleep," agreed Fjorn. "I'll tell Vidurr that the delivery is coming. I worry about him. He hasn't spent one night inside since he joined us."

"It is the way of wolves," commented Audun.

Minutes later, they sat in a back corner of the inn where Ragna and Sigurlina met. A few skatt had abolished the memory of earlier events. The inn's finest fare now filled their bowls and drinking horns.

"Tell us your grandmother's story," insisted Fjorn.

Sigurlina nodded, but her lips were thin and her cheeks pale. Her voice trembled despite the warmth of the room.

"Years ago, there was a karl of Finnmark named Hovi. He was a wicked man who, unwilling to make the sacrifices it takes to learn the ways of Seith Magic, captured true Seithkona and tortured them for their secrets. It was said that he even bound an Angel of Death with his Dark Arts. He died a straw death after falling off his horse while hunting to supply his feast hall. So depraved was he that his prey only had two legs.

"Hel decided he was too evil for Niflheim, so she pressed him into her service as a draugar. As a walking corpse, he terrorised the living, bringing ruin to all, blighting the crops and leaving destruction in his wake until a hero born of the line of Frey rose up to challenge the beast.

"For seven days and seven nights, they fought until the champion cast down the monster. As the draugar fell, it thrust its Niflheim ore dagger into the champion, sending him to Valhalla. The champion's beloved was a Seithkona. She took that dagger and sequestered it in a hidden cave behind powerful enchantments so that not even the servants of Hel could reach it."

Fjorn sighed. "The queen has given me an imposable task. When we reach Alvaldsnes, I will be made an outlaw, at best."

"It's not impossible. The practitioners of Seith, in this area, have always known where the cave is. The energy within hums to us and cannot be hidden. The danger is that when the dagger is taken out of the cave the draugar will sense it and seek to retrieve their property. That, and the bats that live in the cave." Sigurlina pulled her robe tight as Munin rubbed the underside of his beak over her mistress's scalp.

"Draugar. Well, good luck. Been nice knowing you. Thanks for the food," said Ragna. "Siggy, let's go. There will be other ships."

"It is foolhardy." Audun stared into his mead cup.

Kjorn looked at Fjorn. "The queen wants you dead."

"Why would she?" demanded Audun.

"Reasons that are not my fault, but they are reasons none the less. I have to try," said Fjorn.

"Siggy, come on." Ragna waited, staring at her young friend.

"There might be a way. How fast is your ship?" Sigurlina asked.

"Angrboda's bouncing tits! What are you getting us into now?" Ragna slumped onto the platform.

After sleeping, Fjorn traded for the snow serpent hides then carefully picked through the stores of food he carried keeping back just enough for a full crew, two women and a raven to make Alvaldsnes, trading the rest. Ten stout men accustomed to rowing joined his crew filling out the ship's complement. The queen's cargo was stored leaving the ship light and high in the water.

Sigurlina sat on the bed in one of the inn's private rooms running her hands over an oak box about as long as her forearm. Munin stood on the back of a chair dozing in the warmth.

"This is madness! We're going to steal a draugar's dagger and let one of Hel's servants chase us all the way to Alvaldsnes because you think the karl's son is cute." Ragna settled on the straw mattress but kept fidgeting.

"You wanted to go to the capital, and they are paying us six thousand skatt, and who said I thought he was cute?" Sigurlina continued to inspect the box.

"Please," Ragna rolled her eyes.

"It might not be just one." Sigurlina kept stroking the box.

"One what?" demanded Ragna.

"One draugar. In the stories they come together to get back their equipment. Or maybe we'll be lucky and there won't be any around. We might reach the capital before they catch us."

"Lucky." Ragna buried her head in the blankets. "If I was that lucky, I'd still be a karl's daughter. Tell me again why I'm helping with this?"

"Passage to Alvaldsnes, three thousand skatt." Sigurlina blushed and added, "A chance to find out if things are proportional."

Ragna rolled over like she'd been stung and gazed at her friend. "Siggy, I think I'm rubbing off on you. What's the box for?"

"The legend says the dagger has been sheathed in magic

crystals. I'm hoping that if we fill the box with the crystals and put the dagger in them the draugar won't be able to feel it."

"Will it work?"

"How should I know?"

"Wonderful. Why are you petting it?"

"If I can put my own energy into the wood it might mask the call of the dagger. Like two people talking at once."

"It might. Siggy, do you know what you're doing?"

Sigurlina paused in her stroking. "Do you really want me to answer that?"

Ragna rolled over and buried her head in the covers.

After sleeping, Sigurlina, Ragna, Fjorn, Audun and Vidurr gathered together in the girls' room. Munin perched atop the door and watched to be sure they were not overheard.

"I've gotten everything you said we'd need. Kjorn is readying the boat. Are we ready to do this?"

Vidurr grunted.

"Thank you for helping us," remarked Sigurlina.

Ragna shook her head at the girl in silent warning.

"If their living to tell their jarl of the crusader's cowardly use of beasts to do their slaughter will bring death to those swine, then I must needs see they survive to tell their tale." Vidurr gestured towards Fjorn and Audun. "Do not thank me for this." He turned his gaze to Sigurlina. "I will tell you this, girl, as I told these Aesir lovers. My foe is Hakon and his foreign slaughterers. I bear no love for the enemies of Surt, but even Odin would not do things so low as these invaders. Until they are foiled, we are allies, and not a moment beyond that glorious day."

"On that happy note, we should set off. If we're lucky, there may be an offshore breeze later. It's hard to tell, but I feel a wind shift in my bones," said Audun.

Fjorn led the way from the inn then paused.

"What are we stopping for?" asked Ragna.

"How do we get to the gate?" Fjorn grinned sheepishly.

Ragna sighed. "Men! This way." Moving to the front of the group she led the way through the streets to the landward gate.

Just outside the gate they donned snowshoes and collected a sled that was waiting for them. Lighting several candle lanterns they headed up the main trail.

"Munin, please fly ahead and make sure the way is clear," Sigurlina spoke to the raven who launched itself into the air.

"That is an amazing talent. I've seen some falconers with such command of their birds, but it is a rare gift," Fjorn moved to Sigurlina's side.

"It's friendship." Sigurlina shrugged. "So are you really a karl's son?"

A shadow seemed to cross Fjorn's features. "Yes."

They trudged on until they came to a side trail that moved up a steep incline towards a jagged, barren patch of ground.

"This is it. The stories say that this is the path to the cave. Hide anything shiny." Sigurlina pulled her cloak closer about her and started up the trail.

"My legs hurt," griped Ragna.

"You could have waited with the boat," remarked Audun.

"And leave you alone? Someone has to watch out for Siggy, and I don't trust you lot to last five minutes without me." Ragna tossed her head, but her hood hid the effect.

"Shush," whispered Sigurlina. "They might hear you."

Munin landed on her shoulder and spoke into her mind. "I didn't see anything but a big cave mouth. The snow is yellow out front of it. You're almost there."

An opening loomed out of the hillside. It was high enough that Audun could have stepped through without stooping and as wide as a small house. The snow in front of it was trampled flat and stained with yellow and brown streaks.

Sigurlina clutched her forehead. "This is it. The magic is so powerful."

"Ragna, Audun, set up. Sigurlina, Vidurr, and I will go in as planned. Vidurr, how do you want to do this?" asked Fjorn.

Vidurr snarled, took a deep breath and released a blood curdling howl. He shuddered and a moment later the red wolf stood where he had been.

"That is just not right," commented Ragna.

"It is his way," said Audun.

"Good choice," commented Fjorn.

"Munin, you wait here and do it just like we discussed," ordered Sigurlina.

"Let's go." Fjorn drew his sword and led the way into the cave.

They crept forward removing their snowshoes when they reached solid rock. The air warmed as they descended and an acrid stench assailed them. The light of their lanterns reflected off veins of crystal in the rock walls. Water dripped from the ceiling making puddles on the stony floor. The ripples from the drops reflected the lantern light to make wavering patterns on all sides.

They came to a place where the passage narrowed so a man with arms outstretched could touch both walls at once.

"I don't like--." Fjorn threw himself against the wall, barely avoiding the snapping jaws of a dreyri. The five-foot tall bat turned to strike again. Vidurr leapt smashing it to the ground. The huge wolf's jaws closed on the dreyri's neck and there was a crunching sound. Blood bubbled around the wolf's jaws and he drank it down.

"Thanks," whispered Fjorn. "This is a good place."

Opening his pack, Fjorn pulled out a jug of oil and spilled it, forming a puddle on the rocky ground where the passage narrowed, before leading the way deeper into the cavern.

Sigurlina's light reflected dimly off something by the wall and she moved to investigate. A short sword, mostly covered by something black, lay clutched in a skeletal hand with the forearm bones attached. She prodded it with the end of her staff and the hand shifted revealing a ruby ring.

"Over here," came Fjorn's hushed summons.

Sigurlina turned to look. Fjorn's lantern illuminated a place where the cave expanded so much that the light was lost before reaching the other side. On the edge of the illumined area was an altar. Magical lights gleamed around it making a sphere. As she drew closer Sigurlina could see that the altar was bowl shaped and filled with clear-quartz crystals. In the midst of the crystals was a black dagger with a skull-shaped pommel.

"This is it," she whispered.

Fjorn glanced at the dagger then about the chamber's vaulted ceiling. At least three-score dots of light reflected back towards him from above. Swallowing in a dry mouth, he hissed, "Hurry."

"What? Why? This is a delicate spell. I have to."

"HURRY!" Fjorn leapt forward brandishing his long sword, driving back a dreyri.

Vidurr leapt catching another of the beasts in mid-flight and bringing it to ground. A tremendous shriek went up and the cavern was alive with black wings and darting bodies. The noise was incredible. Several dreyri collided in mid-air.

Sigurlina wrenched the wooden box out of her backpack and scooped some of the altar's crystals into it before snatching the dagger. It felt like ice in her hand as she threw it into the box and covered it with more crystals.

A dreyri flew at her. She barely had time to grasp her staff before she heard Fjorn singing.

"The Shields of Asgard are shields of might.
"Turn the wrath of giants to flight.
"Shields to hold a warrior's might.
"The Shields of Asgard are shields of might."

The dreyri attacking her was deflected by a dome of sparkling lights.

"Go," yelled Fjorn as he fended off another dreyri.

Vidurr caught a glancing blow to his side and snarled in pain.

"Shadows to me, I invoke thee." Sigurlina stepped away from the altar. To her nothing seemed to change, except that the dreyri seemed oblivious to her. She stowed the wooden box with the dagger in her bag and started up the passage.

Vidurr moved with near imposable speed, almost as if his wounds spurred him on. Another dreyri fell to his jaws as Fjorn's long sword dripped with blood. Wolf and man slowly backed towards the passage out. A dreyri, larger than the rest, charged them. Its black wings filling their vision. It spat at them then flew back. The spit splattered

Fjorn's cloak which began to smoke and dissolve. A quick slice with his blade and the cloak fell to the floor. They were in the narrower passage now. The large dreyri charged them again. As the creature spat at him, Fjorn lunged forward, driving his sword home in the hideous form. The dreyri backed away squealing while Fjorn and Vidurr raced up the passage.

Sigurlina stood by the oil puddle, her lantern open and candle to hand. The noise below was dulled in the passage. There was a glimmer of light quickly followed by Fjorn and Vidurr running towards her. They jumped over the oil. She put the flame of her candle to the floor.

The oil caught creating a wall of fire and smoke. Beyond the fire, hideous bat-like forms filled the cavern. One released a bark of noise, and then seemed to focus on her despite her spell. She joined her comrades racing towards the cave's mouth.

They emerged to find an open barrel of oil at the cave mouth with Audun and Ragna standing by the now empty sled. Audun was tracing runs on his battle axe.

"Did you get it?" asked Ragna.

"We got it. Move!" Fjorn toppled the barrel, spilling oil over the cavern floor then tossed his lantern into the puddle which roared into flame.

"Munin, now," called Sigurlina.

The raven lifted into the air carrying a miniature candle lantern that sparkled in the darkness.

Everyone doused their lanterns and jumped onto the sleigh. A scorched dreyri shot from the cave and lunged at them. Audun swung with his battle axe. There was a sound like a hammer striking rock. The dreyri fell to the ground as the force of the blow pushed the sleigh onto the steep slope. The sleigh careened forward just as several more scorched dreyri emerged from the cave. The beasts looked around; seeing Munin with her lantern they took to the skies after the raven.

The sleigh sped down the slope. Vidurr was at the front, mouth open, tongue lolling, revelling in the wind on his canine face. The others formed a tight packed line behind him. They picked up speed and, in moments, were on the main trail hurtling towards a tree.

"Lean right," cried Fjorn.

With the weight all to one side the sleigh shifted direction, sliding along the icy path towards Ekenas.

High overhead Munin dropped the candle lantern and swept noiselessly towards the harbour. Her pursuers followed the twinkling light towards the frozen forest below.

The sleigh slowed then came to a stop and everyone tumbled off it laughing. Vidurr released a howl and a moment later was a man. A faint glimmer of a smile graced his face. They all took a moment to breath.

"Do you think the crystals are hiding it?" asked Fjorn, as the seriousness of the situation pushed into his consciousness.

There was a bone chilling screech.

"I think that's your answer, bright eyes," remarked Ragna.

They ran along the darkened trail reaching Ekenas' gates. Seeing their approach the guard opened the gate. Fjorn tossed the guard a bag of coins as he passed that was added to the one he'd received earlier.

Ragna took the lead; guiding them through the maze of streets.

"There she is," called a rough voice from the side of the road.

"Angrboda's bouncing tits!" snapped Ragna as Dorrund and Ginnarr started chasing her group. Both brothers sported black eyes and Dorrund's nose was swollen.

Fjorn's group turned a corner and the docks became visible at the end of the street. Torches burnt on the gunwales of their Kavi which sat broad side to the end of the pier, ready to cast off.

"Stop them. She's a thief," Dorrund called from behind them.

Ragna tried to sprint, but short legs simply aren't as fast as long ones and the smiths were gaining. Her companions jogged beside her full out run.

"My apologies." Audun reached down one handed and picked her up, throwing her onto his back like a child. The group sped up and pulled away from the smiths. Reaching the docks, they leapt onto their ship, falling amongst the crew waiting at the oars.

"Cast off." Kjorn called as he pulled at an oar.

The brothers raced onto the dock as the ship pulled away and the new arrivals took their stations. The smiths tried to stop, hit an ice slick, and skidded to the end of the pier just as the ship's stern passed in front of their noses. They balanced for a moment, arms flailing.

Ragna leapt up to stand by the rudder oar and struck a provocative pose. "Come on, boys, don't you want me anymore?"

The smiths tipped forward falling into the filthy, icy water around the docks.

Audun watched from his station at the tiller as the two men pulled themselves out of the water and stood shivering and scowling as their quarry escaped. "Did you really steal from them?"

"Would I do that?" Ragna batted her eyes at him.

Audun grunted and corrected course. "Wind is shifting. We should be able to hoist sail soon."

Fjorn nodded from his oar station and continued to pull towards open water.

An hour later they were well into the Baltic Sea and under sail as well as oar when they heard another bone-chilling screech from the shore. Everyone paused for a second then redoubled their efforts at the oars.

CHAPTER 5

RACING DEATH

Hours later, as human muscle reached its limits, the oars were shipped and Audun cut a course to make best use of the wind. Fjorn, wrapped in his spare cloak, moved to the tiller oar and sat beside the big man.

"We made good time," Audun greeted.

"We need to do better. Sigurlina is going to try to mask the dagger's call, but..." Fjorn's speech trailed off.

"She seems young. Would you rather a grey-haired hag with missing teeth dressed in rags?" Audun rested the tiller under his arm and began tracing runes on his axe with his finger.

"You expecting trouble?"

"If you aren't, you're a fool." Audun kept tracing runes on his axe.

Fjorn nodded. "My father told me before I left that I had a store of sense so long as there were no bosoms involved. Did I take Sigurlina aboard because she is a powerful Seith, or because she is a beautiful woman?"

"Both. Fjorn, I've got a few years on you. I don't know much about women but I'll tell you this. They are never just one thing. Don't expect them to be. See the person first, then the woman. After that, she's whatever else she is. Now, there's nothing wrong with some good, honest wenching, so long as everyone has their fun, but that's not all a woman is or is good for."

"It's not that. Well, not mostly. Could a more experienced Seithkona mask the dagger's call?"

"Maybe, maybe not. I don't know that much about the Seith way. But she did right well from what you told me about the cave. Ask yourself, would a more experienced captain be better on this boat? We all are what we are, and we do the best we can with what we have. Now, stop worrying and get some sleep, or you'll be useless tomorrow."

#

Sigurlina sat at the bow with Munin tucked under her cloak so that only the raven's head poked out. She ran her hands over the box containing the dagger.

"We should just toss it over the side." Ragna settled beside Sigurlina.

"That wouldn't help our handsome, young captain much with the queen, dear. I rather like him, though I do hope you will advise Sigurlina as to certain matters. I sense he may be rather experienced for one so young." Sigurlina's voice had a strange timber.

"Are you all right?"

"I'm quite fine, dear." Sigurlina continued to stroke the wooden box. She smiled at Munin. "A raven. Tell her I approve. Cats are good too. Snakes sleep too much in the cold to be much use nowadays."

Ragna looked at her friend and her face went pale. "Who are you, and what have you done with Sigurlina?"

"Shhh, you'll wake her. I told her I'd drop by. I'm afraid that while she was correct about masking the dagger with the crystals and her life energy, she doesn't have enough of either to silence its call. My, it is noisy."

"You give her back or I'll--," began Ragna.

"No need to be like that, dear. She's sleeping. Poor thing has had quite a few days. Still in all, I am proud of her. She's finally getting a handle on her powers. As things stand, soon she won't need my gift anymore, and I can get some much needed rest before the final battle."

"You're the grandmother," Ragna whispered.

Sigurlina's body smiled. "Please call me Inga. Don't worry about my little one. My gift helps protect her. Only I know the way around it. She was always so sensitive, far more potential than one so young can control."

"You should let her go," hissed Ragna.

Sigurlina's body sighed. "I will. It is nice to smell the air again in a young, healthy body, but she is my granddaughter. I'll not hurt her. I've done what I can to mask the dagger's call. It should be harder for the draugar to find you if you keep moving. Oh, and before I go, remember, ship's sink, so don't think that the sea will protect you. Goodbye, dear. Give Sigurlina my love."

Sigurlina's body returned the box to her pack, and then settled itself as if in sleep.

Ragna hugged herself. "I just had to make friends with a Seith. Why didn't I just find a nice merchant and get married? Why?"

"Yura bitch," remarked Munin from the folds of Sigurlina's cloak.

"You shut up you black chicken, or its bread and chestnut stuffing in your future."

"Yura bitch," repeated the bird as its head disappeared under the cloak.

After almost three days filled with nothing but sea spray and shifts on the oars, they were passing through the narrows at the tip of Skane. Sigurlina worked a rowing station while one of the oarsmen, Halfdan, relived himself over the side. Ragna stirred a pot of fish stew over the ship's brazier.

The ship rocked to the side and Halfdan pitched into the water.

"Man overboard, back oar," called Kjorn. The boat stopped and all eyes turned to the sea.

"Munin, look for him," ordered Sigurlina.

The raven took to the air.

"I see him. Starboard aft. I. Arrrrrr." One of the oarsmen released a shriek like a terrified child.

Fjorn drew his blade and rushed towards the man.

"Surt's flaming nuts!" swore Vidurr.

A black hand clutched the side of the ship. A moment later a helmed head with glowing blue eyes lifted above the gunwale. The face looked like it had been charred black by a fire.

"Repel boarders," called Fjorn, as he brought his blade down on the blackened arm.

The arm pulled back and the draugar dropped into the sea.

"Get Halfdan aboard. Watch the gunwales," snapped Fjorn.

A screech sounded from the Skane shore that sent a shudder through everyone.

Vidurr swung at something dark above the gunwale. There was the sound of metal striking metal. The thing continued to rise.

Audun threw a line over the stern to Halfdan, who grabbed it.

Sigurlina clutched her staff.

"Watch for it." Fjorn snapped at her as he leapt across the boat and brought his sword forward in a clumsy, amateurish ark. A dark blade rose up to block the blow, opening the draugar's defences. Sigurlina thrust the base of her staff into the draugar's throat; driving it into the water.

"Get that man aboard," yelled Fjorn.

Audun released the rope, reached into the water and hauled Halfdan over the gunwale; leaving him jackknifed at the hips half in and half out of the ship. Halfdan spewed his guts into the Kavi then dragged himself forward.

"Halfdan's aboard." Audun grabbed the tiller. Bracing the steering oar in his armpit, he traced a series of the runes tattooed on his forearm.

"Man the oars. Move. Move. Move," ordered Fjorn.

Ragna slipped the short sword she'd 'acquired' out of its sheath and watched the gunwale. A black hand appeared on the edge of the ship. "Here," she screamed and chopped down on the fingers. A gantlet, blacker than night, turned the blow. The horrid, scorched form of a draugar scrambled into the ship and lashed out with a claw like hand at Ragna, who dodged the worst of the blow, but still fell unconscious. The draugar seemed to grow in strength as if it had given its wounds to the diminutive woman.

"Get away from her, you beast of Hel." Audun brought his battle axe forward with a furry worthy of Thor himself. The draugar struck, but the big man's skin turned the blow as if it was made of iron. The axe struck home with a thunderous retort. The draugar was blasted into the water.

"Row, by the gods, row," bellowed Fjorn.

The crew drove their oars into the water. The longship jerked forward.

Audun dove for the tiller oar and steered them into deeper water.

Vidurr watched the gunwale on one side while Kjorn watched the other.

Munin flew in and landed on Sigurlina's shoulder. "It's falling behind, but there are two more on the shore."

"We're clear for now, but there are two more on the shore," relayed Sigurlina. "Freya!" She rushed to where Ragna lay in the bottom of the boat.

"Is she?" asked Fjorn who moved to her side.

"She's still breathing, but it's shallow."

Fjorn closed his eyes and sang.

"Youth to the gods, golden apples of grace.

Idun's power, heal mortals of faith."

Sparkling light enveloped Ragna. Her breathing deepened but she was still unconscious.

"Let me try." Sigurlina laid her hands on her friend and breathed deeply. It was like the hundreds of times she had practiced with her grandmother, only now the stakes were her friend's life. A light dew seemed to cover Ragna as her breathing grew deeper. Her eyes fluttered open and she looked blurrily about.

"Why do I let you talk me into these things?" She glowered at Sigurlina, and then slipped back into sleep.

Fjorn smiled at the women. "I'd best see to Halfdan."

Hours passed. Halfdan sat at his station wrapped in a blanket pulling on his oar with a fury while his clothes hung from the mast over the brazier. The wind had died. They all watched the gunwales nervously. Ragna slept curled up at the bow.

"Here." Sigurlina held a bowl of fish stew out to Fjorn.

"Can't, have to keep rowing." Fjorn demonstrated by driving his oar into the water with added fury.

"I'll take your station while you eat. I can keep up for a little while. I've proved that already." Sigurlina positioned herself beside him.

"You are quite the woman." Fjorn yelled, "Pause." The rowing stopped just long enough for him to take the bowl of stew and let Sigurlina grasp the oar.

"Stroke," called Sigurlina and the rowing started.

Fjorn made his way to Kjorn, who was taking his turn at the tiller.

"That is a lass. Look at her, slender as a reed, but she'll give it her all to keep up."

"But she can't for long. Still, it's oars in the water. I thank her for that. That draugar was a chance I'd rather not take again. We were lucky not to lose anyone."

"How close a thing was it with the pixy woman?" asked Kjorn.

"Too close. She'll recover." Fjorn slurped at his stew.

"Best she does it quick." Kjorn sniffed the air. "Smell that?"

Fjorn sniffed the air. "What?"

Kjorn shook his head and groaned in disgust. "Learn to use your nose boy, or we'll never make a sailor of you. Storm's coming. Be here in two, maybe three hours."

"Four, if we're smart about it." Audun folded down the blanket he'd wrapped over himself.

"Watch is only half done. Go back to sleep. I figure two. My shoulder is throbbing and my knee is swelling up. We need to make harbour," Kjorn stated.

Fjorn stared at his friend. "We can't. Wherever we go we'll draw the draugar to us. We have to keep moving until the dagger is in the queen's hands. I'm hoping she knows what to do with it."

"You don't want to weather a sea storm." Kjorn's voice was adamant.

"We have to, or give up the dagger," remarked Audun. "To our benefit, the wind should start picking up soon. If we hoist sail, we may give ourselves another hour or two before the storm catches us." Audun stared at Kjorn. "That would be four hours."

Kjorn scowled at Audun.

"Hoist sail," ordered Fjorn. "Audun, keep us ahead of it as long as you can. Kjorn make sure everything is tied down. Do whatever you know to get us through. I need both of you for this."

"As you command, captain. You should let the men take a break from the oars and everyone should eat. It may be our last chance for a while," suggested Kjorn.

"We'll have wind in an hour," added Audun.

"We'll ship oars when we have wind. I want to keep moving." Swallowing the last of his food Fjorn moved to relieve Sigurlina at his station.

The men muttered as the wind picked up and they shipped oars, but made no move towards going ashore.

Halfdan retrieved his clothing from the mast and dressed. The ship sped forward, cutting through the increasingly choppy seas as the crew ate their fill of the supplies and readied for a fight.

"This voyage is cursed," was the oft heard complaint along with, "We should go ashore."

Fjorn ignored the whispers as he walked up and down the ship speaking to his crew as he'd seen his father speak to men going into battle.

The sleet came in, driven by the wind, soaking into cloaks and forming a sheet of ice over everything. The sail strained at its ropes with each gust as Audun and Kjorn both fought the rudder oar to keep them on course.

"If we die before my vengeance is complete, I will hunt you on the Plain of Vigrid, Aesir lover," remarked Vidurr when Fjorn approached him.

"Good to know. I wouldn't want to be at the end of all things and not see a friendly face. Tie yourself off." Fjorn passed the Ulfhednar a length of rope.

"You'd dare trick me into wearing a leash!" Vidurr tossed the rope to the deck.

"If you want to be swept off the ship by a wave, feel free!" Fjorn held up both his hands. "You're not Fenrir and I'm not Tyr, so do what you like."

Vidurr snorted and secured the rope around his waist.

Fjorn moved to the bow where Ragna was tucked away wrapped in blankets drifting in and out of consciousness. Sigurlina sat beside her friend with her staff by her feet. The box with the dagger was tucked under her. Munin was snuggled under Sigurlina's cloak with only her head showing.

"Scared?" asked Fjorn as sleet beaded on his hood and dribbled down his cloak.

"No, not at all," lied Sigurlina.

"Funny, I am." Fjorn smiled.

Sigurlina smiled and blushed. "Maybe I'm a little scared. I... There was a storm when my grandmother took me to Finnmark. I... Look." She pointed to where a dark shape was scrambling over the gunwale.

Fjorn leapt up with a cry. A draugar was half way over the side of the ship. The wind caught at the tattered remains of its clothing and barnacles had grown into its skin leaving dots of off white against the black. Vidurr sprang to his feet drawing his blade as he did so.

The draugar glowered towards Fjorn and hissed, "Mine."

Fjorn fell back with a cry.

Vidurr swung with his sword separating the draugar's head from its body. The undead thing fell into the fast mounting waves.

Munin slipped out from under Sigurlina's cloak and gently pecked at Ragna's ear.

"Are you hurt?" asked Sigurlina.

"Give me the dagger. This has..." Fjorn trembled all over, swallowed hard then continued. "We must go to shore. We'll throw it overboard." His movements were jerky.

Sigurlina stared into Fjorn's eyes. The ship tossed on the waves.

"Fjorn, we should reef sail now, while we still can," called Kjorn from the stern.

"Give me the dagger." Fjorn repeated as he took a deep breath, almost as if tasting the air.

"Fjorn, Kjorn's right. We need to reef sail," called Audun.

"We'll all be better off. This storm could kill us if we don't g... g... go to harbour."

"And what about Jarl Hakon's mission?" Sigurlina looked over Fjorn's shoulder into Vidurr's eyes; silently beckoning him forward.

The Ulfhednar crept closer.

"There are other jarls to serve. What does Hakon need with a Death Bone dagger?" Fjorn shifted taking on a predatory stance foreign to his normal movement. "We could be outlaw together. Think of the riches."

"Fjorn?" called Audun from the tiller oar.

"Reef the sail," called back Sigurlina.

"But--." Kjorn's objection was cut off.

"Just do what you have to." Sigurlina stood in front of Fjorn. The boat pitched to the side tossing them both hard against the gunwale. Fjorn recovered first and dove past Sigurlina.

"Get him. That isn't Fjorn," Sigurlina screamed as she clawed at Fjorn's cloak.

Vidurr lunged at Fjorn, who spun aside sending his attacker into the side of the Kavi head first.

"It would have been so much easier if y... y.... you had j... j...just done what I t... t... told you." Fjorn's body hissed as he lunged for the bag in the bow. Before anyone could block him he threw it over the side and laughed.

Behind him the crew struggled to stow the sail in the heavy wind.

"We could have had some f.. f.. fun, you and I... I... I. Stop it. Stop it." Fjorn's body jerked then was still. "No reason to struggle. I've d... d... done my service to my l... l...lady." Fjorn's fist slammed into his own head. "Stop it, fool. This body will be my r... r... reward. To t... t... truly l.. l.. l.. l ...l.. l.. live again. I."

Vidurr clutched Fjorn's legs toppling him to the deck before pouncing on him.

"You cannot win wolf. I was slaying your kind when your grandfather was a pup." Fjorn's voice took on a cruel quality as he rolled over and aimed a blow at Vidurr's throat. Fjorn's arm jerked to the side missing the Ulfhednar just before his fist contacted.

Sigurlina knelt by the wrestling pair breathing deeply.

"By Hel, thy mistress, by Freya, Queen of Seith, by Odin and Surt, with their warrior bands; I command thee leave this stolen form. Remember the death that took you."

Fjorn's body screamed and arched on the deck.

"Remember the cold of Niflheim. This form is not yours. You are a thief in the night. I banish you to the darkness, return to Hel and know her freezing embrace. Your time is done foul shade. BE GONE!"

It was as if all the light from the torches was sucked into Sigurlina, leaving the storm tossed ship in absolute blackness. That light congealed and burst out of her hands into Fjorn who screamed again and collapsed panting on the deck. Sigurlina crumpled her back resting against the bow as the light from the torches returned.

"Surt," breathed Vidurr.

"What in Niflheim happened?" Audun stumbled forward from reefing the sail. The ship still tossed but not as much.

"Possessed," panted Sigurlina. "I drove out the spirit."

"Can a draugar do that?" asked Vidurr.

"Evidently so," said Audun.

"We lost the dagger," stated Sigurlina.

"This is why I can't let you out of my sight." Ragna looked out from a pile of blankets. "Bird brain..."

"Yura bitch," commented Munin looking offended.

"Right. Munin woke me up just in time. I figured the dagger was better off under me than sitting out in a bag where anyone could grab it, so." She produced the box containing the dagger from under her blankets.

"What did the draugar throw over the side?" asked Audun.

"A half empty sack of charcoal. He wasn't really paying attention." Ragna smiled.

"Audun, I need you at the tiller," screamed Kjorn.

Audun rushed to the stern.

The wind howled as hail the size of a woman's fist pummelled down. Sleet came in sideways and every oar was manned as they tried to ride the waves. Fjorn recovered, and though foggy headed, was put to work on an oar while Sigurlina and Ragna scooped endless buckets of water and ice from the ship.

The stars were gone and the shore lost in the storm. There was little Audun and Kjorn could do save follow the wind and try to keep them from capsizing.

Sleet soaked through all their clothing and hissed against the torches. Soon the oarsmen were trembling with cold and exhaustion, and the struggle went on. Halfdan, still cold from his previous soaking, collapsed into the middle of the ship. Sigurlina took the oar, but all too soon her strength waned.

Wind spun them around and a rouge wave caught the oars snapping five of them like toothpicks. No one aboard held their guts in the tossing sea. Ice sheeted on the deck; making footing treacherous.

Hours had passed when a wave crested over midship's. Vidurr, Ragna and three of the oarsmen were thrown overboard as the ship tipped on it's side then crashed back down half full of water.

"GRAB THE LINES." Fjorn released his oar and pulled on the closest safety rope.

Sigurlina stayed out of the way in the bow scooping out buckets of water as fast as her cold, aching arms could manage. Audun and Kjorn fought with the tiller oar; keeping the bow into the waves while the remaining oarsmen hauled their comrades from the sea.

#

Water closed over Vidurr's head. The taste of salt filled his mouth. He clutched the line and kicked with his legs, driving himself to the surface. His lungs were burning when his head crested into air. He took an enormous breath. Only the sheltered candle lanterns on the bow and stern of the ship could be seen in the churning darkness. Two pale dots of light. Grasping the rope about his waist he pulled himself towards that dim light. His arms screamed with fatigue. The waves threatened to tear his grip lose. He reached the side of the boat and felt his half frozen arms grabbed. A jerk and a twist and he sat with his back to the gunwale and water over his hips.

#

Ragna felt the wave take her and twisted as she went over the side. She rode the wave. The rope around her waist jerked her up sharp but her head stayed above the water. Sleet and hail hissed down around her. The rope jerked again. Grabbing it in frozen fingers she pulled herself towards the pinpricks of light that had to be the ship. Something bumped her leg under the water. She ignored it. Her arms were screaming from the effort of holding on to the rope. Something bumped her again, this time in the small of her back. She felt herself pushed towards the ship. Moments later cold hands grasped hers. Fjorn pulled her over the side to sit in the half-flooded vessel. She looked back and thought she saw a dark, streamlined shadow in the water by the ship.

"BJORN'S LINE BROKE. HE'S LOST!" One of the oarsmen yelled over the storm.

"Get back to the oars. If you don't have an oar, find something and help with the bailing," ordered Fjorn.

Hours later the storm subsided. The sleet and hail petered out and the wind steadied.

CHAPTER 6

THE FINAL SPRINT

Fjorn shipped his oar and held his trembling, blistered hands in front of his face. He could barely see them in the dark. The glimmering light of the bow and stern lanterns had been extinguished. Only the red-hued light of Muspelheim's fire on the horizon entered the world under the invisible clouds above.

"We made it," remarked Kjorn.

Fjorn left his oar and moved, by feel, on trembling legs to the stern. "Where are we?" Fjorn gazed over the dark ocean.

"I can't see the stars, but if we make north we should hit a coast line." Audun took off his cloak and wrung the water out of it over the side.

"Which way is north?" asked Fjorn.

Audun slowly turned a full circle, shrugged and sat. "We'll have to wait for the clouds to break."

Fjorn stared into the dark sky. "Keep an eye out. I want to hoist sail as soon as we can. For now, we need to light the brazier and try to get dry before we freeze."

"How? Everything is soaked." Kjorn stomped his foot down into the ankle deep water in the Kavi.

"Wwwere dddoing our bbbbest," stuttered Ragna's voice from somewhere forward followed by the sound of a bucket being emptied over the side.

"I can make a fire," Vidurr's voice intruded. A moment later he appeared out of the darkness. "My tinder stayed dry." Even the Ulfhednar was hugging himself against the cold.

"Do it. Do you need help?"

"The Seith girl has some sense." Vidurr vanished into the darkness.

"Sigurlina, help Vidurr set a fire in the brazier." Fjorn slumped against the gunwale.

"What is wrong?" Kjorn rushed to his captain's side.

"Dizzy. I'll take the tiller oar. You two check for damage. Once they have a fire going warm some mead for the crew, and start on something hot to eat. This isn't over until we're dry and warm."

Sigurlina used her hatchet to split pieces of a food crate then shaved them into kindling while Vidurr prepared the kindling on a plank they'd placed in the brazier's bowl to keep it dry.

"You follow Freya?" he asked as they worked.

"Yes, she is my lady." Sigurlina fought to keep her teeth from chattering.

"I have no quarrel with the Vanir."

Sigurlina smiled despite the chill. "I'm glad."

They worked in silence for several minutes, laying the fire, before Vidurr pulled out his flint and steel and tried to strike a spark. He couldn't get his hands to hold the tools correctly.

Sigurlina blew on her hands and flexed her fingers. "Let me try." She took the flint and steel from Vidurr and struck sparks. One hit the kindling. A gentle breath from Vidurr brought about a lick of flame that quickly spread. They fed the flame bits of the packing crate. The water in the bottom of the brazier hissed and bubbled away. Fjorn brought a soaking torch over just as they were adding damp charcoal from the ship's fuel store.

"Give it time to grow," grunted Vidurr.

"We need light," objected Fjorn.

"We need the fire to stay lit more." Sigurlina warmed her hands against the growing flames.

Ragna moved close to the flame. She was pale as death and her lips were tinted blue. "C...C...C...C...Cold," she stuttered.

"We all are." Fjorn hugged himself.

"The charcoal is catching. You can light a torch now." Sigurlina took one of the ship's soaking blankets and held it up to the flame.

Fjorn held the torch over the flames as the crew men huddled in.

Audun loomed behind the group. "I checked Halfdan. He froze."

Fjorn stared into the flames and sighed. "We'll see to the living first... Tie up the body, just in case."

Audun nodded and vanished into the darkness.

The torch caught and Fjorn carried it to the forward gunwale returning with another sodden torch.

The torches and lanterns were all lit and the crew slept with bellies full of warm mead and hastily-boiled salt fish by the time the clouds had parted enough for Audun to know the direction they were traveling.

Raising the sodden sail was a challenge, but finally it was in place, and they sped through the dark waters.

Fjorn released an enormous yawn as he moved to Audun's side. The big man slumped by the tiller oar nodding in exhaustion. In the distance to starboard there was a spot of light.

"Can you say where we are?" Fjorn slumped to sit on the bench by the oar.

"That's the tip of Vestfold. We're less than a day out from Alvaldsnes, so long as the wind holds." Audun Bear Friend released a huge yawn and scratched himself like his namesake.

"And no other disasters strike."

"With you back here, who's on the ice watch?" Audun nodded and caught himself.

"Kjorn. His blankets are still drying."

"You should get some sleep." Audun closed his eyes and his breathing became deep and steady.

Fjorn smiled wearily and took the tiller oar leaving the big man to curl up in his too short cloak. "Don't you know, Audun? Captains and karls never sleep." He settled himself, released a yawn and sat the tiller watch.

Sigurlina lay curled at the point of the bow in her damp cloak and blankets. Kjorn smiled down at her. "Good lass. Brave lass."

"Why Kjorn, you old dog." Ragna wrapped in cloak and blankets moved to his side.

"Done baking yourself by the brazier?"

"I was cold."

"There's more than one body aboard that would warm you up."

Ragna snorted. "That was mean."

Kjorn nodded and sighed. "Truth, I'm sorry. There were no call for it, especially with you saving the dagger and all."

Ragna nodded. "She's young."

Kjorn smiled. "Fjorn's not more than three summers on her."

"There's young and there's young. I figure we both know that.

Sometimes I wish... Never mind."

"Go on. Ice watch is tiring business. I could use something to prop my lids open."

"Fine. I was a karl's daughter once, you know?"

"I'd heard, but I thought it was a story."

Ragna shook her head. "It's true. My father sided with Athelstan when he took Wessex. At first it wasn't bad. My father welcomed druids, godi, and the priests of the White God. I loved it. The way they would argue. Father Michael taught me the church speech. Then the crusaders came. They took my father's lands and cut off his head because he wouldn't expel the heathens or follow the law that made people go to the White God's church whether they wanted to or not. They made me a thrall in my own house. Father Michael did what he could for me. He didn't much like the crusaders either. Then raiders from Horland attacked and I was taken as a thrall to Karl Geldnir Oar Snapper's hall."

"I met him. Seemed a good man in a scrape."

"He was the greatest man I ever new." Tears brimmed in Ragna's eyes. "He made a law in his lands. No man could take a girl until she'd bled at least thrice, or a boy until his beard could be scraped away twice in a moon. Thrall or noble, it was the same."

"It's a good law." Kjorn nodded.

"It is. Crusaders pretend to be all noble but..." Tears spilled from her eyes. "I haven't been young in a long time. At least Geldnir's law made it stop." She sniffed and blotted her eyes on the edge of her blanket. "It is all past. I was serving mead when a couple of the White God's godi came to visit. Geldnir gave them hospitality but the things they were saying in the church speech were so rude. I told him and he avenged the stain on his honour.

"After finding out I could understand the speech of the White God's godi, he had me serve whenever godi of the White God came. I'd tell him in private what they said to each other after the godi were asleep.

"Geldnir and Asdis, his lady, cared for me. Asdis explained it to me when I started to bleed. She was more a mother to me than the tart that bore me. That whore left me behind so she could become a crusader's strumpet in Winchester when they murdered my father."

"I've known the type."

Ragna smiled but it didn't reach her eyes. "I bet you have."

Kjorn patted the small woman's shoulder.

"Asdis died of a fever when I was sixteen summers old. She made me promise to look after Geldnir, to give him something to live for. I... He was weeping, and so was I. I missed her and... He was gentle, and it felt good to be held. He loved me, in a way, and I loved him, and I loved Asdis, so I kept my word to her. People whispered about the young thrall who beguiled the old karl. I didn't mind. I was happy with Geldnir, and he was as happy as he could be without Asdis. Do you think I was evil?"

"I've seen too much to think that girl. You say he was happy, what more can a man ask?"

"You're not so bad, after all, you old goat." This time, Ragna's smile reached her eyes.

"Much the same, harlot." Kjorn returned the smile.

"Geldnir spent his time with me letting his son take over his duties more each day. Then one night, while we..." Ragna blushed. "In any case. His arm started hurting and he couldn't breathe. I put a sword into his hand. He smiled at me, then he was gone. I thought I'd take ship with him, but he left instructions that no one was to. That he would sail with his Asdis and no other. He also left instructions that I was to be made a free woman."

"How did you end up in Finnmark?"

"Geldnir's son was a lot like his father. I'd always liked Harr, and he liked me back. His wife felt that traveling far away from Horaland might make it easier for me to accept the karl's loss."

"But, why Finnmark?"

"It was the last stop of the first boat leaving the village."

"Probably for the best." Kjorn nodded sagely.

"Probably." Ragna smirked then yawned. "Warm and dry now. Time to sleep." She settled herself next to Sigurlina. Munin poked her head out from the folds of Sigurlina's cloak and gently stroked Ragna's hair with the underside of her beak.

"Good bird," she said very softly as she petted the human.

Hours later the quiet of the exhausted crew was broken by the oarsman manning the tiller watch shouting, "Ship to starboard. Ship to starboard."

Fjorn threw off his blankets and jumped to his feet; immediately wishing he hadn't as everything cramped at once.

Audun rose more slowly from his rest as did Kjorn.

"It's too small to be a proper ship. More like a sloop," commented Audun, as he gazed at a darker form on the water revealed by the dim light of stars.

"Probably not the kraken ship." There was relief in Fjorn's voice. The vessel continued to bear towards them.

"Wake the crew. I want oars in the water. We've had enough for this trip." Fjorn stretched trying to prepare himself for another session of rowing.

Minutes later, sore, exhausted men pulled at the oars. The smaller vessel continued to close the distance between them.

"Nothing can move that fast," remarked Audun from the tiller. His battle axe was out and he was tracing runes on it.

Fjorn had surrendered his oar station to a crew man and stood by the tiller staring at the oncoming boat. Cupping his hands around his mouth, and using skaldic voice tricks, he yelled. "Stand too. We don't want to meet. You will be repelled."

On the small ship there was a spark and a torch flamed to life. Three charred, black bodies pulled at the oars. A fourth draugar stood in the boat's bow, its glowing blue eyes turned towards Fjorn.

"Surrender what is ours and you will be spared." The voice was like an icy wind from the grave. A shudder ran through every mortal that heard it.

"My queen has given her command. You may treat with her for the dagger." Fjorn loosened his sword in its sheath.

"Your queen is nothing! I serve Hel, Queen of Niflheim. You are free to treat with her when I suck the life from your mortal shell." The draugar's voice was chillingly clear to all over the distance between the boats.

Fjorn spoke softly. "Audun, how close are we to Alvaldsnes?"

Audun stood and pointed to lights forward and starboard. "Less than an hour."

Fjorn looked to his exhausted crew pulling at their remaining oars and spoke in a whisper. "Kjorn, bring me the queen's shopping list and a charred stick. Sigurlina, come here and bring Munin."

Moments later Munin flew towards the lights of Alvaldsnes with a message clutched in her talons. The draugar's vessel continued to close the distance.

"Keep rowing men." Fjorn gauged their speeds.

"They are going to overtake us. Any help that comes will have to sail against the wind," advised Kjorn.

"Sigurlina, is there anything a Seith can do? They are dead." Fjorn eyed the young woman.

"I can hit them with my staff. Until they do something, that's about it. I mean, there is dead, and then there is *dead* and draugar are definitely of the *dead* type." She looked sheepish.

"You did plenty driving that one out of our captain here," comforted Kjorn.

Fjorn smiled at her. "You did and if we live through this, I'll thank you properly. For this fight, stay clear."

Sigurlina made to object but he cut her off.

"We'll need you in case they possess anybody. You're to watch and undo any tricks they pull. We don't have to win; we just have to delay them long enough for help to reach us."

"I can help with that." Ragna popped her head into the group.

"How?" asked Audun.

"Just give me some rope."

Moments later Ragna and Kjorn were laying rope on the deck while Sigurlina sat at the bow mustering her courage and strength. Audun had surrendered the tiller oar to an oarsman and stood beside Fjorn, weapons drawn, watching the approaching vessel.

"If nothing else, it has been a voyage worth a song," commented Fjorn.

Audun slapped the young captain's shoulder. "Save your throat, you'll need it. When we make port I know this mead hall where--."

There was a bloodcurdling screech from inside the Kavi. The oarsmen faltered and stared at Halfdan's corpse. The skin seemed to be burning away and the eyes glowed with a cold, blue light. The body strained at the ropes binding it.

Vidurr drew his blade and calmly decapitated the body before it could break its bonds. "He deserved better." He remarked as the oarsmen stared at him.

The ship jolted with the draugar's boat's impact. The draugar swarmed onto the deck drawing weapons as soon as they were aboard.

The lead draugar howled and its cohorts joined in. Five of the crew were overtaken with fear and threw themselves into the sea.

Fjorn and Audun huddled back from the undead menace. The draugar stepped forward. One held up a bony finger, pointed at Audun and spoke in a hissing voice. "Mi wouaaaa."

Ragna pulled on a rope from her place in the bow causing it to shoot up under the draugar's legs, toppling it to the deck.

Fjorn sang as Audun leapt forward.

"The Shields of Asgard are shields of might.

"Turn the wrath of giants to flight.

"Shields to hold a warrior's might.

"The Shields of Asgard are shields of might."

Audun slammed his battle axe into the side of a draugar. There was a retort and the creature toppled over the gunwale. The draugar clutched at the side of the ship and began to haul itself up. Another draugar's sword skittered off a sphere of sparkling lights that surrounded Audun.

Vidurr pounced forward driving his sword into a draugar which lashed out with its short sword, leaving a gash in the Ulfhednar's stomach.

Fjorn pushed forward driving his sword into the draugar that had wounded Vidurr. Vidurr snarled in rage and with near impossible speed swong his blade catching the draugar's ankle and toppling it to the deck.

Oarsmen fell on the fallen draugar driving home their blades. The draugars attacked with spell and steel wounding several of the humans.

"Mine," hissed a voice. One of the oarsmen backed away from the battle and aimed his blade at Vidurr's back.

"By Hel, thy mistress, by Freya, Queen of Seith, by Odin and Surt, with their warrior bands; I command thee leave this stolen form. Remember the death that took you," commanded Sigurlina with her hand outstretched towards the oarsman. He screamed and collapsed to the deck.

Sigurlina continued the spell. "Remember the cold of Niflheim. This form is not yours. You are a thief in the night. I banish you to the darkness, return to Hel and know her freezing embrace. Your time is done foul shade, BE GONE!"

The torches dimmed as the oarsman exploded with light then groaning crawled away from the fray. Sigurlina waited at the bow for when she'd be needed again.

Audun turned to the draugar scrambling over the gunwale. Before he could take action the undead thing jerked as if something was dragging downwards. It tried to rise but jerked down again then fell into the sea with a splash.

"Fall back," bellowed Fjorn. Two draugars remained. Five oarsmen were either dead or injured enough to be useless. One of the draugars was nothing more than rendered pieces and a stain on the deck.

"You can depart," called Fjorn as the battle lines were redrawn.

"Surrender," hissed the draugar. The voice sent a shudder down Fjorn's spine.

"No." Fjorn swung with his blade cutting one of Ragna's ropes. The sail dropped pulling a line around that lifted a plank and slammed it into the lead draugar's side. Fjorn lunged while the beast was off balance, forcing it to the side of the Kavi. The draugar teetered on the gunwale. A seal leapt up caught the draugar's arm in its teeth and overbalanced it into the sea.

The remaining draugar lunged forward driving its short sword into Fjorn's stomach. Audun and Vidurr charged, forcing the draugar back as Fjorn sank to the deck. Ragna pulled on a rope from her place at the bow and it pulled up taught behind the draugar's knees. The undead warrior stumbled over the rope, grapling at Audun who stumbled back bleeding from a deep gash across his chest. Vidurr pressed the assault, but was repelled by an aura of intense cold. The draugar gained its feet and stepped forward.

"Now," gasped Fjorn, who then slumped unconscious on the deck. Four oarsmen pushed forward with their oars ramming them into the draugar's chest. Ice formed on the oars but didn't reach down the shaft. Pushing together they drove the draugar to the gunwale. The frozen wood shattered but they pushed the broken ends forward like spears driving the beast over the side. It fell into the water and sank in its heavy armour.

Audun, grimaced as he traced a series of runes on his arm. A light dew formed on all aboard. The wound in his chest stopped bleeding. Fjorn remained unconscious.

"Please no," Sigurlina moved to Fjorn's side and placed her hand on his chest. A light dew covered him and those around. Audun pushed himself to his feet and Vidurr sighed with relief. One of the fallen oarsmen opened his eyes.

"We need to get him ashore." Audun staggered towards the tiller oar.

"Maybe I can help." A slender, dark-haired woman of maybe thirty stood naked at the stern where the draugar's boat was tethered. Something like a hide was draped over her arm.

"Is this a trick?" demanded Audun.

"I swear by Aegir, no tricks. Your raven proved a worthy messenger. My sister and I came as swiftly as we could. I have some skill as a healer. Let me help."

"How did you get here?" demanded Ragna, as she eyed the stranger.

"I swam. Now, may I help your friends?" Lean arms gestured towards the wounded on the deck.

"Please," pleaded Sigurlina.

The strange woman moved amongst the wounded and sang in a beautiful, soprano voice.

"Youth to the gods, golden apples of grace.

"Idun's power, heal mortals of faith.

"From the deep sea, comes life to this place.

"Idun's power, heal mortals of faith."

A moment passed, Audun touched his stomach through the rip in his shirt. The area was covered with fresh tender skin.

Fjorn opened his eyes and looked around, his gaze falling to the beautiful, naked woman.

"Hello," he smiled then grunted in pain when he tried to move.

Behind Fjorn, the wounded oarsmen were waking up, but two lay lifeless on the deck.

"Thank you. Who are you?" Sigurlina tried not to sound petulant and failed.

The woman smiled. "They call me Halla Sea Born. Jarl Erik asked me to aid you when we received your message. The queen is preparing to receive your cargo. We should get to Alvaldsnes before the draugar can plan another attack. They sink in all that armour, but that only means they have to walk to shore and find another boat."

"Right. Oarsmen to your stations." Fjorn tried to stand and slumped back to the deck.

"You, my good captain, must rest. It took three healings to keep you from Odin's hall. Now give your body time to finish the job."

"As my healer commands." Fjorn closed his eyes in pain.

Halla spoke softly. "So I command, son of Geldnir of Orkney, for the sake of the father who loves you. Why don't you see to him?" She smiled at Sigurlina. "I'll tell them you're coming."

"How?" asked Ragna.

Vidurr donned a rare smile. "We should speak later, sea sister."

"I look forward to it, land brother." Saying this, Halla unfolded the hide over her arm revealing it to be a seal skin.

"Wait, seal maiden. Please, tell the jarl I must speak to him. Tell him we know what is happening at sea." Fjorn's voice was strained. He sat clutching the wound in his side.

Halla nodded to him. She pulled the skin on like a dress, transforming into a huge seal. She barked once and dove into the ocean and swam away.

"That just is not right," commented Ragna.

Sigurlina tucked blankets around Fjorn and the other wounded men.

Shortly, a large longship pulled alongside them and escorted them to a pier at the fabled docks of Alvaldsnes. A sleigh, with a contained passenger compartment and ornate scroll work over its outer surface, drawn by two large horses, waited at the end of the pier. Fjorn forced himself to stand and carry the dagger in its box off his vessel. Kjorn and Ragna volunteered to stay back and put the ship to rights.

Royal guards crowded the dock and shoreline. Queen Gunnhild stepped out of the ornate sleigh and strode to meet Fjorn on the pier.

"Do you have it?" she demanded as she approached.

"The full order, but this, I think, might be what you are referring to, my Queen." Fjorn dropped to one knee in a seeming show of respect and presented the box.

Sigurlina bit her cheek and hoped that she was the only one to see the grey cast to Fjorn's features, or how his jaw clenched with suppressed pain.

"Impressive." The queen scanned Fjorn's companions. Her eyes stopped when they fell on Sigurlina and, for a moment, uncertainty crossed Gunnhild's features. "You and your crew are guests of the jarl. Rooms are being prepared. My guards will bring you and the rest of your cargo." Taking the box, she strode back to her sleigh and raced away.

"I think she's impressed," commented Audun.

"I hope whatever she is doing is worth the price." There was a waver in Fjorn's voice as he looked back over his diminished crew.

Sigurlina took his hand and braced against his weight as he stood using her for support.

\#

Ragna glance around to be sure she wasn't being watched then pulled the boots off one of the dead men. Using a dagger, she cut off his toes and stowed them in a bag.

"What are you doing?" demanded Kjorn.

"We don't want Naglfar to be completed too soon."

"For that you trim the nails." The old sailor walked up beside her.

Ragna looked nervous. "Fine, to the right people these are worth a warm bed and a hot meal." She looked at her dead crewmates. "They don't need them anymore."

"Half." Kjorn held his hand out.

Ragna tentatively shook the hand. His thumb tapped twice, hers tapped once, his tapped twice again.

"You really are an old scoundrel." Ragna smiled.

"You don't know the half of it. Now move. I think the guards will be unloading us right quick."

CHAPTER 7

A DEEP BREATH BEFORE THE PLUNGE

Sigurlina stood beside Fjorn to one side of the end of the pier as royal guards carried the rest of the cargo from their ship. She wanted to see everything at once. In land bridges spanned a frozen river. People had built rude shelters on the ice, but the buildings on land were all of fine quality. Looking inland she could see a massive tower of stone. Fires burnt in braziers at its top and human figures, looking no bigger than dolls in the distance, stood beside them. There were people everywhere. Around the dock Sigurlina saw more people than had lived in her entire village. The city seemed to stretch on forever.

"What do you think?" Fjorn's voice held pain, but Sigurlina was too a gasp to notice.

"I... It's... There are so many..." She looked around trying to take it all in.

"Audun says we're staying at the palace. What did I tell you? Royal guards here we come." Ragna's voice intruded. The diminutive woman clapped her hands and eyed some of the men carrying cargo ashore with an appraising eye.

A group of guards piled the cargo on a sleigh, made of a flat platform of planks on runners pulled by a large horse and pulled away. Another sleigh, of the same kind, pulled up to the end of the docks.

A guardsman, nearly as tall as Audun, stood beside Fjorn and gestured towards the third sleigh. The big man was smiling, but something in the way he moved made it plain that boarding the sleigh wasn't a request.

"The jarl is most gracious." Fjorn grit his teeth against the pain that made him want to shuffle and walked with dignity.

Sigurlina rushed up beside him and slipped her arm around him, lending support without appearing to. Fjorn leaned on her as if she were a conquest letting her take his weight.

"You need to heal," she whispered.

"Thank you. Stay close. I need to stand right now more than I need to heal." Fjorn whispered back.

"Honestly, the first handsome karl's son, she meets and she's all over him. I have to have a talk with that girl." Ragna commented in a voice that seemed like it was meant for her shipmates, but was loud enough to carry to the royal guards.

Several of the guard's eyes scanned Sigurlina's athletic form and they snickered.

Sigurlina mounted the sleigh, smiled and reached a hand down to Fjorn. Audun slipped behind his captain and braced in case the younger man fell backwards. Fjorn took Sigurlina's hand and half pulled himself onto the open sleigh. Pulling his cloak tight around him he sat with his legs dangling over the side while the rest of his crew climbed aboard, then they were away.

Town's folk stopped and stared as they made their way through the city streets lined with shops and houses. They crossed several bridges spanning frozen rivers crowded with huts made from whatever was available. The smell of wood smoke, sewage and cooking meat filled the air.

Sigurlina snuggled close to Fjorn with her arms around him in the way that she'd seen women who were courting in her village hold their men. Really she was holding Fjorn up as he drifted in and out of consciousness.

"How is he?" Audun asked from Fjorn's other side.

"Not good. He needs warmth, food and sleep in that order. Why can't he just lie down?"

"He has his reasons. He'll share them as he will. Right now, we must help him look strong before the jarl and queen."

#

Vidurr sniffed the air, a disgusted expression filling his face. "Human filth."

Around him, people were crowded into the city so close he wondered that there was air to breathe. The frozen rivers were covered in waste of every kind such that he thought if they ever thawed they would poison the sea itself. Babies cried and children screamed while their parents rushed in all directions with seemingly no purpose. Torches and lanterns fouled the air with dark, heavy smoke that lingered and seemed to stick to the inside of his nose. A discordant racket of voices, songs, and instruments issued from an inn they passed.

#

"This is amazing," remarked Ragna. She smelt foods of all kinds, saw items from lands so far away she didn't have names for them. Everyone was busy building and trading. The houses on the land were the finest she'd ever seen. Voices were raised everywhere in a thousand discussions about a thousand things. Lights burnt such that they turned night into day. The sounds of music came from inns scattered along the streets they traveled.

#

Kjorn looked at the city and his heart broke. Fimbulwinter had fouled it as it did everything. When he'd visited before the rivers flowed, carrying away the filth. Shallow barges had carried goods from all of Midgard to the shops and bazaars. Skalds had sung on every street corner.

#

"Freya!" gasped Sigurlina as they turned a corner and the palace appeared at the end of the street. Its towering walls stretched into the dark sky and seemed to reflect the light of the torches around it. The gate was large enough for eight men to walk through abreast and it stood open. Heavily armed guards flanked the street before the gate. They moved into an arched passage that led to the palace's courtyard where the sleighs from the pier waited, filling only one corner of the space. The temperature seemed to rise as the wind was blocked. Arrow slits in the walls surrounding the courtyard glowed from the light within. The gate closed behind them and an iron portcullis dropped on the inside end of the passage. Stillness filled the air.

Munin flew off the battlements and landed on Sigurlina's shoulder. "I did what you said. I gave them the message."

"You did very well," commented Sigurlina.

"This place is amazing. Rooms everywhere, and there are ravens here. The queen's familiar is a raven. He's really nice. He showed me where I could get food, and a really nice perch close to a brazier so it's warm and..."

Sigurlina half listened to Munin's babble in her head as she tried to care for Fjorn.

A fastidious looking man in an expensive cloak shuffled out of one of the many heavy, wood doors opening into the courtyard. He walked up to the sleigh and eyed the dirty, exhausted sailors with distaste. "Which one of you is Fjorn, son of Karl Geldnir of Orkney?"

Sigurlina gently shook Fjorn who blinked then cleared his throat.

"Well?" demanded the bureaucrat.

"I am Fjorn, son of Karl Geldnir." Fjorn slid off the sleigh, and remained leaning against it.

"Jarl Erik Bloodaxe greets you. I am to see you to your rooms."

"I must speak with the jarl." Fjorn felt Sigurlina slip down on one side of him and Audun take position on the other. Vidurr and Ragna moved to stand behind him. The oarsmen watched uncomfortably from the sleigh.

"That will be quite impossible. The jarl is busy." The bureaucrat seemed to puff up and his cloak parted. Sigurlina couldn't believe her eyes. The man was plump. Not solid like almost everyone else was, since fimbulwinter, but carrying an actual layer of fat.

"I must insist. I have important information to share."

"Well, well, well. Then you can tell me. I am his Majesty's ears, eyes and voice."

"We must insist we speak with the jarl himself." Audun glowered down at the man.

"You are most ungracious. This is no way for a royal guest to act. I will..."

"I can take Fjorn from here, Geldnir. Why don't you show the crew to their room?" said Halla, wearing a rich gown, as she stepped out of a side door.

"Ambassador." Geldnir's tone was just this side of rude as he gestured to the oarsmen to follow him.

"Bureaucrats, they are a constant nuisance around the capital. Still, someone has to keep track of things. I have spoken to Jarl Erik. He will receive you, Fjorn. The rest of you should go with Geldnir."

"I and Vidurr have first hand knowledge of the matter at hand," explained Audun.

"Very well, but, the women." Halla gestured at Sigurlina and Ragna.

"Where he goes, I go," said Sigurlina, eliciting a smile from the beautiful selkie.

"I'm part of this mess too," added Ragna.

"Very well. Come this way."

Fjorn leaned on Sigurlina and grit his teeth as they were led into the palace and down a long corridor of dressed stone.

"Are you unwell?" Halla paused in the passage examining Fjorn in the torch light.

"He needs time to recover. You said that yourself," remarked Sigurlina.

"Sadly, that is true. Magic can only do so much. Try to be brief. It will be welcomed by the jarl and better for you." Halla opened a wooden door and led the way into a room as large as a great hall in most towns. On a raised dais at the far end, Jarl Erik Bloodaxe sat upon his thrown surrounded by men holding scrolls who all seemed to be jabbering at once. Armed guards stood along the walls.

Fjorn and his companions walked towards the dais across the empty room. Erik noticed them and motioned for the jabbering men to leave him. He nodded to a child in the corner of the room and the boy carried forward a large horn. Curls of steam came out of the horn's mouth.

Three, large, armed guards stepped forward. The middle one spoke. "We will hold your weapons."

Fjorn bowed his head, unstrapped his long sword and passed it to one of the guardsmen.

Sigurlina held out her staff.

"Do you walk the shadow road?" the guard facing her looked from the staff to Munin on Sigurlina's shoulder and back nervously.

Confusion crossed Sigurlina's features then she remembered how her mother and grandmother had acted with strangers most of her life. She pulled herself up to her full height and spoke with quiet authority. "I follow the ways of Seith. However, we have no quarrel. Hold my staff against my return without fear." She allowed a slight smile to touch her lips. "I need it not."

The guardsman swallowed and gingerly took the staff. "I will keep it as if it were the queen's own. Your raven may wait on the perch behind the throne." He gestured to a wooden railing close to the ceiling that spanned the width of the room behind the throne. A large raven was already perched there.

Sigurlina dipped her head. "Munin."

"Squawk, pretty bird, pretty bird." Munin launched herself off Sigurlina's shoulder and landed beside the other raven.

"And she criticized me," muttered Ragna, as she watched the ravens begin to groom each other.

Audun handed over his battle axe and Ragna the short sword she'd 'acquired' from one of the oarsmen that had leapt overboard at the start of the last battle.

Vidurr gripped his sword and scowled. "Only because this is his house, and it is a proper request for a host to make. Erik Bloodaxe is no jarl to me."

"It is not for me to challenge your reasons, I need only hold the weapons," the guardsman said coldly as he took the sword.

"Come." Halla led the way to the jarl's feet.

Fjorn, Audun, Sigurlina, Ragna and Kjorn all dropped to one knee before the throne. Vidurr stood with his hands in view at his sides.

Erik scanned the battered, wounded and weary group before him. His face soured when he looked at the Ulfhednar. "I accept the obligation of the host, wolf's son."

"I accept the obligation of the guest, jarl of my companions." Vidurr's posture relaxed and he dipped his head.

"Halla said you had news about the sinking of my ships," prodded Erik.

"Yes, my Jarl. For your ears." Fjorn looked up at Erik as blood from his wound seeped through his cloak and dripped to the floor.

Erik noticed the red splatter. "One moment." Erik clapped once and the boy who'd brought him the horn rushed to his side. "Fetch my healer and be quick." The jarl turned back to Fjorn. "Have you strength to speak. All I have brought to this chamber can be trusted."

"Hakon has a horn that can summon kraken. He is using the beasts to attack your ships." Fjorn grunted in pain.

Erik rose from his throne and brought the steaming horn to Fjorn's lips. "Drink, the warmth will help. Have you seen this horn?" he looked at Audun as Fjorn drank.

"I have been on two ships attacked by kraken after it was sounded, and I have seen the ship it was on. Hakon and his crusaders slaughtered my first ship's crew. Fjorn saved me from shipwreck. We were attacked during our voyage and barely escaped."

"I saw the kraken attacking them. Two of them working together, and I heard the horn that called them off when the battle went our way," added Vidurr.

Erik passed the horn to Audun. "It is a horn of greeting, drink all of you. When the healer comes for Fjorn, I will have you shown to your rooms. It would seem you have had an eventful voyage. This is dire news you bring. If it is true."

Audun quaffed from the horn and passed it on. "I can only report what I have seen and heard."

Fjorn collapsed and Erik caught him as he fell, lowering him to the floor then pulling back his cloak. The tunic revealed was soaked in blood.

"Freya!" Sigurlina rushed to his side. Breathing deeply she called her magic. Warm dew beaded on the blood stained tunic and Fjorn's breathing steadied.

"Nicely done, but he will need more. I've seen this wound, it can be survived. He has proven himself loyal to me, and a loyal man is more valuable than gold. I will not see him squandered." Erik drew a dagger and began cutting away the tunic. A moment later three men rushed into the room and hurried to Fjorn's side.

"Care for him as if he were me." Erik rose, took the horn form Ragna and finished it before tossing it to the boy and resuming his throne.

"I will think on this matter. Ambassador Halla Sea Born, please see my guests to their rooms. I will keep you informed about Fjorn." A smile graced Erik's lips. "It would seem he has made a jarl smile more than once."

Halla led the group from the great hall, through a maze of corridors to a large room divided by wooden walls into private chambers. Just inside from the door was a chamber containing a table and hearth. A fire burnt in the hearth and the table was laid with bowls of steaming stew, loves of bread and a platter of meat.

Ragna raced from the door into a seat at the table and began ladling stew into her mouth.

"How can you eat when Fjorn may be--?" began Sigurlina.

"Starving ourselves won't help him," Audun interrupted her as he took a horn from a peg in the wall and lifted the wooden cover on a keg of mead by the door. He scooped out a horn full, took a long drink then moved to the table. "Better than ship's fare, I'll say that."

"They're right. I've known Fjorn for a long time, and he'd say the same." Kjorn filled a horn.

Sigurlina felt a hand on her shoulder and turned to look at Vidurr. "This isn't over. You'll need your strength. We all will."

Sigurlina nodded and sat at the table. The stew and meat were venison, while the bread was the best she'd ever tasted. When the table was barren they moved to the private chambers finding that each contained a sleeping platform dressed for the night.

Sigurlina stripped off her salt crusted clothing hanging it on pegs in the wall and slipped under the blankets. Despite her worry, exhaustion, warmth, and a full belly conspired against her and she was asleep in seconds.

#

Fjorn groaned and his eyes fluttered open.

"Can you speak?" demanded an elderly man that leaned over him.

Fjorn swallowed. It felt as if his mouth was stuffed with rags. He whispered, "Drink?"

The old man vanished and a moment later returned with a horn that he held to Fjorn's lips. Fjorn drank tasting weak mead and bitter herbs.

"You gave us quite a time," remarked the old man.

Fjorn sighed. "Draugar are not gentle creatures."

"So that part was true?"

Fjorn nodded. "My friends?"

"All well fed and sleeping. That big one can eat, no surprise there, but the little one. Where she puts it all?" The old man smiled. "I am Geldnir, Healer to the Jarl, and whoever the jarl decides he likes, or he has a use for. I don't know what you told him, but you have put a falcon in the dove croft. I've not seen the court this busy since the fire."

Fjorn settled on the cot. "Good."

"We need to get some food in you, then more rest. With luck, in a day or two, you will be back with your friends."

#

After sleeping, Sigurlina ate then walked the corridors of the palace. There was a strange sensation, almost like an itch. It was both like and unlike what she'd felt at the cave where the Death Bone dagger had been kept.

"If it please you, my lady, these are private chambers." The young, handsome guardsmen that had been assigned duty as her guide smiled pleasantly as he spoke, but the set of his jaw told her that his implication was no suggestion.

"Can't you feel it?" asked Sigurlina.

"Feel what?" replied the guard. "These are the queen's private rooms. None may enter save by her or the jarl's command. I must--." The guard's eyes went wide and he dropped to one knee.

Sigurlina felt someone behind her and turned to face a stunningly, beautiful woman nearly half a head taller than her.

The woman smiled, but her blue eyes stayed cold. "Hello fellow seeker. I was planning to invite you to dine with me, but I suppose it is not surprising that a Seithkona would be drawn to my efforts."

Sigurlina swallowed hard, averted her eyes and fell to one knee. "Your Majesty."

Gunnhild chuckled and stroked Sigurlina's cheek. "Come, you are invited. Ragnar, I'll have one of my ladies show her back to her room. You have done your duty by me, so have no fear."

The guard dipped his head lower and stood. "Thank you, my Queen." He backed away three steps then turned and strode down the corridor.

"Men, always a balancing act. Push too hard and you unman them, and then they're useless. Push too lightly, and they forget their place. Training them is an art." Gunnhild examined Sigurlina. "What is your lineage? Who taught you?"

"My grandmother, Inga, daughter of Asdis, of the line of Jarl

Ingvarr, Your Majesty.

"We are sisters. Asdis taught in my lineage as well. I've heard of your grandmother. She was great in her time. Whose company does she now keep?"

"She made the final voyage a few days before I joined Fjorn." Sigurlina bit her lip and tried not to cry.

"I am sorry; it is never easy, though it need not be as hard for us as most." The queen patted Sigurlina's shoulder.

"Thank you, Your Majesty."

"It is I that owes you thanks."

"I'm sorry?" Sigurlina looked up startled.

"It was not for nothing that I ordered Fjorn to retrieve the Niflheim ore dagger. Come, there is that which I would show you." Gunnhild led the way down the passage into her personal section of the palace. "You may never speak of what you see, but as a Seithkona I have need of your aid. You can recognise what I will require if you come across it, and I foresee travel in your future."

"What?" began Sigurlina.

The queen threw open a side door. A blast of cold entered into the hallway. Sigurlina followed the queen into a square courtyard five strides to a wall. A circle of braded silver and gold was set into the floor marking a space four strides across. Inside that circle was another circle of dried ash berries. In the centre of that circle grew an ash tree. The tree was in full leaf. Nine skulls hung on the tree, seven of them were unmarked. Precious metal and gems encrusted one of them. The remaining skull was pierced by the Death Bone dagger so that the handle rose from its top and the blade protruded from its bottom.

"The draugar--," gasped Sigurlina.

"Are blind to it. The walls of this courtyard are wrapped in spells so no being, be they mortal or immortal, can sense what occurs here. What you see is my greatest working. Nine skulls taken from those who carried the blood of gods to focus the powers of creation." Gunnhild smiled at the top most skull. "It's a pity really; I rather liked Baleygr, such a polite man, no designs against my husband's throne. He was a great voice of reason at the meeting. That is why I used him for Asgard.

"It's Yggdrasil! Well a sculpture of Yggdrasil." Sigurlina looked confused.

"Feel it girl," commanded Gunnhild.

Sigurlina closed her eyes and reached out with her senses. Her eyes flew open and she stepped back against the wall.

Queen Gunnhild's eyes flashed and her demeanour became crazed. "Do you understand? Can you understand? The gods care not! We are pieces on a gaming board to them, nothing more. Once I am done though; then let Surt's fires rage, let the worlds collapse. My land will yet stand, and when the new world forms; we will be first. I will rule all, and my power will stretch over the nine worlds. So, at the least, I will rule as queen of a living realm in a world trapped in a season of death. At most, I will be a goddess more powerful than Odin himself, reigning over a new and vibrant Midgard. And it is not just for me. Think of the thousands that will live because of my craft. Now are not you proud to have played a part in my undertaking?"

Sigurlina swallowed. "It's amazing. But how?"

"We are but started, sister. I must link the other seven skulls. I need a piece of each of the nine realms to draw the energies of creation and feed them into my lands. From Orkney to Sverland, Sogn to Jutland, I will bring back the spring, and all will fall down before me and worship. Think, a green and growing land that is free of the tyranny of gods who squabble and fight like spoiled children. Think of how the White God's minions will desert him when they see real power. A living realm."

"This is greatness, but how can I help you, my Queen. I can barely comprehend the majesty of your effort. Why even bring me into your confidence?" Sigurlina tried to keep a waver from her voice.

"You already have helped me. Bringing the dagger to be sure, but the way you shielded it with the crystals, and the very life of your body. That showed me ways to refine my spell. I realise that the raw energy of Yggdrasil isn't enough. You are a young, fresh mind to see the problems. I have worked alone for too long. I need your eyes and your thoughts. It has been lonely work, as has been being queen. I see in you another seeker, and perhaps, a kindred spirit. I have dreamt of you. You are destined for great things, my dear. Great things indeed."

"I am honoured by your interest," said Sigurlina. The skin on her neck crawled.

"As you should be. Now, as your queen, and your friend, I call on you to watch for the remaining seven parts of my spell. An item from each of the realms. Bring them to me as you are able. I believe you are well meant for this task. Of five ships I sent around Midgard to retrieve Niflheim ore, only yours was successful. Thus I charge you to continue as you have begun." The queen stared at Sigurlina with an insane intensity.

"Of course, Your Majesty. May I ask, what happened to the other ships?"

Gunnhild shrugged. "Two were lost at sea, likely sunk by draugar, one returned without the Niflheim ore I sent them after. They lost half of their crew and their captain in the attempt, so Erik showed them mercy. The last, the captain and half his men went renegade. It wasn't a great loss; their ship was old and leaked."

Sigurlina suppressed a shudder at Gunnhild's dismissive tone. "I'm glad we were up to the task."

"You did wonderfully." The queen hugged Sigurlina like a long-absent friend. "It is so nice to have someone who understands. Erik is wonderful but he's a man, and you know what they're like. Even the ones that study Seith never really understand creation as we women do."

Sigurlina pushed down on the sick terror rising from her gut, smiled and nodded.

"This just couldn't be better. We must celebrate. Have you ever tasted wine? It's like mead only made from a fruit called grapes. It's very nice." Taking Sigurlina's arm Gunnhild led her from the courtyard and down the hallway.

\#

Audun drained his mead horn as his free hand pulled a dusky-skinned woman with hair as black as night into his side. She laughed and played her fingers across his chest.

"And then I tossed the bear a fish. I guess she thought a meal that didn't fight back was better than one that did. I miss Lady White and her cubs. They were good companions. I suppose the White God's godi I left on the iceberg will keep her company. Or supply a meal. Either way, I wish her well."

"You were so brave," cooed the dusky woman.

Ragna sat at the table in their common room and rolled her

eyes. "Please."

Munin nodded her head vigorously and squawked. "She's a bitch, she's a bitch."

"I'm agreeing with a black chicken." Ragna buried her face in her hands.

"Yura a bi--."

Ragna's hand shot out and held Munin's beak closed. "Sorry. You aren't a black chicken." Standing, Ragna strode to the end of the passage between the private rooms. A heavy drape separated a small, stone room. The stone had been cut so it made a low shelf at the back. An oval of wood lay in the middle of the platform.

"I wish my father could have seen this. Fit for a karl." Ragna moved the wooden cover revealing a hole in the rock shelf. Shifting her clothing she squatted over the hole. Moments later she reached for the wooden cleansing spoon hung on the wall. She scraped, swished the spoon in the bucket of water kept on the shelf for that purpose and returned the spoon. While readjusting her clothing, Ragna heard a distant plop come through the hole followed by a faint voice. Picking up the cover to return it, to stop the stink form coming into the room, she paused, listening.

"Why does she have to be like that? By the gods, I'm the jarl, not her! I should just..." Jarl Erik's voice was faint and echoed but unmistakable.

Ignoring the smell, Ragna brought her ear close to the toilet hole. Below her the hollow inner wall of the palace fell away to what had once been a stream. With fimbulwinter the water was frozen, but the depth of the hollow was such that it would take years for the refuse to pile up.

"Deep breath, Erik. Deep breath. None of it means anything if Hakon isn't stopped." The jarl chuckled. "Send a bastard to stop a bastard. She might like that."

There was a bumping sound and Erik's voice was cut off. Ragna put the cover over the hole and left the toilet alcove.

"Better than hanging off the side of a ship, I warrant?" Kjorn met her in the corridor. The man's smile left his face when he saw Ragna's expression. "What is it, girl?"

Vidurr paced in his small, private chamber. The air was too still. The only light came from the stinking oil lamps in the hall. The stone around him felt unnatural and the stench of human was everywhere. A subtle waft of air reached him through a place where the mortar between the stones in the wall had fallen out. He sniffed. A puzzled expression came to his face. Howling he transformed into the wolf. He lost the nuance of colour in his vision while his other senses came alive. He sniffed. On the breath of air through the chink, he could smell smoked meat and garlic. He listened and the sound of chewing reached him.

The door to his room opened and Audun appeared. "I heard you howl? Is there a problem?"

Vidurr pointed his muzzle towards the gap in the mortar then scratched at his ear.

Audun looked confused, then nodded. "I understand, if I had a nose like yours, I'd want to smell this place too. It is a magnificent abode. If you could just warn us in future, friend Vidurr."

Vidurr bared his teeth and growled a little as Audun closed the door.

#

Audun stroked the back of the dusky woman as she sat up from his sleeping platform.

"Bjork, where are you going?" He tried to pull her to him.

She stood turned and smiled at him.

"I have duties other then bringing you food and mead." She brushed the wrinkles out of her dress where it hung from a peg in the wall.

"Duty is easy to forget when faced with an exotic, beauty such as yours."

Bjork blushed. "What are you going to do now? I mean they say your captain is almost healed, so you won't have a reason to stay here anymore."

"I'm a navigator. I'll take ship. There is still a lot of Midgard I haven't seen. And I've a score to settle."

"With who?"

"Crusaders. They murdered my friends, my ship mates. They

didn't even have the decency to put a blade in their hand. To kill a man in battle, to send him to Valhalla, that is the way of things. To condemn a good man to Niflheim? I cannot let that spread in the world. It is an evil too foul."

"So, you won't stay with your captain... Fjorn was it."

"If our ways run together, and if he'll have me, I would take ship with him again. He is young and still learning, but there is that in him I would follow to the ends of the earth. Have you heard anything about him that the king's messenger didn't tell us?"

Bjork dropped her voice. "Well. Frida, she's one of the queen's maids, told Jora who mentioned to me that Jarl Erik and Queen Gunnhild have been heard arguing in their private chamber. The name of Fjorn came up. Jora thinks that the queen has taken him to her bed, and the jarl is angry about it. It's just a rumour." Bjork pulled on her dress.

"Just a rumour?" Audun looked to where he had stuffed a piece of rag into a chink in the wall's mortar to 'stop a draft.'

#

Munin leaned against the queen's raven on his perch in the royal's sleeping chamber. Below the floor was covered in carpets and a canopy bed dominated the centre of the room, surrounded by wardrobes and paired desks, both covered in hide scrolls. She absently groomed her companion's feathers. The door opened admitting Erik and Gunnhild.

"Nothing has changed!" snapped Gunnhild.

"Will you listen? We need to do something about that accursed horn. It will be a perilous mission." Erik sighed. "Probably one doomed to failure. It's a chance for the boy to die with a sword in his hand. He got you your Niflheim ore, we owe him that much."

"And suppose he succeeds?" Gunnhild glowered at her husband.

"Then the kraken problem is solved. Do you think this will be the last task we will have to select men to die for? We are fighting a war."

Gunnhild sighed. "You made a mistake when you ordered your healer to save him."

"Maybe I've lost enough brothers. Maybe I've had too many men under me find their way to Valhalla." Erik's voice sounded tired. "It's not the boy's fault my father would pull up his tunic for an ogre after draining a horn or two. The lad doesn't want to be a karl; let alone a jarl."

"He is yet young. Give him time and his desires will change. Though, I suppose it will be easier for Sigurlina if he goes to Valhalla. She is smitten with him, and she has been prominent in my visions. I can't fault her taste in men, he looks like you." Gunnhild smiled seductively. "When will you tell him to take ship?"

"In the morning, wife. In the morning." Erik half growled then pulled her to him and kissed her hard.

#

Fjorn, Sigurlina, Audun, Ragna, Vidurr and Kjorn entered the jarl's private office. It was three strides to a wall with a large table dominating its centre. A map depicting the great isles was rolled out on the table. Miniature, wooden swords in various colours were scattered about and model ships of various sizes and types were set on the surrounding seas. A fleet of ships was crammed into the area around Isle of Wight. Erik and Gunnhild stood studying the map.

"Fjorn, tell me. What do you think will happen when Hakon sails with his crusaders if our ships are trapped in harbour?" Erik gestured towards the fleet by Isle of Wight.

Fjorn studied the map and answered in a grave voice. "Odin will need to build new feast halls."

Erik looked directly at the others in the room. "At the least. Fjorn, son of Karl Geldnir of Orkney, I command thee, as my bondsmen, to undertake a mission that may save us all from the White God's savagery. None save those in this room know of it, or may know of it until it is done."

"Of course, Your Majesty."

"Dear as sister, will you aid him?" asked the queen.

"Yes, Your Majesty." Sigurlina bowed her head respectfully.

"You others, I would have you for this task. If you would depart, do so now without loss to your honour. If you stay, you are bound to this mission." Erik eyed Audun, Ragna, Kjorn and Vidurr.

"I am sworn to Fjorn, Great Jarl. I will not surrender that duty," said Kjorn.

"Will I get to kill crusaders?" Vidurr glowered at the royals.

"You will bathe in their blood," answered Gunnhild.

"Then we are of common cause."

"I will serve my Jarl," said Audun.

"Someone has to have some sense in the group, so I better go along," agreed Ragna.

Erik smiled. "I am glad. I have ordered your ship repaired and provisioned. None of the crew that came with you wishes to voyage with you again." Erik chuckled. "The general comment was that you couldn't spend skatt in Niflheim. I will have one of the bureaucrats give you a list of able seamen who will take ship. They will know nothing of your mission."

"What is the mission, Jarl Erik?" asked Fjorn.

"The selkies have brought word. The same storm that you sailed through went out over the Orse Sea. It nearly sank several of Hakon's ships. These ships are limping back to Winchester for repairs. My spies in Wessex report that Aethelstan has been building a great treasure house. Since he received word that the ships were coming to port he has ordered it finished before they arrive."

"Jarl Erik, how could you get word so quickly? It's only been three days since we arrived." Sigurlina blushed a little after speaking.

"Come sister. Selkie are faster than any ship. Did you think our young captain here was the first to think of using a Seithkona's raven as a messenger? Our sisters in the lands stolen by the White God's forces languish under their rule. Tortured, beaten and burnt for no reason save they will not grovel before their men, or forsake their gods and deny the art they have gained through long effort and practice. We have many allies. A message passed from raven to raven is swiftly carried."

"We will need gear, skatt that is struck in Wessex and a little time to plan." Fjorn looked at the map.

"Four days hard sailing, give or take. Then the over land portion," remarked Audun.

"You have not heard." Erik pointed to a place on the map over marked with black ink. The runes spelt out Winchester. "After the first year of Fimbulwinter Aethelstan ordered Winchester moved to his summer hall on the shore to give him quick access to his fleet. He changed the town's name for reasons of his own. His capital is now located near the mouth of the South Hamm Tun Water. "

"That makes things easier. We'll still need gear," observed Fjorn.

"Buy what you need." Erik tossed over a large sack of coins. "I will see a bag of skatt bearing Aethelstan's image is placed aboard your ship. Plan during the voyage. You sail before you sleep again. There is another task I will charge you with."

"Yes, Your Majesty." Fjorn weighed the coins in his hand.

"Towns on the coast of Northumbria have been set to the torch. Survivors speak of a jotun in a castle on the sea throwing flaming spears. As you must follow the coast anyway, investigate. King Cuaran is a staunch ally and I would offer him such aid as I can. But don't take too long about it," commanded Erik.

"I will do what I can, Your Majesty."

Gunnhild smiled at the group. "Die well, if die you must. Bring the horn to us; or at the least see that Hakon and his puppet master, Aethelstan, are deprived of it."

The royals left the room.

"How do we get into Aethelstan's court without getting killed?" demanded Ragna.

"That's the easy part," said Fjorn.

"If that's the easy part, I'm not sure I want to talk about the hard part."

CHAPTER 8

ONCE MORE TO THE SEA

"I name thee *Apenhet.*" Halla painted the name onto the front of the vessel. The runes looked flat until Audun passed his hand over them. The runes glowed for a moment and the small longship seemed to ride a little higher in the water.

"It's a good name," remarked Sigurlina.

Audun smiled. "A very good name for our vessel. It is what we fight for."

Fifteen oarsmen sat at their stations waiting to push off.

"I'll swim ahead and make sure the way is free of ice and other ships. With the sea safe for the moment, Jarl Erik is trying to get all his shipping done while he can. I'll come aboard when I need to rest." Halla slipped out of the traveling dress and cloak she wore and passed them to Fjorn. There was a collective gasp from the oarsmen. She donned her seal skin and slid into the water.

"I still say that is just wrong." Ragna walked the boarding plank and took her place in the bow.

Vidurr watched the large seal leap through the waves. A smile touched his lips as he boarded.

"It is her way." Audun boarded and moved to the tiller. Fjorn, Sigurlina and Kjorn followed.

"Cast off and make course. We'll hoist sail as soon as we have a favourable wind," ordered Fjorn.

The oarsmen pulled and the ship moved away from the dock.

Ragna opened her sea chest and brushed her hand over the rich clothing it contained.

"You should keep that closed so they stay nice. We'll need to look good when we reach Winchester." Sigurlina looked through the food chest, taking out the ship's cauldron. "We should heat some water for a stew to go with the journey bread. The oarsmen will like something hot."

"I'm sure they would, but I haven't given up on getting a royal guard yet." Ragna grinned wickedly.

Sigurlina blushed. "Ragna!"

"We can't all get the first karl's son we see. Lucky girl. I didn't even get to find out if things were proportional."

Sigurlina sputtered and carried the cauldron to the ship's brazier supporting the cauldron on the steel tripod above the charcoal. Using a bucket she filled the bottom of the pot with sea water then half filled it with fresh from the water barrel before dropping dried meat and some diced, preserved, root vegetables into the water. "In a few hours that will be stew."

"For which we all thank you. Nothing like a bit of hot food after a shift on an oar." Kjorn walked up the midship's plank. "Audun wants us all at the tiller before Halla comes back." He faced Ragna, "I think he has some privy talk to share... if you get what I'm saying."

Sigurlina looked confused but went with Kjorn and Ragna to the aft of the ship. Audun sat holding the rudder oar with Fjorn and Vidurr flanking him. They all moved close and spoke softly so the oarsmen couldn't overhear.

"Your jarl cannot be trusted. They were listing to everything we said when we were at the capital. Spying on us," blurted Vidurr.

Sigurlina went wide eyed. Everyone else shrugged.

"It's the capital. Jarls and karls spy if they want to keep their seat. I expected it. That's why we couldn't talk before now. And we still have to be careful." Fjorn gestured towards the oarsmen. "Audun, Ragna, Kjorn, keep a look out and let me know who you think might be a spy?"

"We also need to figure out who they are working for?" said Ragna.

"You mean Hakon?" breathed Sigurlina.

"Or the jarl," added Fjorn.

"They were all picked by one of the jarl's bureaucrats. We can't be sure of any of them." Kjorn laid his finger beside his nose.

"Or the queen. I heard the jarl. They were fighting about something. The jarl didn't want to do something, but she was nagging him," remarked Ragna.

"What were they fighting about?" Fjorn stroked his beard which had grown in enough to hide his jaw line.

"It was you. The rumour was running through the servants. Some of them thought that she'd taken you as a play thing. Bjork told me."

"So, that's what you were doing with that hussy, getting information." Ragna glared at Audun daring him to deny it.

Audun smiled. "Among other things."

Ragna sniffed.

"I... I think the queen may be mad." Sigurlina's voice came out as a barely audible whisper.

"What, just because she's the competition? He's not that bad looking, even with the fur on his face," quipped Ragna.

Sigurlina blushed crimson and Fjorn shifted from foot to foot.

"It's not that." Sigurlina dropped her voice even lower "She... She's working a spell that she thinks will turn her into a goddess."

"Will it?" asked Fjorn in hushed tones.

"Maybe. I don't know. She's used nine of the jarl's brothers' skulls as part of it. Whether she killed them for their skulls or just picked them out of the ashes, I don't know. She frightens me."

"How close is she to completing her spell?" Audun closed his eyes as he thought.

"Years away, I think."

"Then we'll worry about it later. What I want to know is what they decided about me." said Fjorn.

"Pretty bird. Pretty bird." Munin hopped from the gunwale to Sigurlina's shoulder.

'*I know. I know,*' the raven spoke into Sigurlina's thoughts.

"What do you know?" Sigurlina turned her head to face her familiar.

'*I was in the royal chambers with... Well, I was in the royal chambers and the jarl and queen came in. The queen said that the jarl shouldn't have saved someone. She was mean. I think she meant Fjorn. I like him; he slips me meat sometimes when you aren't looking. Don't tell him I told you because he might stop, but I know you wouldn't mind and--.*'

"Munin," hissed Sigurlina.

'*Sorry. The jarl said they should send Fjorn on dangerous missions. That he should at least get to go to Valhalla. The queen was happy with that. Of course after that the queen was very happy with.*'

Sigurlina tried to erase the image that Munin projected into her mind while her face turned beat red.

"What is it?" demanded Fjorn.

"The jarl and queen decided to send you on dangerous missions until you go to Valhalla."

Fjorn sighed. "I guess it's better than the straw death."

"Munin thinks it's mostly the queen. She wanted to kill you. Jarl Erik was just trying to keep her happy."

"Why does she hate you so much?" asked Vidurr.

"She doesn't hate him. She told me she likes him." Sigurlina turned her gaze to Fjorn. "She said you remind her of Jarl Erik. I... Oh my!"

"Took her long enough," remarked Ragna.

"The beard does hide it a little," observed Audun.

Vidurr shook his head. "You couldn't tell from their smell? Humans!"

Fjorn buried his face in his hand. "I'm going to die because I look like a man I never met."

"You will die, captain. But not today, and not alone." Audun scanned the faces around him. Everyone nodded. Munin hopped, landing on Fjorn's shoulder and began grooming his hair.

Fjorn took a deep breath and straightened. "We will not speak of this to Halla. I think she is safe to include in all our plans for the jarl's task."

"Agreed, she is the jarl's ear." Audun replied.

"She is a creature of the sea. He does not own her, although they have common cause," corrected Vidurr.

"As you say. We will plan for what is to come with her return. For the moment, the wind is shifting in our favour. I think we should hoist sail and get some sleep," ordered Fjorn.

Kjorn nodded and turned to the crew. "Ship oars and hoist sail. Gaut, get back here. You said you had experience with a tiller oar, now you can prove it."

#

Fjorn lay wrapped in blankets at his oar station near the stern. Water dripped onto his face. He murmured, "Sigurlina." A hand grasped his shoulder and shook it violently. His eyes flew open and he blinked stupidly at a very wet and naked Halla.

"I need your help, now!" The beautiful seal-woman looked panicked.

"What?" began Fjorn.

"A drifting net. Selkies are trapped in it. They'll drown."

Fjorn drew in a lung of air and bellowed, "All hands to stations."

The ship exploded into activity as the crew sprang to action. Audun rushed to the tiller oar then sat blinking stupidly awaiting instructions.

"Where are they?" Fjorn scanned the dark waters.

"Follow me." Halla slipped on her seal skin and dove over the gunwale.

"Follow that seal." Fjorn pointed in the direction she swam.

"What is happening?" demanded Vidurr, as he pulled on his oar.

"Selkies trapped in a drifting net," explained Fjorn for all to hear.

"We're racing to rescue devil spawn," snapped one of the oarsmen.

"Stow that bilge!" Fjorn glared at the oarsman pulling a name from memory, "Grimnir."

Ragna tied a coil of rope to a grappling hook from the ship's supplies.

Halla leapt from the water, did a summersault and dove.

"Munin, fly up and try to see the net," ordered Sigurlina.

The raven took to the air, skimming over the waves. Moments later she circled close to where Halla had disappeared. Oars drove into the sea and the ship came alongside the wooden sphere of a net float.

"Here," Ragna passed Fjorn the grapple on the line. He threw it, snagging the float the first time.

"Ship oars and pull on this line. Get things to cut the net." Fjorn bellowed.

The oarsmen began hauling the net into the ship. Muscles strained as they raced to drag the sodden hemp from the sea. A writing body crested the surface. Fjorn swung with his blade slashing the cords entangling the selkie. Ragna slit the cords entangling its tail. With a splash the seal-like form fell into the water, swam a little away and dove. Another selkie crested the surface. This one didn't writhe in its bonds. The net was hauled up. Audun and Vidurr lifted the selkie over the gunwale and lay it on the deck. Blade and axe made quick work of the net binding the creature, but it still didn't move.

Sigurlina moved to its side and pressed her hands against its chest calling her power. A light dew covered the still form. She pushed in on the chest, then released. Squeeze and release, while the men pulled two more selkies into the ship. Squeeze and release. The end of the net came into view. The first selkie they'd freed gnawed at the ropes holding one of its brethren. The rope gave way and the two selkies dove again.

The seal-like form in front of Sigurlina vomited, then its chest expanded and it started breathing.

"Youth to the gods, golden apples of grace.

"Idun's power, heal mortals of faith."

Fjorn's voice carried over the ship.

Audun traced Runes on the two selkies that just came aboard. One of them shifted on the deck.

"Youth to the gods, golden apples of grace.

"Idun's power, heal mortals of faith.

"From the deep sea comes life to this place.

 "Idun's power, heal mortals of faith."

Halla, naked with her seal skin over one arm, sang as she raced to kneel between her fallen kin.

The last of the rotting net pulled above the water. Two selkies gnawed the ropes holding a final one of their kin. The trapped one took a huge breath of air and barked weakly as the last of the ropes gave way dumping her into the sea.

The hide of the selkie closest to Halla parted down the front and a stunningly, muscular and handsome, young man slipped out.

"Thank Aegir you found us." He stood and took Halla's hands in his own.

A groan riveted Sigurlina's attention to the selkie in front of her, who was revealed as a girl of maybe thirteen. She could have been a younger version of Halla in looks.

"My grandfather? He pulled us up net and all so we could get another breath of air, but he..."

Sigurlina looked to the remaining selkie on the deck. It didn't move.

Halla knelt by the still form and felt for a pulse. She hung her head.

Fjorn looked over his crew. Most of the oarsmen bowed their heads. Gimnir sat in the stern scowling at the selkie. One of the men stepped forward and bowed. "Sister, beloved of the fallen. My skin was taken from me. Would a great heart grant me the sea while he swims with Aegir and Ran?"

"What happened to your skin, brother?" asked Halla.

"Crusaders captured me. They called me abomination and burnt it. They clamed to be saving my soul. But as we are as the gods made us; I knew that to be a lie."

"You are his kin," stated Halla turning to the other selkie.

"He was a great heart and lived a long life. Rejoin the sea, brother," said the male.

Tears welled in Vidurr's eyes as he watched the oarsman move to the side of the dead selkie. Half singing the oarsman stroked along the front of the seal-like form. The hide parted and peeled back from a grey-haired man who fell out onto the deck.

The oarsman removed his clothes and slipped into the seal skin. He barked twice then dove into the sea.

The young selkie raced to her grandfather's side and knelt hugging him.

"Why do you travel with these?" The male selkie gestured at the human ship's crew with anger and distain.

"Times change and it is necessary. Of the evils we face, they are the lesser," explained Halla.

"You are foolish to think so."

"We just saved your life," snapped Ragna.

"Humans made the net?" The male selkie scowled at her.

"Did I not say the lesser of evils," commented Halla.

"Are there angel of death duties you require?" Audun's voice was a soothing rumble.

The male selkie jerked around and found himself looking straight into the bottom of the big man's neck. His eyes tracked up to a mane of wild red hair, half wet from retrieving the net, then down to the battle axe held casually in a hand that could nearly envelop his head.

"The selkie inhaled deeply. "That is not our way."

"I am a death singer. I can do the calling."

"I would appreciate that, Yifa come. Lady, if you please." The selkie girl obeyed her brother's command and stood by the gunwale of the ship. Halla and the male selkie picked up the body and tossed it over the ship's side. It hit the cold water and floated. Halla spoke.

"To the deep places, the flesh, while he swims the nine realms freely.

"Come, great harvester and take this one forward to rich seas without end.

"May he know boundless fish and warm beaches.

"May all his days be blessed by Aegir, Ran and Njord."

"Goodbye grandfather," whispered Yifa.

Halla released a high-pitched cry that rose until it became silent. The body floated in the icy water.

Fjorn and the others watched the display. Fjorn noticed that Gimnir remained huddled by the tiller oar scowling and muttering to himself.

Halla repeated the cry.

Ragna turned to Audun. "What's supposed to happen?"

"I don't know. Perhaps it is like the keeners that cry at funerals. I--." Before he could finish, an orca swam through the icy water, devoured the body, and dove into the inky deaths.

"The great harvester is come; your grandfather now swims with Aegir." Halla took the other selkie's hands.

"Thank you," they both said as tears fell down their cheeks.

"Captain, what should we do with the old net? Toss it over the side?" asked an oarsman.

Fjorn looked at the mourning selkies. "No. Cut it up fine and burn as much as you can. I don't want a piece longer than your forearm going into the sea. Its killing days are over."

"The lesser evil," remarked the male who turned to Halla. "Call if you need us, we will come." Donning their hides brother and sister dove into the sea and vanished.

"Are we really going to chop up this net?" asked Gimnir. His face looked like he had eaten something sour.

"Every bit of it. Get your knife; you're on the first team." Fjorn turned to Halla. "Are you all right?"

"No. Thank you for asking. Your mother would have been proud of your work this day."

"You knew her."

"She would come and 'dance' with us on the beach because your father couldn't. We met. I should dress and get some sleep."

Fjorn realized that he had forgotten Halla was naked.

#

The wind died and they all had to man the oars, so it was nearly a day as the stars made it before they hoisted sail and Fjorn and the others could gather at the stern. Fjorn ordered Gimnir to the ice watch while they spoke.

"I don't trust him," said Ragna as she gestured towards the bow.

"I agree with you, but we can't just throw him over the side," said Fjorn.

"If he is with the crusaders, it is better than he deserves," snapped Vidurr.

"And what if he is simply unpleasant, lazy and cruel? You don't have to be a crusader to be nasty," said Audun.

"I don't like the way he looks at me." Sigurlina shuddered.

"It's unnerving, but you get use to it," Ragna and Halla replied in unison.

"What?" queried Fjorn.

"You try not to be a pig about it. Not all men do," remarked Halla.

"Am I supposed to understand that?" Fjorn looked confused.

Ragna rolled her eyes.

Halla sighed. "I suppose it's nice when it is so foreign to them that they don't even see it."

Fjorn still looked confused. "Right. In any case, if we make port, I'll pay Gimnir out and put him ashore. He's less than half a hand when there's work to be done, and he stirs up trouble with the crew. That's reason enough." Fjorn looked at the stars. "Are we drifting east?"

"Good, you're learning. We need to cut east to come between

Wessex and Saxony, so I'm not fighting the current," explained Audun.

"Keep hugging the Northumbria coast. We still need to investigate the burnt out villages."

"What's the plan when we reach Winchester?" Kjorn looked over the side to where an iceberg drifted by. "Did anyone hear that fool announce?"

Fjorn shook his head and sighed. "Half wages and if we even come close to land, he's off."

"I'll see to it. Should just throw him overboard. Could you do that whale call if I did?" Kjorn looked hopefully at Halla.

"It is only for the worthy dead. I would not want to give the great harvester indigestion." Halla smiled but it didn't reach her eyes.

"Too bad." Kjorn stomped to the front of the ship.

"What do we know about Winchester?"

"I was in the old city once when I was little. It was like the village I lived in, only bigger, except for the ghosts," said Ragna.

"Ghosts?" queried Fjorn.

"They may still be a problem. There were settlements along the coast from when the men of Rome tried to take the Great Island. The Romans liked to use stone to build." Audun adjusted the tiller oar. "I had a captain during my apprenticeship who told me about them. The stone works are falling. Some folks say giants built them, but the Romans were clever with rock, so I don't know. The new town is beside one of the old Roman settlements. Folk say the old ruins are haunted."

"That might help. We need to get into town undetected and scout things before we walk up to Aethelstan and ask him to open the front gate."

"I still don't like your plan. It violates the obligations of the guest," objected Vidurr.

"Aethelstan and Hakon violate the obligation of the host every day. They refuse hospitality to anyone who hasn't pledged to the White God," snapped Ragna.

"It's true. My father told me how the monks overcharged for their goods and cheated everyone who followed the Aesir. That's why he went Viking against them, to remove the stain to his honour when he found out he'd been cheated." Fjorn nodded sagely.

"The White God's people cheated in business and did not expect retribution?" gasped Vidurr.

Everyone nodded.

"Fools! Very well. They are not deserving of the laws of hospitality if they so betray them." Vidurr leaned back against the gunwale.

"This doesn't get us into the treasure hall," commented Audun.

"That is why we need to go in quietly first. Once we've seen how things are, we will make a plan." Fjorn looked over the icy sea.

"Land fire, starboard," called Kjorn's voice.

They looked forward. The torch showed two silhouettes, one was holding the other half out of the ship. When they listened carefully, quiet, intense words and whimpering could be heard. Several of the oarsmen sat watching the show. Judging from their postures, they seemed to be enjoying it.

"Make for the fire. If it's a port, I'm putting Gimnir ashore before someone kills him." Fjorn turned back to his associates.

"What I want to know is, how are we going to get by Hakon's fleet? The jarl's reports said that there were a lot of ships in the waters around Winchester?" Audun adjusted the tiller oar to take them towards the distant light.

Fjorn drummed his fingers on the gunwale.

"Really? You've never played the Game of Shadows. It's hard for them to catch you if they can't see you." Ragna shook her head in disbelief.

"I was too old for it when Fimbulwinter started," said Fjorn.

Ragna smiled and a twinkle came to her eyes. "I meant the grown up version. I've never been caught." She looked at Audun and winked. "Unless I wanted to be."

Audun shifted uncomfortably at the tiller oar.

As they neared the shore the firelight revealed the remains of a burnt out village with the figures of men, women and children silhouetted by the flames. Fjorn loosened his sword in its scabbard and ordered the crew to arms.

"What happened here?" whispered Audun.

Vidurr closed his eyes. It was as if he aged years in an instant.

"Crusaders like fire."

"Drop sail and set oars," ordered Fjorn.

The oarsmen obeyed and in minutes the *Apenhet's* bow scraped up on an icy beach. Five people in soot-stained clothing bearing torches rushed towards the *Apenhet*, swords drawn.

Fjorn looked at them as they drew near. They all had burns and hastily bandaged wounds. Rage and hopelessness were mirrored in their features.

"We come in peace and with offer of aid. What happened here?"

A woman with half-burnt braids stepped forward. A burn line cut across the right side of her face. "Who are you, and who do you call lord?" she demanded.

"I am Fjorn, son of Karl Geldnir of Orkney bonds man to Jarl Erik Blood Axe, and, had I had time when I saw your fire, I would have raised the white shield."

The woman's posture relaxed. "Anina, I lead... led this village."

"What happened?" asked Sigurlina who moved to Fjorn's side.

"I'll tell you what happened." An older man holding a battle axe limped forward. "It was a crusader's cog, ungainly, stupid, slow vessel for warm seas. I know it cause I sailed the south in me younger days. It dropped anchor two hundred strides off shore and threw fire at us. They didn't even land to loot us. They just wanted to burn us out."

"It threw fire at you?" Vidurr moved to Fjorn's side.

"I'll show you," offered the older man.

"Show my companions. Vidurr and Ragna, go with him. Kjorn, see to the ship and unload any supplies we can spare. After that, I want everyone helping to salvage the town. Audun, Sigurlina you're with me. We'll see to the wounded as best we can. Halla, scout the water and make sure nothing sneaks up on us."

Anina looked at Fjorn with wonder and a tear came to her eye. "Orkney has made a friend this day."

The next six hours were spent in feverish activity. Of the twenty-three surviving townspeople, seventeen required healing. Fjorn sung himself hoarse while Sigurlina had to be carried back to the *Apenhet'* where she collapsed exhausted from the magic she had expended. Between the oarsmen and Kjorn, a crude communal shelter was erected using the village debris. Halla came ashore leading seven selkie. Each carried two large fish that were added to the merger stores the *Apenhet* could spare.

When what could be quickly done was finished Fjorn and his crew gathered by the *Apenhet*. Anina, the burn on her face reduced to a slight reddening of the skin, faced Fjorn.

"Thank you. You have proven Orkney's worth this day. It will not be forgotten." She stared into Fjorn's eyes and smiled. "And thank your witch woman for me when she wakes up." She touched the newly healed skin on her face. "Another kindness that I will not forget."

"I wish I could do more." Fjorn looked over the camp that had been a village.

"You have turned death into life. Not bad for any mortal. We have a start to build from. I sent people to Jorvic with some skatt to spread the word and buy supplies. We should last until they get back now."

"May your gods walk with you," offered Fjorn.

"And yours." Anina returned to the temporary shelter.

"You need to see this." Ragna's voice came from behind Fjorn.

Fjorn turned and saw her standing beside Kjorn and Vidurr, who was holding a shaft of wood as long as Fjorn was tall and about as thick around as Ragna's wrist. The front of it was wrapped in cloth while the back had fins like an arrow, only larger.

"It landed in a snow bank. It's the only reason it survived. Shift it so he can see." Ragna stepped aside so Vidurr could stand the shaft on its end. Fjorn moved close. The cloth around the shaft's head stank of oil.

"Part the folds," said Ragna.

Fjorn pulled back the cloth revealing a clay pot twice the size of a man's fist held to the shaft by a bronze ring that circled the pots neck and was secured to the shaft with wooden pegs.

"What is it?" Fjorn stared at his friends.

"It's a ballista bolt. I saw them in my younger days. It's like a bow, only bigger," said Kjorn.

"It's made to carry fire. See the scorching on the cloth and that jar's full of oil," added Ragna.

"Crusaders, they're not even looting. Just burning towns then letting the cold do their work for them," spat Vidurr.

Fjorn closed his eyes for a long moment. He opened them and looked at the village that was. "They will pay. By Odin, Surt and all the powers, they will pay!"

Vidurr let his lips curl back from his teeth in a smile.

"We're ready to cast off." Kjorn moved to Fjorn's side and whispered. "What about Gimnir?"

Fjorn sighed and shook his head. "These people have enough problems. We'll have to keep him aboard."

Kjorn released a displeased grunt and nodded.

They boarded and moved to the stern where they were joined by Audun and a still unsteady Sigurlina.

"What I don't understand is why they haven't used this weapon before," said Ragna gesturing towards the burnt out village.

"Because their cogs are leaky tubs. In a fight, the 2 could sail circles around one," stated Kjorn.

"It makes sense. Use the kraken horn to force us to keep our ships in harbour. Then send the cogs out to destroy the towns. If your goal is just to kill town's folk, destroying their shelter and letting the cold do it is craven but a solid plan," said Fjorn.

"No honour," snarled Vidurr.

"No honour," agreed Fjorn and Audun in unison.

#

Five days out from Alvaldsnes, Fjorn finished his bowl of stew and watched as the final coals in the ship's brazier turned to ash.

"Last hot food for a while," remarked Audun.

"I don't mind. The journey bread is good. The jarl had it made fresh the day we left, so it isn't too hard yet, and..." Sigurlina trailed off as she felt all eyes on her.

"I'll douse the torches as soon as we stow the sail. I still say we should keep the lanterns." Kjorn moved to the mast and began working the ropes.

"Only the one we cover. We need to be invisible. Halla, you are our eyes now. Find a good landing in the ruins." Fjorn turned to the beautiful selkie who was already removing her clothes.

"I'll find you a spot. Just don't hit any icebergs before I get back."

Fjorn smiled at her. "We'll do our best. Vidurr, we could use your nose and ears as well, if you don't mind."

Vidurr nodded then howled. A moment later the giant, red wolf stalked along the deck to the bow and gazed over the side.

"It's going to be cold without any fire," complained Ragna.

"Warmer than being striped and tied to a mast. This was your idea. Are all your ropes set?" whispered Audun.

"Set and ready to tie you down," Ragna winked suggestively.

"I'll never be tied down." Audun moved to the tiller oar and slipped a loose loop of rope around each ankle.

Kjorn snuffed the torches and the darkness closed in. He shipped and doused the aft lantern, brought the fore lantern midship putting it in a barrel that had held salt cod and closed the lid. The darkness of fimbulwinter closed in. The stars were dim. The fires of Muspelheim on the horizon were a distant, red glow. The Bifrost Bridge danced in the northern skies, but it did little to light the eternal night.

"Someone is fighting a battle," observed Sigurlina, as she watched what looked like ants because of the distance travel over the Bifrost Bridge.

"Someone is always fighting a battle. It's just a matter of if it's your battle or not." Fjorn, going by sound and feel in the dark, reached out and cupped her cheek. "When we are off this ship, I want to show you things," he whispered.

Sigurlina felt her heart flutter. "When we are off this ship." In the dark, she risked nuzzling his hand.

Fjorn pulled away ending the moment. As he looked out over the gunwale, he could see the sea was alive with points of light. A creaking sound reached his ears. "Muffle oars." He hissed.

The oarsmen wrapped rages around where the oars passed through the oar locks and started pulling with long, slow strokes.

Time stretched on in the dark as they steered away from any of the seaborne lights. After a seeming eternity, there was a seal's bark. Lowering a platform into the sea, Fjorn and Kjorn reached over the side. Wet, slender arms first brushed then gripped their own. Silently, they helped Halla aboard.

"I found a spot. I think it's an old harbour. It's silted in and gone to marsh, but we have a shallow enough draft to get in. Hakon's ships are everywhere, but they are giving the old town a wide berth," whispered Halla.

"Thank you. I'll toss you the rope and you can guide us in." Fjorn whispered in reply.

Halla climbed over the side. A moment later there was the sound of a splash. Fjorn and Kjorn pulled the platform aboard then Fjorn moved to the bow. Vidurr greeted him with a growl.

"Do you know how unnerving that is in the dark?" Fjorn took a length of rope with the fishing float they'd recovered tied to one end and threw it into the sea. The rope was attached at the other end to an oar handle they'd cut off and secured to the gunwale at the bow with a single spike. A moment passed and the oar handle pulled to starboard.

Grasping a rope on the deck Fjorn tugged it.

At the tiller oar, Audun felt the rope around his right ankle tug and he steered starboard.

The wood secured to the forward gunwale pulled straight. Fjorn tugged both the ropes in his hands and the tiller straightened as the oarsmen slowly brought them forward. A line of what could only be torches grew nearer. The crew shipped oars and held their breath as a huge longship cut across their course. When it was a distant spot of light they rowed again. Twice this pattern was repeated before they neared the coast.

The land began to close in on either side of the *Apenhet*. The oar handle pulled starboard and Fjorn tugged the rope in his left hand. The *Apenhet* steered starboard. The oar handle straightened, Fjorn pulled both ropes and the *Apenhet's* course trued. Minutes passed before something loomed ahead of them. The sound of dry reeds brushing against the side of their boat filled the air. There was a seal's bark.

"Ship oars." Fjorn took the mooring line and leapt forward onto a dark shadow. He landed on a stone pier thrust into the marshy water and pulled the line to what proved to be a crumbling pillar of stone. As he was securing the line there was a thud and a colossal shadow moved on the pier. There was the sound of wood bumping stone as the shadow pulled on something then moved to another shadow.

"Ship secured fore," hissed Fjorn.

"Ship secure aft," replied Audun's voice.

CHAPTER 9

A GHOST OF A CHANCE

Fjorn went back to the ship, which was little more than a shadow against shadow. "Kjorn, you're in charge until I return. Wait five days and if I haven't come back, leave and tell the jarl that we failed. No lights, no noise unless you can find an old building that will hide them. Scout the area, but be quiet," commanded Fjorn.

"Yes, captain," replied the old sailor's voice.

Fjorn turned to the shadowy form of a seal on the pier. "I am in your debt, Halla. This is a perfect landing. If you could search the coast for hidden inlets and bays where we could hide if we must, I would appreciate it. Return here in two days, as the stars make it, if you would."

The selkie barked once and slipped into the water.

Vidurr stepped onto the pier and curled one of his wolf lips.

"You should remain a wolf, your senses are sharper, and we'll need that," remarked Fjorn. "Just remember, we don't want a fight today."

"Here." Sigurlina passed Fjorn his pack and the stern lantern draped in a wet piece of cloth then mounted the dock Ragna followed. Munin circled in the blackness above. A moment later, the raven landed on Sigurlina's shoulder. "Munin didn't see anything but a strange light in the ruins."

"Torch or lantern?" Fjorn's voice was concerned.

"She says it was nothing like that. Just a glowing spot. There wasn't anyone there."

"Everyone, get your snow shoes and we'll get started. We move north and west whenever the streets allow. We want to scout the new town's defences and maybe find a way we can sneak in." Fjorn donned his snow shoes and, looping the end of a rope around his waist, led the way into the runes with Vidurr walking at his side.

The crumbling, stone walls to either side of the street loomed as darker shadows against the night. Before fimbulwinter, vines and weeds had taken hold leaving fibrous robes to trip the group. The snow had drifted against obstructions. In some places they had to force their way through chest-deep snow piles while in other places the ground was nearly bare.

"Can we have some light now?" whined Ragna, as she walked clumsily in her snowshoes past a drift taller than herself.

"No. We keep the lantern covered until we reach the new village. Right now, the darkness is our friend. Only speak when necessary," hissed Fjorn.

Sigurlina tried not to look at the spirits they passed. On the crumbling remains of a stone house, a woman in a toga sat holding an infant to her breast and weeping as she rocked back and forth. Soldiers in strange armour, carrying huge shields and short swords, marched in straight lines down the street carrying a fallen comrade on a bier.

A man in rags knelt beside the foundation of what once must have been a fine home begging. A mounted man in armour made of metal strips with a horse's mane on his helmet thundered down the street, his lance poised to strike. A matronly woman in fine clothing walked past clutching the bloody stump of her severed left-hand.

All manner of death and sorrow surrounded Sigurlina. She knew if the ghosts discovered she could see them, she would be swarmed by them. She stepped closer to her living companions and kept her eyes forward.

Turn followed turn as they zigzagged their way through the maze of crumbling city streets. Foot sore and chilled, they came to a place where the road ended in shadow. Fjorn motioned for them to hide and whispered, "Vidurr."

The huge wolf stalked forward, vanishing into the darkness and rubble.

Vidurr sniffed the air. He could smell the waste of humans. Before him rose a palisade made up of piled stone interspersed with wood. The snow was covered in foot prints, some of them recent. He found a place by a wall where a man had relived himself. The smell told him that is was close enough in time that the urine was still warmer than the surrounding ice and snow.

Vidurr crept back to his companions and silently led them away. Two streets back from the palisade, behind the shelter of a crumbling building, he howled, resuming his human form.

"They have a wall the height of two, tall men. It probably

encircles the landward side of the village. Men patrol it. If we tried to climb it we'd be seen." Vidurr flexed the fingers on his hands as if they were stiff from the cold.

"And if we kill the guard we'd have to make it look like an accident or give ourselves away," remarked Audun.

"Wolf attack?" suggested Vidurr.

"And have every hunter with a bow scouring the area. No." Fjorn's voice was thoughtful.

"Can we have some light while we talk?" There was an edge to Ragna's voice.

"We're sheltered here." Fjorn uncovered the lantern.

The light of the lamp reflected off the snow revealing the world to their dark adapted eyes like a full moon once would have.

Vidurr scowled. "Too much stone. It reminds me of the palace."

"Look." Sigurlina pointed to a dimly glowing sphere just down the abandoned street. The light seemed to pulse and change colour.

"It's pretty," said Ragna.

"So is a wild cat. I still wouldn't want to see one if I was a rabbit," observed Audun.

"What is it?" asked Fjorn.

Everyone shrugged.

"Should we follow it?" Ragna took a step in the direction of the light.

"EGO haud operor ut si EGO eram suus," spoke a ready voice.

Sigurlina whipped around. The voice had sounded like a shout to her. A slender man in a ragged toga with long, unkempt hair wearing a wooden pendant in the shape of a fish stood at the edge of their lantern's light.

Fjorn and the others squinted in the direction of the voice and drew weapons.

Fjorn saw a wispy, transparent form. It was a scruffy man in a strange draping robe. He sank into the snow to his knees without disturbing it. A pendant in the shape of a fish hung around his neck. The voice had been just on the edge of hearing.

Sigurlina stepped forward. "Who are you?"

The Haugbui stared at her, its face puzzled.

"I don't think it understands me," said Sigurlina.

"Quisnam vos?" asked Ragna.

"Abselema." The Haugbui gestured towards the light and spoke in heavily accented Orse. "Willow Wisp. A bad creature." He bit his lip as if in thought and continued slowly. "It will lead travelers to danger and then eat their life."

"Thank you." Sigurlina un-slung her pack and took out a loaf of journey bread. Breaking off a piece the size of her thumb she set it on a protruding rock. "I make offering to you helpful shade in thanks for your guidance."

Abselema seemed to puff up and half floated through the snow to the offering. "Accipio." He seemed to take on substance as he hovered over the bread.

Sigurlina could now see other shades at the edge of the lantern's light. They crowded in, their voices pushing into her mind, more voices arriving by the second.

"Meus infantia, Meus infantia."

"Is erant a bonus Pusio. centurion haud res transporto eum."

"EGO sum fames."

"Nos mos coegi illud puteulanus pictoratus spurius tergum."

"Ingratus parvulus. Vos mos requiro mihi iam."

"I think he said thank you," translated Ragna.

"So, we don't follow the light. We still have to know if he is dangerous or not?" Audun gestured at the Haugbui.

"I know that." Sigurlina snapped; her voice was like a whip. She clutched her head and fell to her knees from the jumble of spirit voices. The invisible spirits crowded in closer to her. Her companions shivered if one stepped through them.

Audun took half a step back. "What?"

"It's the others. Discedo vos sors. Per Niveus Deus quod suus valde abbas discedo," said Abselema.

"What's he saying?" demanded Fjorn.

"He's telling the spirits to go away." Ragna looked at Sigurlina, who knelt in the snow clutching her head. "I don't think they're listening."

"I don't see any spirits other than him." Vidurr glowered at Abselema.

"You're not a Seithkona." Ragna scowled at Vidurr then moved to her friend's side and hugged her. "Think of the living. We're here. Keep them out. You are Sigurlina, you are a Seithkona. You can control them."

Sigurlina pulled her hand away from her head, reached into her belt pouch and clutched the three stones her grandmother had given her. Her body jerked then she slowly straightened.

"Thank you, dear. That helped." Sigurlina's voice had an odd timber. "Oh my, there are a lot of them. You shouldn't feel bad, dear. This would have challenged me, but we're together now."

"Thank you, grandmother. I just couldn't keep them all out." Sigurlina's voice returned to normal.

"Sigurlina?" breathed Fjorn.

"He is a handsome one. You just be good to my granddaughter." Sigurlina's lips moved, but the voice wasn't hers, nor was the provocative posture.

"Grandmother!" Sigurlina blushed crimson.

"It's her grandmother. I think she's here to help. Aren't you?" asked Ragna.

Sigurlina's body turned and smiled at the diminutive woman. "It's a little different than before. Sigurlina is awake. I suggest we get her out of this place. It's not good for two spirits to share one body. It becomes hard to know where one ends and the other begins. And I wouldn't want to do something my granddaughter would rather do for herself." Sigurlina's body trailed her fingers over Fjorn's chest in a suggestive manner.

"Grandmother!" Sigurlina jerked her hand back and blushed.

"I... It's a pleasure to meet you, Ma'am." Fjorn sounded confused and intimidated.

"My name is Inga. I must say, a karl's son, handsome, and seemingly honourable. You're lucky and have good taste, little one. And Fjorn, the pleasure is mine. Or would be, if this were my form."

"Grandmother!" Sigurlina looked horrified. "I'm so sorry. I..." her voice trailed off.

"Come. I know a place the shades will not go," remarked Abselema.

"It would be for the best," agreed Inga. "Young, healthy flesh offers too many temptations." She eyed Fjorn and sighed.

"Can we trust a Haugbui?" challenged Audun.

Abselema eyed the big man unpleasantly.

"Please," pleaded Sigurlina. "Grandmother, stop looking there."
Sigurlina's blush deepened. "Is this what you were really like when you
were young?"

"How do you think I netted your grandfather?" replied Inga.

"I like her," remarked Ragna.

"Thank you. The Haugbui will behave himself. Sigurlina and I are
here to make sure of it," added Inga.

Fjorn shifted uncomfortably. "We need to make camp anyway.
Please lead us to your safe place, Abselema."

The shade moved to a crumbling building at the side of the
street, drifting through snow banks as if they weren't there, until it came
to a set of stone steps leading downwards. They followed the Haugbui
down the steps into a stone walled room five strides long by three wide.
A crude fish had been carved into the wall opposite the entrance door
and a stone block erected. A wooden cup stood on the stone with a small
brazier suitable for burning incense and a chipped porcelain plate.

"They won't follow you in here. It is consecrated to the White
God," said Abselema, who became more tangible as he drifted towards
the altar.

Fjorn stopped at the door. Sigurlina pushed past him.

"It is quiet," she remarked as her tension eased.

"If feels like Baldur. Not surprising really." A wicked smile came
to her lips. "Be good dear, but not too good. Have some fun."

Sigurlina lurched and leaned against the wall. She slipped the
three stones back into her belt pouch.

"Are you...well... you?" Ragna pushed into the room.

"I'm fine. Grandmother left. Fjorn, I'm... well." Sigurlina blushed.

"I would have liked to have known your grandmother when she
was young. She seemed... interesting," Fjorn entered the room. "If this
place was the White God's, where is the cross?"

"Cross? The instrument of death? This is a place of life. A place
for fishers of souls," Abselema sounded confused.

Vidurr's nose twitched as soon as he entered the chamber. He moved behind the altar. A mouldy blanket covered something. "Who was this?"

Abselema drifted next to the blanket. "My mortal remains. My son came back and covered me before he escaped. My brethren never returned. I hope they got away."

"What happened?" Sigurlina sat with her back against the wall.

"That is a long story." Abselema moved about the chamber tidying it.

"We have time before we sleep," observed Audun.

The Haugbui moved in front of the altar. "If you insist."

Ragna settled beside Sigurlina. "You see what you've done? Now we get to listen to his life's story. Literally."

"Yura bitch," commented Munin from her place under Sigurlina's cloak.

"What I want to know is, why do you look more solid and your voice is stronger?" asked Audun.

"He's taking strength from our presence. The more he is with the living the more like the living he becomes," explained Sigurlina.

"You understand a great deal. Are you a priestess?" Abselema eyed her with curiosity.

"I follow the ways of Seith. I am what that makes me." Sigurlina smiled benignly.

Fjorn sat on Sigurlina's free side while Audun and Vidurr settled themselves across the room. Journey bread was pulled from packs and Audun produced a skin of mead.

The room grew quiet.

"Abselema please tell us. Why are you here and is there a way we can aid you?" opened Audun.

The Haugbui took on more substance and his voice became stronger. "I was a fool. I marched with Caesar's legions, spilling blood and bringing pain wherever we went. Then I met a fisher of souls. He was a simple man in worn clothing but he spoke of peace and love. He said that all men were brothers, and that the White God was for all.

"When I returned to Rome, I remembered his words, but searched other ways. Mithra had been my god in the legion but I was tired of battle and strife. I went to the temple of Jove, but it had lost its way and was too much a tool of the state, supporting whatever our rulers wanted. For a time I followed Lady Isis, but then I found her in Mary, blessed be her name, and her son was not a warrior, justified or not, which meant much to me. So, I became a fisher of souls. I was not a fanatic like some. I paid my taxes and gave lip service to Caesar's divinity, so none came to drag me to the coliseum for the games. My wife and I had good years before she was called to the Lord.

"I raised our son, but the day of his coming of age was approaching. I knew they would come to take him for the legion. This, I could not bear to see. The White God is a god of peace, and to see the peace I'd raised my son in shattered and twisted, no. My choices were few. Deny Caesar and have my son and myself taken for the games because he would not kill for the glory of Rome. Surrender my son to a life of bloodshed that would taint his very soul, or run.

"I sold all I owned. My son and I took ship to the furthest reaches of the empire where we hoped to vanish. For a span of years it worked. I founded a chapel, found others who embraced the White God's message of peace.

"Then, we were betrayed. Legionnaires broke down our door demanding the taxes we had withheld in protest to the ways of conquest and bloodshed. A legionnaire grabbed my son by the hair and dragged him towards the door. Then came my shame. I seized a legionnaire's sword from his scabbard and struck him down. I fought, spilling blood, betraying my vow of peace. The others fled, but I was run through and fell behind the altar."

"You were defending your people. It was a good death," comforted Audun.

"I broke my oath. I took a life. I am cursed because of that. I cannot leave this place and rejoin my Cloelia and son until I am forgiven by a priest of the White God. I must confess and be granted absolution."

Fjorn looked at Sigurlina. "Can you help him?"

"I follow Freya. All I know of the White God's way is what the crusaders showed me when they betrayed the obligation of the guest and slaughtered my parents."

"There are always those who will take something good and twist it to evil," said Abselema.

"Then maybe those who want it to stay good should stand against them," snapped Vidurr.

"Be this as it may. Do we want to live up to the best in our gods or down to the worst?" Audun met Vidurr's gaze and held it until the Ulfhednar looked away. He then turned to Abselema. "How can we help you?"

"Only a priest of the White God can grant me absolution from my sin."

"Angel of Death duties, I understand." Audun nodded.

"We need to enter the new town. Can you help us with that? If you do, we may find a priest that we can bring back here," said Fjorn.

Abselema paced the room in thought, his image passing through objects as if they weren't their. "Why do you wish to enter the town?"

"Fjorn looked at the Haugbui, he was no judge of spirits, but he was a good judge of men. "A false pretender to the throne has a weapon of incredible power. He has been using it to slaughter innocent seamen. We want to take the weapon away from him so the killing stops."

Abselema hung his head. "Man still kills his brother. When will it stop? Tell me, is it these crusaders you spoke of that hold this weapon?"

"This is ridiculous. We speak with a Haugbui and expect it to aid us," snapped Vidurr.

Fjorn glared at the Ulfhednar then turned to Abselema and answered. "Yes."

"Than I will do what I can. Yours is not the first tale of their misdeeds I have heard. The teachings of the White God should not be perverted into an excuse for bloodshed and war.

"It is beyond where my curse permits me to walk. I have heard from other shades that a bath on the edge of the city, closest to where the new village has grown up, has been restored. It may offer you access. I know of one who can tell you more. I will seek him for you while you rest."

"Thank you." Fjorn glanced around the room. Reaching into his pack he pulled out a tallow candle that had nine rounded bits forming its length. "Each of us will take a watch. We'll light the candle and when a sphere has melted it is the next person's turn."

"I could watch for you," suggested Abselema.

"That is not going to happen," remarked Ragna.

"I agree," added Vidurr.

"Have I not offered you my hospitality?" The Haugbui glowered at Ragna and seemed to suck the light out of the room while its image became cadaverous.

Hands went to weapons but Sigurlina's voice halted them short of being unsheathed.

"I'm sure what they mean is that, while you seem very nice, we only just met you. People aren't always what they seem. That's all it is. You must remember what it was like to meet new people."

Abselema seemed to shrink in on himself and the light returned to the room. "You have fair words, sighted one. Set your watch, though there is no need." With that he drifted from the chamber.

"You can't trust him. He's, well..." Ragna searched for the right words, "he's dead!"

"Yura bitch," squawked Munin.

"Just because someone is dead doesn't make them a bad person if they were good; or a good person if they were bad. My great, great grandfather took my grandmother and me in when all the living people turned us away. This is Abselema's home. The least we can do is be polite." Sigurlina glared at her companions.

Audun took a deep slow breath and looked at Ragna. "Sigurlina's right. If he were a living man, it would only be fitting to use fair speech."

"Fine, as long as we set watch." Ragna snuggled down in her cloak.

"We will, and I believe you are first up." Fjorn smiled at the diminutive woman and lit the candle from the lantern's wick.

The candle burnt away casting its flickering glow into the chamber. Abselema appeared at the door several times but never stayed until Sigurlina was sitting her watch.

"May we speak?" asked the Haugbui.

"If you like." Sigurlina eyed the dead man as he sat on the floor in front of her.

"What are you that you see the others, and that I don't have to shout for you to hear me?" he asked.

"I told you, I follow the ways of Seith. We walk the borders between the nine realms; tasting of them all; being in part of all of them and fully of none." Sigurlina quoted her grandmother.

"But you follow Pagan gods," said Abselema.

"The gods watch over the worlds. I respect them for their service, which benefits us all."

Abselema wrinkled his brow. "But they are not all powerful."

"Is a jarl all powerful? He may give commands that are followed, but let him command the grass to stop growing and who will heed him. Yggdrasil itself is all things. Even Surt is but part of a greater whole."

Abselema nodded. "You are strange to me, but I think we use words differently to say the same thing. You sound much like a priestess of Isis I once knew. I saw no evil in her."

Sigurlina nodded. "Evil is what evil does. Many call a thing evil because it is painful but a person chooses to do evil."

"Or good. Will your friends truly seek to bring me a priest of the White God?"

Sigurlina smiled as her eyes swept over her companions. "If they have said it, they will do it or spend their lives in the attempt. That is our way."

"That is a fair way."

They sat in silence until the bulb on the candle burnt down and Sigurlina woke Fjorn to take her place. Abselema left the chamber to prowl the dark streets.

Sigurlina awoke to Fjorn's gentle shaking. She opened her eyes and saw Abselema standing by the chapel's doorway with a transparent, dark-haired youth of maybe thirteen. The youth was dressed in a tunic and trews.

"Abselema says he's brought the one he spoke of, but none of us can see or hear him." Fjorn stepped back.

Sigurlina sat up and rubbed the sleep from her eyes. "I see him."

"Where?" Ragna stood up and practically walked through the young shade who was only a finger's breath taller than her.

"Right in front of you."

"She really can see me," breathed the shade.

"Yes. Tell her your tale," suggested Abselema.

The youth drifted to Sigurlina's side. "I'm Banning, son of Daegal."

"Sigurlina." Reaching into her bag she took out some journey bread, broke off a piece as big as her thumb and set it as offering.

"Oh," the young shade leaned against the wall. "That is wonderful."

"I'm glad you like it."

"Young Banning here may be able to help you get into the village unseen," prompted Abselema.

"How?" asked Sigurlina.

"Before I died I was a singer. King Aethelstan enjoyed my voice and didn't want to lose it when I grew up. I overheard him telling his priest to... to... to cut me, so that my voice wouldn't change." The young spirit hung its head and bit his lip. "I didn't want to be cut. I knew what some of the crusaders did to the half men in the choir. I had to get away.

"My father worked in the baths. I'd played there when I was small. There is a tunnel where they pour the dirty water. It washes down and takes all the dirt from the privy holes with it. It leads out into the old city. I slipped through the hole they pour the waste down and followed it. I got into the old city. I hoped that if I could hide until my voice changed; that King Aethelstan would forget about me. Only I..."

The shades features turned grey and what looked like water bubbled out of its mouth.

"It's all right, Banning, You've said enough." Abselema spoke in soothing tones. "Banning followed a willow wisp. I cannot blame the creature, it does what it does, but this King Aethelstan is no better than Nero."

"What's he saying?" asked Fjorn.

"There is a tunnel that carries waste water out of the baths that we might be able to use to get under the wall." Sigurlina pondered a moment. "Banning, how big is this tunnel?"

"It was big when I was little but when I escaped, I barely fit."

Sigurlina nodded. "It won't work."

"Why?" demanded Audun.

"Banning is just a boy, and he barely fit. He isn't much bigger than..." Sigurlina turned her gaze to Ragna. All the others followed the direction of her eyes.

"What?" Ragna paused in her 'inspection' of the temple's contents.

"Could she?" asked Fjorn.

Sigurlina's gaze swept from Banning to Ragna. "She's a little smaller than him in general."

"We don't all have to go into the town to inspect it. One could do it and report back."

"What are you talking about?" Ragna marched up and stood with her hands on her hips.

"Banning, could you show us where the tunnel you used lets out?" Sigurlina smiled.

"If you'll do something for me." The shade hugged himself as if he was cold.

"What?"

"Tell my father why I ran away. I don't want him to think it was because of him. I've tried but he can't hear me."

"We can do that."

"Stop talking to the spirit and tell me what's going on!" Ragna stomped her foot.

#

After a heated argument followed by a short walk, they stood as the opening of an arched passage. The passage ran into a gully that spilled into a frozen stream. A pile of semi-frozen waste had collected below the tunnel.

"Take these. It's some of the skatt bearing Aethelstan's face that Jarl Erik gave me. When you get through, we need to know the general way of the town. How many guards and most important where the treasure hall is and how it is guarded. Also, how far the hall is from the docks and the fastest route between them."

"I know, I know," snapped Ragna. "I'm buying myself a nice, new dress and cloak after I crawl through this privy."

"Do what you need to. We'll wait at the chapel for two days as the stars make it," said Fjorn.

Sigurlina was ignoring the shade that was lurching drunkenly down the stream bed, a clay amphora clutched in one hand, calling, "Hic piscis piscis. Hic piscis piscis." The spirit fell into the ice so only the back of his head was visible, then appeared up stream again and repeating the act.

"Sigurlina."

Fjorn's voice caught her attention. "What? Oh. Yes. I'll send Munin along so you can send back messages."

"Great, I have a black chicken to help me." Ragna rolled her eyes as she took off her cloak and sword and passed them to Sigurlina.

"Yura bitch!" Munin hopped away from something she'd been pecking at on the stream bank.

"She'll wait for you on the roof of the bath. Try to stay out of trouble." Sigurlina looked at her friend with quiet resolve.

"Me, cause trouble?" Ragna smiled in a way that made all her companions cringe, took the dagger Fjorn held out to her, then pulled a candle from her pack, lit it from the lantern, and slipped into the tunnel.

"You do realise she is going to get us all killed," remarked Vidurr.

"I heard that, wolf breath," echoed out of the passage.

CHAPTER 10

UP THE PIPE

Ragna started into the passage. For the first five strides she was stooped over, but standing, then the passage stepped up and narrowed. She was forced to duck walk. The floor was moist, and there were occasional soft lumps left along its length. The air stank of waste and was cool, but warmer than outside. Occasionally side tunnels would open off the main way, but there was no mistaking the primary conduit. After another twenty or so strides, the passage stepped up and narrowed again. Cringing, Ragna dropped to her hands and knees.

"Ragna, you're the only one that will fit. Ragna, we need you. Ragna, there's no other choice. I'd like to see them crawl through a privy. I'm buying myself the nicest, most expensive dress in the town when I get out of--."

There was a thud; the sound of voices speaking in Anglic, then the whoosh of flowing water.

"Angrboda's bouncing tits!" Ragna braced herself as a rush of filthy water careened down the tunnel and slammed into her. She was thrown into complete darkness. When the water was passed she spat and opened her eyes. Maybe ten strides ahead she saw a dim light. The tunnel narrowed again. Fighting to keep her stomach down she crawled forward on her belly. The arch of stones above her gave way to a cover of wooden planks high enough to let her stand in the stone trough below. Holes, slightly larger than her head, were cut in the passage's ceiling.

Water splashed through two of the holes.

"I'm telling you, this thing is as big as a horse, and vicious. It killed two of the men pulling its cage, strangled them with its webs."

"The Pope should like it. Way I hear it; he loves to watch the animals go at each other. The more exotic the better."

"Seems wrong to me, making them fight like that."

"Just animals. They don't feel pain, priest says so."

A bell sounded three times in the distance. "We'd better hurry. The royal guards will be in soon."

"Have to give themselves something to confess for the next mass. Speaking of things to confess. You seen the new lot of slaves that came in?"

"The big blonde? Udele would make my life hell if I brought something like that home."

"Might be worth it."

"It might, but it's hard enough to pay for the indulgences as it is. Have you heard, the Church declared another seventeen days of chastity? I figured that when I got married it was right in the sight of the Lord, but nowadays it seems the church has more days that you can't then you can."

"Do it anyways, then do a few hail Marys. Father Wallace is a soft touch."

There was the sound of retreating foot steps. Ragna shook her head, stood and continued along the passage trying to avoid the trickle that flowed by her feet. After the privy holes, there was a stone arch followed by a wooden ceiling. Light crept in around a cover over a large hole in the ceiling. She pushed up the wooden cover a crack and looked out. The room was lit by a red glow that came from one side. Pushing the cover up higher, she slipped out of the sewer. Stifling heat hit her. The red glow came from a fire that blazed in a stone chamber about a stride in height. Beyond the flames she could see pillars supporting an upper platform. A trough came through the ceiling over the hole she crawled out of. There was wood stacked against the wall.

She slipped to the heavy, wooden door in the wall and listened. There was silence. Cautiously, she opened the door and slipped into a stone corridor. A stair rose from one end and on the other was a platform with privy holes cut into it.

Moving to the stairs she crept up them and found another corridor with doors opening off the sides.

"Honestly, if he wants to keep taking our workers, he can't expect us to keep the baths operating." A new voice spoke.

"He's the king, appointed by god. That means he can expect anything he likes."

The voices came from around a bend in the passage.

Wrenching open one of the side doors Ragna threw herself into the room beyond and mostly closed the door.

"I guess. It's only until the treasure hall is completed."

Two men walked by carrying bundles of wood.

Ragna closed the door and scanned the room she'd entered. A pool of water big enough for six people to sit in filled its centre. Wisps of steam rose from the water. Towels were laid out on a wooden bench at the end of the room, and there were hooks on the wall to hold clothing. An oil lamp, burning scented oil, hung on the wall giving a wavering illumination. Sniffing herself she curled her nose. Stripping out of her dress and boots; she stepped into the tub. She immersed herself waving her hair about to clean it. The warm water felt wonderful. She rinsed off her boots then grabbed her dress and pulled it in, waving it about until the worst of the filth came off. Hanging the dress up on a peg, so it hid her dagger, and putting her money pouch into her boot she took a towel and dried herself.

The door creaked open and a dark-haired, slender, young woman entered carrying a tray of oils.

"What happened?" she gasped.

"I...I had to get clean."

"I know most of the guests prefer that, but what were you doing? And why didn't you use the common bath."

"I'm new. They told me to go in here." Ragna looked contrite.

"They did, did they? Well, I'll have a few words about that! Not your fault if this is where they told you to go. For the future, the only time we use the private tubs is when we are with a guest."

"I'll remember that." Ragna made her voice earnest.

"See that you do. What a mess. I'll have to get Daegal to flush the tub. It smells like a privy. Now, you get to the dressing room. We'll have bathers soon."

"Thank you."

Ragna lifted her dress off the peg wrapping the dagger inside it as she did so, grabbed her boots, and left the room. She moved down the hall taking a moment to open the door in the wall opposite to the one she'd slipped through. Past the door was a pool of water as big as a small longship. Benches lined the wall sitting on a narrow deck about the water. Moving on, she felt a chill. She turned the corner and saw another corridor that had a door in its side opposite an open cubicle of a room. At the end of the passage was another door.

She fingered her dress, which was still wet. Taking a deep breath she straightened her back and strode to the door at the end of the hall, pulled it open and stepped through.

"You must be the new girl. I'm Daldis," A tall, attractive woman of late-middle years weareing a revealing dress sat at a desk in the room behind the door.

"Ragna." Ragna put on an ingratiating smile of her own.

"I know you're probably nervous, but it isn't so bad. We get mostly nobility here, some wealthy merchants, and I'm sure a tiny thing like you will be very popular. I see you've had your bath. You didn't need to wash your dress; we'll give you new clothes. Don't worry about it; I did the same thing when I first started. Let's see about getting you something to wear. After all, the guests like to leave something to their imaginations, at least for the start. I think maybe from the youngsters section. Oh yes, you will appeal to some of our guests. Your size with your curves, they'll eat you up."

Ragna felt her stomach churn.

Daldis led the way along the corridor to a side room and opened the door. The room was filled with dresses.

"Now, how can we accommodate your attributes?"

Ragna took a simple dress off a peg. It would fit her for length. The upper section was padded to give the illusion of breasts. "What if we pulled the padding out of this one? That should make room."

"It's a little drab, but until we can get you something better... If you can play the innocent it will work into that. Now, get dressed. After that we'll have to comb your hair. I have to check some things, but I won't be long. Can you do the alteration yourself? There is a sewing kit." Daldis gestured at the corner then left the room.

Ragna moved to the small, wooden box sitting on a stool that was the sewing kit and opened it. A sharp knife for splitting seams gleamed at its top. Moments later the padding was gone and she'd squeezed herself into the dress. Putting on her belt she thrust the dagger through it and hung her money pouch on it. Her boots were damp, but she couldn't help that. Slipping through the door she hurried from the bath's back rooms. In the main passage, she heard Daldis' voice.

"I certainly didn't tell her to use the private bath. You know how the girls like to play with the newcomers. I'll have a word with them."

Ragna opened the door to the outside and slipped into the welcoming darkness.

She hugged herself against the cold as she let her eyes adjust to the sporadic torch light.

"Caw." Munin dropped down from the bathhouse's peaked, clay-tile roof and landed on the icy street.

Ragna turned and examined the squat building. The back of the bathhouse was incorporated into the town wall and its walls were mostly stone, patched in places with wood.

Ragna looked across the street to a great hall that bore a sign with a mead horn over its door. The wall facing her was solid. Streets ran deeper into the town on either side of the great hall. The street she was on seemed to circle just inside the palisade.

"Stay close, black chicken. It's cold." She draped her old dress over her shoulders like a shawl.

"Good bird, good bird," commented Munin.

A bell tolled four times.

Ragna started down the avenue that cut across the front of the great hall. Houses lined the way. A thousand strides later a palisade rose to her right. Torches burnt along its length and armed men patrolled the area.

"What is your business?" demanded a rough voice in Anglic.

Ragna looked up into a scowling face. "I... I'm trying to find a place to buy a cloak and a dress..." She thought for a moment. "My sister stole all my things when she ran off with my man. I need to buy clothes." She gestured to the dress she was wearing in a seemingly innocent way that still drew attention to her cleavage and curves. "This is all I have, and it barely fits. It's not fair. I was a good wife. I have a little skatt to pay." She snuffled and forced tears to her eyes.

The guard's features softened and he looked uncomfortable. "It's not so bad. You still have your looks. I'm sure the priests will grant an annulment. You're new to town, so you don't know this, but with the crusader garrison and all, there are a lot more men here than women.

You'll find a new husband to look after you."

"Thank you, that's kind of you to say." Ragna looked up with a tear streaked face.

"You should move on. I have to get to the guards' mass, and you don't want to catch a chill. Two streets down and turn left. That is Tradesmen Street. Go to the fifth shop on your right; tell them that Lister sent you. If you hit the crusaders' halls by the docks you've gone too far."

"Thank you. Are you a palace guard?" Ragna swished her hips.

"I am pledged to King Aethelstan's service. You'd best run before you freeze."

Ragna smiled and hurried along noting that half the guards she passed were moving into the enclosure defined by the palisade. The palisade looked to be a man and a half tall. Archers could be seen over its top, their eyes scouring the surrounding town.

She reached Tradesmen Street and went to the fifth shop on her right. The cold had stiffened the damp dress she was using as a shawl and she could feel the chill creeping into her bones.

"Fly around and look at the town. When you're done, wait for me on the roof. I'll be a while. Find out what you can about those bells." Ragna instructed Munin.

"Yura bitch." Munin eyed her companion.

"I know its cold but I can't take you with me, and I need proper clothing before I freeze."

A person walking down the street looked at the small woman talking to a raven oddly but kept moving.

Munin snorted. "Yura bitch." She leapt into the air.

A bell tolled five times.

Ragna opened the door and stepped into the warmth inside. A fire sent smoke into the thatching above. A stall with a pig and several piglets in it occupied the space to the left of the door. A woman, working a loom, sat on a raised platform surrounding the fire pit at the back of the single room. A man sat opposite her, stitching a half-finished boot. Clothing and leather works occupied shelves to the right of the door.

"What can I do for you?" The man came to his feet.

"I need to buy clothes. Lister sent me."

The man smiled. "Any friend of Lister is welcome here."

"Thank you." Ragna reached into her pouch and pulled out a handful of coins. "It's all I have. My husband ran off with my sister and took everything I had. I asked my mother to hold onto our money because my husband likes the dice cup. The coins she held for me are the only reason I'm not freezing in a snow bank." Ragna made her lip tremble.

"You poor thing." The woman got up from her loom and hugged Ragna.

"I'm Wanda, and I'm sure we can set you up right." Wanda, who was almost skeletal, dark haired and a full head taller than Ragna, held the smaller woman at arm's length and pursed her lips. "You are a hard fit. I may have something. Does the chest have to be that tight?" Her voice became disapproving for the last.

"It's an old dress from before I finished growing. My other dress got dirty." She held up the dress she was using as a shawl.

"You poor little thing." Wanda sighed. "What you're wearing looks like something those harlots at the bath would wear. I think we can do better." Reaching into the garments beside her she pulled out a blue dress. "It will be too long, but I can hem that up. Try it on and we'll see. "Patton, start looking through the children's cloaks and keep your back turned until I say you can look. We can't have her catching her death when she goes outside."

#

Munin flew over the town. All the streets came in from the street that circled the inside of the town wall, connecting to the road that circled the royal compound in the middle of town like the spokes on a wagon wheel. The landside gate was almost perfectly opposite the docks and heavily guarded. The entire town sloped gradually down towards the sea.

Flying back to the clothing shop, Munin perched on the roof. A group of crusaders marched up the street beside a small wagon. A large cauldron of water sat on the wagon. A metal cage, containing a human-looking creature about the size of a cat, was suspended over the cauldron by a metal tripod. The creature had red and orange wings, rust-coloured hair and golden eyes. Many of the crusaders had burns on their hands and faces. As Munin watched the creature glowed and the bars of its cage turned orange. A crusader shouted and several of the warriors took up pails that waited on the wagon and doused the little creature with water. The creature released a shriek of agony then they continued on their way.

#

Wanda hummed as she hemmed the dress while Patton and Ragna sat on the platform chatting. Ragna was running an antler comb through her hair while Patton sipped from a steaming mug.

Patten smacked his lips and continued his story. "Lister was glad that he wasn't selected to guard the king, he hates traveling. I personally think that if the Witemagemot want to meet they should come to the king, not him to them. All they do is argue anyway. I can't see what good any of their advice would be, bunch of spoiled, fat land owners, but I guess King Aethelstan has his reasons for humouring them. The upshot of it is, he's out of Winchester and has left Hakon as his steward. Personally, I'm guessing he wanted to give Hakon a taste of running a kingdom before he takes the north. Bit of an apprenticeship so he doesn't make a muck of things."

"That's fascinating," oozed Ragna.

"Hot air is what it is. It's not our place to be gossiping about kings, princes and the like." Wanda tied off the thread she was sewing with and using the scissors dangling from her dress broach cut it. "Try this on." She passed the blue dress to Ragna. "Patten, get some more firewood."

Patten bit his lip. "We haven't the skatt."

Ragna noticed that the fire they did have barely filled half the fire pit. "You've been so kind. Please let me." She pulled several coins from her purse.

"That's good of you." Wanda eyed the coins. "Patten, take the coins and go. Be sure to remind Gar that he has to pick up his tunic on the way to mass this Odinsdagr."

"Yes, my love." Patten turned to Ragna and took the coins. "Thank you."

When he left the little house Ragna squirmed out of her tight dress and pulled on the new one. It fit well, and was a thick, warm material.

"Now that's a sight," said Wanda. "You are a pretty little thing.

Now try this on, so I can set the length." Wanda held up a wool cloak.

Ragna slipped into the cloak and Wanda started pinning the hem. She hummed as she worked then went to her sewing box and pulled out a length of pale thread. "You can take it off now."

"Thank you. That thread is different?" Ragna watched as the seamstress straightened it between her fingers.

"I got it a few days back. Strongest I've ever seen. That giant spider they pulled up to the treasure hall shot it out. I collected it. It t-ain't right keeping those beasts in the town, I say, but I guess that if King Aethelstan's treasure hall can keep thieves out; it can keep the beasts in. At least until they're ready to ship them on. I'll say this much, things I've seen pulled along this street. Week before last there was a snake long as a kravi and covered in fur. I swear it talked plain as you please. I've no desire to leave town, even on pilgrimage. Nasty beasts."

"A giant snake. That would scare me to bits," remarked Ragna as Wanda started sewing.

There was the sound of a screech from outside.

"I don't even want to look. Just t ain't right to bring such things into town." Wanda shook her head.

Patten returned and started bringing in armloads of fire wood. The first armload was added to the fire and the next few stacked in the little house.

"Gar said he didn't have the skatt to pay for his tunic. It's been a trial for him since the king gave the lands he was harvesting to the church. He can barely keep up with the tithes, and him with mouths to feed. He said he'd trust us with the price of the tunic until Odinsdagr if I took it in trade. I couldn't say no, Wanda. I just couldn't."

"Of course you couldn't. I swear, I'll not speak against the White God, but between the king's taxes and the church tithes, they're fit to make paupers of us all." Wanda kept sewing.

Patten turned to Ragna and held out the coins she'd given him. "Here's your money back."

"Keep it. You've let me stay warm by your fire." Ragna looked over the simple furnishings of the hovel and thought to herself that her hosts were probably one tithing from starvation themselves.

Wanda smiled. "All you've been through, we couldn't."

"Then I'll take a pair of fur boots. You can make them over the next week or two, and I'll pick them up when they're done." Ragna pulled out coins adding them to the ones in Patten's hands.

Patten smiled broadly. "Can't ask fairer than that. You've made our day, that's to be sure." He pulled a piece of decrepit, shaved, sheep skin out of the pile. "Let me get a tracing of your foot, and I'll have them ready before Sunnudagar Mass."

Ragna pulled off her boot and Patten traced around her foot with a charred stick.

Minutes later Wanda passed Ragna her new cloak. Ragna fastened the simple C clasp at the shoulder and pulled it tight around her.

"I should go. You've both been so nice." Ragna slipped out the door to a chorus of warm farewells. Munin flew down and landed on her shoulder making Ragna stumble .

"Yura bitch!" said Munin.

"I know it was a long time but I learned a lot, and look at these clothes. I'll tell you everything as we walk. How about you?"

"Good bird. Good bird." Munin fluffed her feathers.

"I need to get something to eat and a place to sleep. Once I've found an inn, you can fly back to Sigurlina and tell her what we've found out. Tell her I'll be coming out the landward gate in one day as the stars make it from now, and that I may need help."

"Good bird. Good bird." Munin used her beak to part the folds of Ragna's cloak and push her way under the material. Ragna automatically raised her arm creating a perch for the raven that pressed tight into her chest. Munin was shivering.

"Poor bird. I'm sorry you got so cold." Ragna patted Munin's head under the folds of her cloak.

"Poor bird, poor bird," agreed Munin.

Ragna started to walk towards the docks. "Now listen, this is what I learned."

After a long sleep, Ragna awoke and scanned the inside of an inn. It was patterned after a great hall. People lay passed out on the platform surrounding the fire pit. She closed her eyes and spent a while listening to the conversations around her until one caught her attention.

"I'm telling you they came like trained dogs. I've seen many a thing at sea and ashore, but to watch that... If we weren't serving the White God, I'd have thought it were the devil himself we'd called."

"Don't talk foolish. The priests say we're doing the heathens a favour by making them take the wafer. Anything we do to make that happen is right in the Lord's eyes."

A bell sounded once. "First bell, we've been up all night."

"Guard's mass ain't till five bells. We have time."

"Good. I'll get another horn. I don't know about using them beast to kill folk being a favour to them. Maybe that crazy, old monk who said people should make their own choice had a point. Remember the one the crusaders ran off."

"He were just a crazy old man. People have to be driven to the faith, like sheep. You need to confess your doubts. This horn is a gift from the Lord to strengthen the faithful."

"Maybe? I overheard some of the crusaders talking. They said they'd taken it from some folk who worshiped false gods down south."

"But the Lord gave it to them. Talk to a priest. You have time. It will be a fortnight before the ship is fixed. Until then the horn is safe in the treasure hall."

"I'll go after the crusaders' mass. I best finish me horn and coast. Them royal priests don't take with drink, unless you hand over the skatt for an indulgence."

Ragna rose, collected a goose leg from the food table and slipped from the inn. Outside little flakes of snow drifted down from a sky of patchy stars. She moved down the street past two great halls that had a stark quality to them. Men in chain wearing cap helms trained in the courtyards and horses occupied large stables between them. The stench of a privy reached her nose. Further along she came to the docks, which were lit with what seemed a thousand torches. Six piers thrust into the water. A line of longships occupied all but the centre pier where two, strange vessels flanked the deep ende. These vessels were as long as a medium sized longship but ridiculously wide. They resembled fortresses on the water, with fore and aft castles creating additional decks. Burly men hauled amphoras and rolls of cloth onto the foreign vessels.

On the shore, teams of men repaired longships that had been pulled onto support frames.

Ragna strode up and tried to step onto the pier where the foreign vessels were docked.

"I help you?" demanded a short man with dark hair, a swarthy completion, and a scar along his jaw, who approached from further up the dock.

Ragna stared at him for a moment. "I...I was hoping my brother's ship would have come in."

The small man nodded then tried to struggle through some words in Anglic. "This... No..." He sighed. "Do you speak the church tongue?" he said in Latin.

"I speak some church tongue. You speak Orse?"

The man smiled and answered in Orse. "I some Orse." He returned to Latin. "I am rumex. You can not exspecto here. The king has ordered us to keep the navale clear. You should go domus."

Ragna bit her lip as she thought through the strange words and constructed her own sentence in Latin. "I buy lamp oil. Mother ill... dark sadness. Lamp light help."

The crusader nodded gravely and answered in Anglic. "Dark sadness bad. I prey for her. Pier five, ship unloading. You buy there. Be quick. You no be here, king's law."

"Thank you." Ragna smiled shyly.

"Go with god." The crusader made a sign of blessing and moved towards the barracks.

The bell sounded three times.

Ragna hurried to the fifth pier. Men were unloading amphoras of oil. From her new angle she could see something that looked vaguely like a bow set on its side on the foredeck of the foreign vessel. She traded some skatt with a sailor for a small pot of oil then hurried back to the street moving into the town. She paused to drop a coin in a beggar's bowl and shook his hand.

Tap, tap. Tap. Tap, tap, went their thumbs.

"What you need, sister?" the skinny man dressed in rags asked through broken teeth.

"Where?" said Ragna.

"Karl's Rest on Fletcher Street. Tolan works the door."

Minutes later, she stood at the entrance to the Karl's Rest. It was a decrepit establishment with a clientele who looked to be in their cups. A heavily, muscled man with brown hair and a squished in nose stood at the door. Ragna walked up to him and held out her hand. It vanished inside the man's hand and they shook. Ragna barely managed to move her thumb enough to tap.

"I'm taking a minute," called the large man.

"Right," grunted another man who moved to the door from inside the inn.

"I'm Tolan ," said the man from the door as he walked Ragna a little way down the street.

"Ragna. I have a harvest." She pulled a smaller bag that she'd kept in her money pouch out and passed it to Tolan.

Tolan opened the bag looked in then extracted a severed toe. "These will be good for two nights' shelter and food."

"Do I look like I need shelter and food?" Ragna donned a haughty stance. "I need to know things."

Tolan stroked his chin. "What kind of things?"

"How many guards are in the royal compound? Who in town to talk with to stir up some trouble. Where can I find a priest of the White God that will stay bought? How can I get something out of the royal compound quietly?"

Tolan smiled revealing two missing teeth. "Aethelstan added guards around that treasure hall of his when he left, so a good hundred. Add a hundred if god's warriors are in the church for mass. As to the other, what you got in mind, and is it worth my while? As to the priest, depends and what you need him to do. I got some names. For the last, only thing that leaves that compound without being searched is shit." Tolan's smile widened. "And that happens 'tween five and six bells. Them royal types ain't nothing, if they ain't regular."

Ragna smiled. "Tell your people you're going to be gone for a while. We need to talk."

The bell sounded four times.

Later Ragna slipped into a chapel, no bigger or ornate than the poor houses she'd seen in the town, and knelt in seeming prayer before an alter bearing a wooden plate and cup. A young looking man with a shaved head, dressed in a priest's robes entered the room and added wood to the scant fire in the pit. She moved to his side.

"Father Wallace?" Ragna's voice was small.

"Yes, my child?"

Ragna stifled a laugh; the man was probably younger than her.

"I need you to come with me."

"I'm quite busy, what?"

Ragna slipped a hand full of skatt out from under her cloak. "Someone needs to speak to a priest. They can't come into town."

Father Wallace looked from pleading, brown eyes in a pixy face to the coins then nodded. "How far outside the town wall must we travel?"

"Just outside of it. Half now, half later. He is devoted to the White God and needs death duties." Ragna held up the priest's hand and dumped the coins in her own onto it.

The priest looked at her and returned the coins to her hand. "I'll get my cloak."

"Thank you."

Minutes later Ragna and the priest passed through the town's landward gate. A raven cawed in the darkness and there was the sound of beating wings.

"Where is the person we are meeting?" Father Wallace sounded nervous.

"He's close." Ragna led the way along the path, beaten by the guards who patrolled the outside of the palisade, toward the Roman ruin.

"I don't like this. These ruins are haunted."

Sigurlina stepped from behind a pile of rubble. "Do tell."

Vidurr stepped out from the piled snow drifts behind them. "We have to get moving, the guard will be here soon."

"I have no money," began Wallace.

"Who is this?" demanded Vidurr.

"Abselema's godi. We promised."

"What is--," objected Wallace.

"Don't make us gag you," said Sigurlina.

With a shove, Vidurr got Father Wallace moving and they passed into the maze of snow drifts and ruined buildings.

"You are just a thief," accused Father Wallace.

"No, someone really needs death duties and once we're done our business, we'll let you go. I... I'll even give you the coins I promised," soothed Ragna.

Vidurr curled his lip.

CHAPTER 11

INTENT IS ALL

Fjorn led them away from the sewer outlet.

"What should we do now?" Sigurlina tried not to look at the naked man, who was floating above a ruined house at the level of what must have been its second story. The spirit seemed to be kissing and caressing someone. There was the sound of a door opening. The spirit looked horrified, and then blood poured from wounds all over it. There was a pause and the scene repeated.

"We should go back to the ship and wait for Munin." Fjorn stopped to get his bearings.

"I don't like sending Ragna alone like that," said Audun.

"He never would have fit," commented Banning from Sigurlina's side.

"Could I have?" she asked.

"Maybe, you're skinny, but maybe not. I barely did. You will tell my father that I didn't leave because of him? You will keep your promise?"

"I'll do my best."

"And tell him I love him."

"I will."

"But don't tell him I'm dead. Just let him think I'm afraid to come back because King Aethelstan might be mad at me."

Sigurlina smiled sadly. "If that is what you want."

"Who are you talking to?" asked Vidurr.

"Banning, the spirit that showed us the passage."

"Can you see all spirits?" Vidurr sounded hopeful.

"Only those trapped in Midgard. If they have moved on, then they aren't here to see."

Vidurr bit his lip and asked in a very soft voice. "Do you see spirits around me?"

Sigurlina blinked and looked closely around her comrade. "No."

Vidurr sighed and a brief smile came to his lips. "Fight well in

Muspelheim, father," he whispered.

They reached their mooring to find the ship deserted save for a single oarsman who pointed them to a trail of foot prints in the snow. Following it they came to an intact building and found a door. Opening it let a blast of light and warmth into the cold and dark.

"Well, come in and close the door. You're letting the heat out," snapped Kjorn.

Entering the room they found the rest of the oarsmen gathered around a fire in a room seven strides to a wall. Kegs of mead and barrels of food lined the wall. Several of the oarsmen were passed out, snoring in their cups.

"There's a stock of wood in the next room and more then a man could eat in a year, furs and weapons too," remarked Kjorn. He paused and his voice took on a worried quality. "Where's the pixy?"

"She's in the town," said Fjorn. "It's a tale to tell around the fire." He looked around with concern. "Who do you think left all this?"

Sigurlina shifted uncomfortably. "I should go to the Apenhet. Munin is expecting me there."

"I'll go with you. Stone walls are no comfort to me." Vidurr led the way out the door.

"I'll send others soon," said Fjorn behind them.

Sigurlina and Vidurr walked in silence until the Apenhet came into view.

"It's funny. This ship feels more like home to me than anyplace since my village," Sigurlina stepped onto the dock.

Vidurr sighed. "My home is in Muspelheim with my father, my bitch and..." He hung his head. "My cub was just a boy. I prey he took up a blade. Do you think Surt would accept a great heart, even if it was in just a child?"

Sigurlina bit her lip. "I don't know. The gods and giants are so far beyond us it is hard to say what they value. All I can say is, if your boy is anything like you, I would be proud to have him as a warrior of my house."

"I like you, Seithkona. You don't tell a soft lie of comfort; yet you are not cruel. My bitch was like that."

Sigurlina smiled in the dark. Boarding the *Apenhet* she moved to the bow and wrapped herself in blankets. Vidurr howled, startling the drowsy oarsman who sat by the tiller oar. The huge, red wolf settled itself by Sigurlina like a friendly dog.

"May I?" She tentatively reached out and scratched him between the ears. His tail thumped once and he laid his head in her lap.

Sigurlina dozed but awoke to Vidurr's cold, wet nose pushed against her face. She sat up. He turned, his lip curling back from his teeth. Five more oarsmen dozed, wrapped in blankets, on the ship. Clear in the distance was the sound of oars creaking in their locks.

"It looks like there's some bugger in our slip," came a voice over the bay.

"Well, that is rude. We'll have to teach them some manners."

"We'll give them a lesson in proper behaviour. Gain a few thralls to sell and add a ship to our little fleet in the process. It's all profit boys. Draw your blades."

Sigurlina moved to the closest oarsman and woke him by covering his mouth and shaking him, then whispered in his ear. "Get Fjorn at the building. We're under attack. Be silent and try not to be seen."

The oarsman crawled onto the dock and, keeping low, raced away in the darkness.

Sigurlina woke the other oarsmen while Vidurr moved onto the dock and sniffed the air.

Sigurlina knelt beside the wolf and whispered. "We won't have enough warriors to hold them until Fjorn gets here."

Vidurr tossed his head in agreement.

"I have an idea. Wait here."

Sigurlina slipped down the dock to the snow-covered ground at its end. Closing her eyes she reached into the cold boarders of death. She knew that with every second she was dying and being reborn; that the cycle was all. She built her power then released it, whispering softly, "Come hither servant, durable symbol of our ending. I summon thee, black one."

The ground beside her bubbled up and a black skeleton rose out of it holding a copy of Sigurlina's staff.

"Follow me," she hissed and her voice was like a breath from the grave.

Vidurr cringed back when the skeleton stepped onto the dock. Sigurlina walked passed him, her creation in tow. Stepping onto the ship, she led the skeleton past the oarsmen, who all huddled back.

Placing her lips where the skeleton's ear would have been she whispered. "You will let no one from the other ship board this vessel. Do you understand?"

The skeleton nodded.

Sigurlina moved to the bow, motioning for the oarsmen to hide themselves, and waited.

A shadow came up on the stern and a rope was thrown. A grappling hook bit into the *Apenhet's* stern post and the other craft slammed into them making the *Apenhet* rock violently.

A torch was lit, casting light over the *Apenhet's* stern. A scruffy-looking man leapt aboard, and was faced with a skeleton that swung ripping boney-fingers across his throat. Two other men, who were about to follow the first, screamed and tumbled back onto their ship's deck. A forth man leapt, his battle axe raised to strike, but the skeleton swung with its staff knocking him so he tumbled onto the dock. Vidurr pounced ripping the dazed man's throat out before he could rise.

"It's a ghost ship. Cast off before Hel takes us all," cried one of the voices.

"It's a Seith trick. Kill it and we'll have our way with the Seithkona that called it."

Three men leapt onto the stern. The skeleton struck against one, but the other two bore down on it until swords flashed out of the shadows in the bottom of the boat. The oarsmen cut deep, hamstringing the intruders. Sigurlina added her staff to the skeleton's, pummelling the last intruder, but now more men were pouring onto the *Apenhet* as others leapt to the dock. Vidurr took the first intruder's arm in his jaws ripping it off and propelling the man into the sea. Two more took the dock behind him and drove the big wolf back with flashing swords.

Step by step Sigurlina, Vidurr and the oarsmen were driven back. An oarsman fell, then another. Sigurlina took a slash to her arm leaving a stain of blood trickling down her sleeve.

A burly intruder was just about to bring his axe down on Sigurlina's head when Fjorn leapt to the deck and, with a savage uppercut, separated the intruder's arms at the elbows. The axe and forearms tumbled to the deck beside Sigurlina while the man's blood painted her in splotchy red. The skeleton drove its staff into another intruder's teeth.

Vidurr bled from several wounds, but they only seemed to enrage him as he swept amongst the intruders on the dock. One of the intruders managed to flank the big wolf and, while another kept him occupied to the fore, was preparing to run him through when a battle axe struck home with enough force to open the intruder's chest. The intruder looked startled for a moment as his heart continued to beat for all to see. Then he toppled off the pier. Audun brought his axe around with a savage, back-handed swing decapitating the man fighting Vidurr.

"Cast off, Cast off," came the cry from the intruding vessel.

Fjorn led the charge, driving the remaining intruders off the *Apenhet* and the dock, then leaping aboard the enemy vessel.

"Board that craft. Kill any who don't surrender," ordered Sigurlina.

The skeleton leapt to the other vessel. Sigurlina followed it. Pulling on the dregs of her power, she opened a vortex beside the remaining crew of the enemy vessel. The portal siphoned away the energy of their souls, feeding a portion of it to her, draining them of courage and will. The wound in her arm began to seal while she became a dark shadow painted in blood.

"Wait," Sigurlina commanded the skeleton when Fjorn didn't press the offensive.

Vidurr leapt to the deck beside her, his teeth bared in a snarl, the pony-sized, red wolf eyed their attackers. Covered in other men's blood, Audun came to tower on her other side with his battle axe poised to strike. Before them, Fjorn, with his sword drawn, stood straight and resolute. Behind them was a band of oarsmen led by Kjorn.

Fifteen men huddled at the stern of the ship.

"We seem to have started badly." Fjorn's voice was as pleasant as if he had been bumped in the marketplace.

Puddles formed beneath two of the men.

"I... This is our pier," stated one of the men with a tremor in his voice.

"I saw nothing to indicate that. I have a proposal. You can surrender. If you do, I will swear by Gungnir to keep you safely and release you when my business is done. If you don't; well." Fjorn smiled. "Bones have to come from some place, and my friend could use some more servants."

Another bladder released.

Sigurlina held her spell and forced her face to remain fixed in haughty anger, but inside her heart shuddered. To think that Fjorn would consider her capable of doing what he suggested, was like an icy fist in her chest."

"We surrender," said the intruder captain.

"Good. My business in this area won't take more than a few days. I am assuming that the place my helmsman found is your warehouse. I apologise that we feasted on your stores, but that is between friends. We will count what we have taken, and will take, against the weregild you owe me for my murdered oarsmen. By what gods do you swear?"

The intruders looked amongst themselves.

"It's like that is it. I had hoped to bind you with an oath. Very well, you will go to your warehouse and be tied up there until I am finished. I will leave men to see to it that you are released, no matter how my business concludes. It should not be more than a week. Will you comply?"

The captain eyed the skeleton that waited on Sigurlina's command.

"Step forward." Sigurlina let all the cold anger she could muster enter her voice.

The skeleton took a step forward.

"We accept," yelped the intruder's captain.

Munin descended to land on Sigurlina's shoulder.

Vidurr howled, transformed into his human guise, and drew his sword. "Must we let them live?" he asked casually.

"You swore by Gungnir," blurted one of the intruders.

"So I did. As long as they behave themselves we have to let them live." Fjorn eyed the intruders.

"Pity," stated the deep rumble of Audun's voice.

"I swear, we won't make any trouble." The intruder captain laid his sword on the ship's deck. The rest of the intruders followed their captain's example.

"I believe them. You'll just have to wait for fresh skeletons, my lady." Fjorn sheathed his sword.

Sigurlina scowled and ended the siphon spell. Her wounds were healed.

"Gentlemen," Fjorn made a courtly gesture to the dock. "Kjorn, moor their boat. They may need it later."

Kjorn smiled broadly and bowed. "Yes, my Karl."

Sigurlina watched with her comrades while the oarsmen searched, disarmed and bound the intruders before taking them to the warehouse.

Tension seemed to leave Fjorn's body when the last one was taken away. He collapsed to sit on the deck.

"That was close," remarked Audun.

Fjorn nodded. "I owe all of you but Sigurlina, Vidurr you most of all. If you hadn't been aboard we all may well be dead right now."

Sigurlina sniffed as she tried to wipe blood off herself.

"It won't work. Hot water for the skin, cold water for the clothes," remarked Audun.

"Is anyone wounded?" Fjorn laid his head back.

"It is just a nick," remarked Vidurr.

"I've cut myself worse during my spring shave," remarked Audun.

"I'm fine," Sigurlina's tone was petulant.

"So you're all gravely wounded. Come closer."

Audun and Vidurr stepped closer. Only now that the battle was over did Sigurlina notice how gingerly they moved or the blood oozing out of their wounds.

Fjorn sang.

"Youth to the gods, golden apples of grace.

"Idun's power, heal mortals of faith."

Sparkling lights enveloped the men and both stood straighter.

"Sigurlina?" asked Fjorn.

"I can look after myself." Sigurlina tossed her hair, but it was matted with blood ruining the effect.

"What's wrong?"

"Nothing!"

"It has to be something."

"I'm fine!"

"Are you injured?"

"I can heal myself. I told you, I'm fine!"

Vidurr shook his head. "You are on your own with this fight, my captain." He stepped onto the pier.

"Poor bastard." Audun followed the Ulfhednar.

"He has to learn sometime." Vidurr started towards the warehouse with Audun.

"What are you two talking about?" Fjorn looked at the retreating backs of his friends. He turned back to Sigurlina and felt a distinct urge to run after the other men.

She was still coated in blood, but there was something beyond appearances that was unnerving.

"We should go!" her voice could cut meat.

"Was it something I did?"

"I'm fine, or rather, I will be when I wash off this blood." Sigurlina swept past him onto the dock. The skeleton followed her.

Fjorn took the intruders' torch in one hand and rushed to Sigurlina's side.

"Was it something I said?" Fjorn looked at her with pleading eyes.

"I'm fine," snapped Sigurlina.

Munin eyed Fjorn from her mistress's shoulder. The raven bobbed its head. "Yura bitch."

In the warehouse the intruders were tied up along the wall and several oarsmen lay on the floor by the fire with strips of cloth wrapped around their wounds. Audun finished tracing runes onto one of the oarsmen's chests. The man gasped, took a deep breath and nodded.

Fjorn moved amongst the wounded immediately.

"Youth to the gods, golden apples of grace.

"Idun's power, heal mortals of faith."

Sparkling lights enveloped a wounded oarsman who stopped coughing up blood and settled into sleep.

Sigurlina moved to another of the wounded oarsmen and

placed her hands on him. A light dew covered him and his breathing became easier.

All three moved on to other wounded.

Fjorn found himself by one of the prisoners. Taking a deep breath he sang.

Minutes later Kjorn and Vidurr pulled Fjorn and Sigurlina, who were limp with exhaustion, to blankets by the fire and lay them down.

"I..." Fjorn tried to order his thoughts but his head was swimming.

"You must sleep now, my Karl. You've done all you can." Kjorn placed a blanket over his young captain.

"Help them," whispered Sigurlina.

"You did brave heart. You did. Now help yourself," soothed Audun.

Both Fjorn and Sigurlina fell asleep.

"They healed three of us," remarked one of the prisoners.

"Yes." Kjorn turned to face the man.

"Why?"

"They needed healing."

The prisoner fell silent, a look of wonder on his face.

Kjorn arranged a rotating watch for the *Apenhet* as the crew rested after the battle. Hours later Fjorn sat eating a breakfast of dried apples and salt meat. Sigurlina sat down beside him and sipped from a cup of mulled mead. A cauldron of water heated over the fire. Audun, Vidurr, and most of the oarsmen had already cleaned the blood from their skin, though their clothes were indelibly stained.

"Feeling better?" asked Fjorn.

"I'm fine!" Sigurlina sounded surly even to herself.

"Not this again. Come." He stood and held a hand down to her.

"I don't--."

"That's an order, captain to crew."

She took his hand and stood. He led her out of the main room into a back area full of barrels, crates and stacked fire wood. He left the door open so light from the fire could reach them.

"Either tell me what it is, so that I can do something about it, or let it go." Fjorn spoke in a low voice.

"I...It's nothing."

"It's getting in the way of our mission. Talk to me."

Sigurlina looked at the floor. "I'd never do it. And it hurts to think that you think I would."

Fjorn stared at her. "Well, that cleared that up."

"I. It hurts that you think I'm a monster. I thought, oh never mind." She moved to step away from him.

Fjorn grabbed her by the wrist, gently pulled her to him, and kissed her. She kissed him back. "Would I kiss a monster?" he asked when the kiss broke.

"But you said I'd strip the flesh from those men's bones and turn them into thralls."

Fjorn sighed and buried his face in his hand while shaking his head. "Siggy, we were done. All of us were wounded, and most of them were fresh. Can you honestly say you had anymore magic to spend on that fight? Vidurr was bleeding from half a dozen wounds, and Audun had a slash in his side as big as my hand. The other men's blood hid it. Half my ribs were broken. I have the bruses to prove it. Most of the oarsmen were wounded as well; some a little, some a lot. I had to make them surrender. They are warriors, or at least were at some point in their lives. Death wasn't going to be enough."

"So you lied," said Sigurlina.

"I lied. I know you'd never butcher someone for their skeleton. Even if you had to, there are enough bones that no one is using anymore."

Sigurlina put her hand with its coating of dried blood on his cheek and kissed him. "All right. I guess I was a little silly, maybe."

"Now that that is settled. You can have the next cauldron of hot water. Once we're clean we need to plan."

Later Fjorn sat on the *Apenhet* with Sigurlina, Audun, Vidurr and Kjorn. The oarsmen were all in the warehouse granting them privacy. A black skeleton stood guard at the landward side of the pier. They sat in the dark and ignored the willow wisp that flitted around coming and going.

"I told you, that is everything Munin said. Isn't it my good friend?" Sigurlina fed the raven a piece of meat where she sat huddled under her cloak.

"Good bird. Good bird," agreed Munin after swallowing.

"It's our only way into the treasure hall," said Fjorn.

"No!" snapped Vidurr.

"It's a good plan. It's the only way we'll be able to open the treasure hall without being seen. If that fire creature is what I think it is, it will also let us give Hakon's fleet a little surprise. Assuming we can get it to cooperate," said Audun.

"You do it. We'll tell them you're a frost giant, you're big enough." Vidurr's voice was nearly a growl.

"I don't like it either. The spell is tricky, and I'll need to see where I'm going, but what else can we do?" added Sigurlina.

Vidurr rumbled low in his throat. "Together we will do this thing. For our families."

"For our families," agreed Sigurlina.

"Way I see it. The problems start once we reach the docks. *If* we reach the docks," said Kjorn. "They aren't just going to let us sail away."

"Leave that to me and Halla," intoned Audun. "They can't chase what they can't see."

"That's if Halla makes it back. I didn't like sending her alone, but she is the only one that could scout the sea," remarked Fjorn.

"Your concern is touching, Fjorn, karl's son." The voice was soft and came from a shadow on the pier. "Where did the other ship come from?"

"Smugglers." Fjorn retrieved a blanket from a pile in the bow and gave it to the selkie.

"Where is the small one who talks too much?" Halla settled herself with the others.

"Ragna is in the town," said Sigurlina.

"Ah. I noticed your skeleton, nicely done. Is it wise to use Gimnir as a guard?"

"What?" Fjorn leapt to his feet.

"I saw him as I was swimming in." Halla stood and pointed to one side of the end of the pier. "Over there."

Clear in the stillness was the sound of snow crunching under running feet.

"Skeleton, Get the man running away, stop him. Keep him alive if you can. Munin, fly ahead and keep track of where Gimnir goes." snapped Sigurlina.

A deeper shadow moved into the gloom accompanied by the sound of crunching snow.

"I guess we have our answer about that son of a snake."

"Vidurr, if you would be so kind," Fjorn led the group onto the pier.

Vidurr howled, and the huge wolf bounded in pursuit of the man.

"If he tells Aethelstan, he will ruin everything. Halla, watch the boat until the guards arrive. Kjorn go to the warehouse, set the guard, and then have the rest of the oarsmen search the area in case Gimnir doubles back." Fjorn stroked his beard as he started after the tracks in the snow. "Sigurlina, we may need to introduce him to your families' reputation when we catch him."

"As long as you know the truth," Sigurlina fell into step beside him.

"Audun, you're fastest, run ahead and help Vidurr if he needs it." Fjorn broke into as much of a run as the snow allowed.

The footprints led between the ruined buildings.

Sigurlina tried to ignore the spirits they raced by. Two children played in the street tossing a ball back and forth their lower bodies lost in the snow. A prostitute plied her trade to clients long dead and gone. A man in Roman armour clutched the body of a child impaled by a spear sobbing. More images of sorrow and death assailed her. She forced herself to look away.

The sounds of battle came from in front of them. Fjorn drew his blade and Sigurlina readied her staff. Moments later the shadow forms of Gimnir, Vidurr, Audun and the skeleton came into view. Gimnir, who no longer stooped when he stood, held a long sword with a master's posture.

"Pro Niveus Deus' palma, absum diabolus ova," he cried as he swept his blade through the skeleton. The skeleton crumbled into dust. Vidurr leapt, Gimnir reversed his blade so it grazed across the wolf's chest allowing Gimnir to sidestep the attack.

Fjorn rushed into the fray and found himself immediately on the defensive.

"Pro senior of totus res EGO offendo." Gimnir cried out in ecstasy as he aimed a savage blow at Fjorn's head. Fjorn barely managed to parry the blade.

Audun traced runes on his arm and rushed Gimnir. Gimnir swung, but the full on blow deflected off the big man's skin leaving only a small wound. Audun swung with his battle axe. Gimnir parried the blow. There was a thunder like retort and the blade of Gimnir's long sword snapped.

Leaping back, Gimnir turned and ran.

"He must be a crusader. We can't let him get away," snapped Audun.

"We have other things to deal with." Fjorn moved to Vidurr's prone form. The wolf weakly raised its head and whimpered. There was a gaping wound in his side.

"Youth to the gods, golden apples of grace.
"Idun's power, heal mortals of faith."

The lights came as Fjorn sang. The wound in Vidurr's side closed. He came unsteadily to his feet.

"Munin, follow the crusader, but keep your distance," ordered Sigurlina.

Vidurr howled and stood pale faced and shaken in his human form. "He is one of the best swordsmen I have ever seen. It was all an act, the laziness, the ineptitude."

"Not the nastiness and cruelty. He must be a crusader," said Sigurlina.

"We have to press the advantage. If he re-arms himself." Audun shook his head.

"Then let us go." Vidurr staggered forward a step and his comrades caught him before he fell.

"You need to recover. Sigurlina, can you get him back to the warehouse?"

Sigurlina nodded and slipped Vidurr's arm over her shoulders.

"Once we get you some place warm I'll heal you again. Right now being damp would probably do you more harm than good." She turned to Fjorn. "Tell Munin that I want her to lead you to Gimnir when she comes back. And stay alive."

"We will try." Audun and Fjorn started following the crusader's prints.

"This is humiliating. My first chance at real vengeance and I am laid low." Vidurr grimaced as they walked.

"You'll get other chances."

Fjorn and Audun followed the tracks until they disappeared into the ruins of a building. Munin circled then landed on Fjorn's shoulder.

"Is he in there?" Fjorn looked at the raven.

"Good bird, good bird," replied Munin.

The willow wisp drifted by casting an enticing glow. Fjorn ignored it.

"Can you see him from above?"

"Yura bitch, Yura bitch."

"I think Sigurlina needs to teach her bird more words," commented Audun.

"I think she makes herself quite plain," countered Fjorn.

Munin nodded, looked at Fjorn and said, "Pretty bird."

"At least they have similar tastes. What are we going to do? This man is deadly and these buildings don't look safe either."

Fjorn thought for a moment then touched his nose before speaking loudly.

"Don't worry about the floor. Follow the willow wisp. They always show the safest path."

The ball of light paused and pulsed where it floated over the floor of the ruined building that the foot prints led to.

Audun smiled, "Those are legends. Are you sure?"

"Positive, they are common up around my area. No traveler ever came to harm following one. Sometimes they even show the way to lost treasure."

The Willow Wisp pulsed brighter and moved over another section of floor.

"Fine, let's go."

Fjorn whispered to Munin, "Fly over and watch for him. Warn us if you see him."

"Good bird, good bird." Munin leapt into the air.

Fjorn and Audun slipped into the ruin. The walls were stone while the ceiling, which consisted of wood beams and planks, was partially intact. The floor was wooden planks and creaked ominously as they walked on it.

The willow wisp hovered over the middle of the room as they hugged the wall.

"We'll bring in the Seith and the wolf as soon as we find him," said Fjorn.

"Right, she'll get answers out of him for sure. Probably use his bones to make a new servant."

"I've asked her to stop doing that, but she seems to like peeling away the living flesh to make them, trapping the spirit so it can't move on. It must be painful walking around without any skin or muscle."

"The willow wisp is showing the safe path. We should--."

A dark figure leapt out from a shadow.

A stirring music played, wind howled in the ruined building accompanying the spell song.

The dark figure lifted impossibly high into the air then crashed down immediately below the Willow Wisp. The floor gave way. The figured screamed as it fell from sight. The ceiling above the middle of the room let lose sending an avalanche of snow and rotting wood into the hole below. Fjorn and Audun hugged the wall and made for the door as snow choked the inside of the ruin. Before the air cleared they had left the building.

"Do you think that killed him?" Audun stared at the destruction beyond the door.

"I hope so. There's no way to check. It is coming up on the time that we have to meet Ragna."

They started back for the warehouse.

"Did you know that the Willow Wisp could sing skald songs?" Audun looked back over his shoulder.

"No."

"But you're a skald."

Fjorn shrugged. "You're a Galdr. Do you know every creature that uses runes?"

"True enough. Do you think it will like us now?"

"I think it will eat us, if it gets the chance. We wanted the same thing just now. I won't take any chances on that happening again."

Audun nodded. "Pity. It is a pretty thing."

Minutes later Munin landed on Fjorn's shoulder and bumped the side of his head.

"What is it?" Fjorn reached for the raven. She dropped something into his open palm.

"I think it worked." Fjorn held up a finger obviously pecked off at the first knuckle.

"Good bird," Audun nodded.

CHAPTER 12

DEBTS PAID

"So Gimnir was a crusader. I never liked him. Is Fjorn sure he's dead?" Ragna plodded through the snow in the snowshoes they'd brought for her.

"As sure as he can be. Munin flew out of the ruin with one of Gimnir's fingers and gave it to Fjorn." Sigurlina got a far away look. "She says that he was nearly torn in half by one of the beams from the roof. Good bird." Sigurlina petted Munin under her cloak.

"You killed one of god's warriors," gasped Wallace.

"He was trying to kill our friends. Maybe if he didn't want to meet people who fight back he shouldn't have come to the north trying to slaughter us," snapped Sigurlina.

"But he was a servant of the Lord. He was trying to save you from your heathen ways."

Sigurlina stopped walking and faced the priest her face going red. "Maybe I don't want to follow your god of blood and death. Your crusaders broke the laws of the guest and murdered my parents when we gave them hospitality. Your monks cheat everyone they trade with who doesn't follow your White God. Maybe if your god wants people to follow him, he should tell his crusaders to help them not kill them. Maybe he should live up to something instead of having his godi spout pretty words then doing the exact opposite. Maybe..."

"Sigurlina?" Abselema's voice ended her tirade. The Haugbui stood beside her.

"Abselema, we brought you your godi. I...I didn't mean you." Sigurlina looked at the snow.

"I know. One is what one does. Words are a poor substitute for action. I still see no ill in you."

"Let us get on with this. Fjorn will have the ship ready soon." Vidurr's voice was nearly a growl.

"Senior servo mihi." Wallace crossed himself and clutched the cross about his neck so tightly that the fish engraving along its length bit into his hand.

"I told you I didn't lie. Wallace please meet Abselema. He needs death duties," said Ragna.

"I have much to confess." The Haugbui bowed his head in front of the priest.

Wallace looked at Ragna. "Why did you bring me here?"

Ragna looked confused. "I told you. We gave him our word we would, and he needs your help."

"Have the chosen fallen so far that they no longer value honesty?" Abselema's voice was sad.

Wallace stared at the Haugbui and took a deep breath. "No. Not all of us. Confess your sins my son, and be forgiven, or would you rather a more private place?"

"I will speak as we walk. My friends know my sins."

Abselema moved to the priest's side and spoke in Latin as he led the way back to the chapel.

When they reached the chapel Wallace pulled back the mouldy blanket covering Abselema's bones.

"And so I have languished here ever since. Tell me Father, what penance may I perform to wash clean my soul?" Abselema finished his confession and stared expectantly at the priest.

"You have done it over these long years, my son." Wallace reached into a bag he carried and took out a clay pot.

Sigurlina stood at the back of the chapel watching. Wallace muttered something, dipped his thumb into the pot and touched the skull in front of him.

Abselema smiled. "Thank you my friends."

Sigurlina saw a bright light at the end of the chapel. A plain woman in Roman dress with black hair and tan skin stood in the light. She smiled and spoke, "Carus."

"Cloelia," cried Abselema.

A thirtyish man dressed in a tunic and trews moved beside the woman. "Pater."

"Meus puer."Abselema strode into the light.

"Where did he go?" asked Ragna.

"You didn't see?" Sigurlina felt tears well up in her eyes.

"See what? He was here, then he was gone." Ragna looked around as if expecting the Haugbui to jump out at her.

Sigurlina smiled, even though her cheeks were wet with tears. "Home."

"What?" asked Ragna.

"That's where he went. His home."

"It could be your home too. The White God will forgive all your si--." Wallace fell silent when Sigurlina turned her gaze on him.

"I will join Freya when my time in Midgard is spent. My home is with her. Foolish godi, Yggdrasil is vast. You look at a twig and think it is the whole, then call the other branches false to try and make your ignorance seem true." Sigurlina shook her head.

"You are Siggy, right?" asked Ragna.

"I am me. I just learned something new. I'm beginning to understand why my mother and grandmother said some of the things they said. We should go."

"What about Wallace?"

Wallace looked from the two women to Vidurr who was scowling at him from the doorway. "I did as you asked."

"We will keep our word. Our work isn't over yet. You'll have to come with us. In three days, I promise you will be free," explained Sigurlina.

"And have the skatt I offered you," added Ragna.

Sigurlina looked at the small woman in surprise.

"I feel bad for him. He came to do his duty. That should count for something."

"I will honour that. To not is to be as bad as a crusader." Vidurr sounded like the words were bitter on his tongue.

Wallace looked shocked.

Sigurlina smiled. "We are not what you have been told we are. Fjorn will be waiting."

After a walk in the cold and dark, they stepped into the warehouse. Six of the smugglers had been untied and were helping to build what looked like parts of a cage. Another group of oarsmen had stretched a white cloth over a ring of metal.

"What are the smugglers doing free?" demanded Vidurr as soon as he saw them.

"They swore by Gungnir to serve me loyally until we reach home. After that, they are free to take ship with another captain or stay in my service." Fjorn smiled.

"You trust them not to betray you?" breathed Wallace.

"They swore by Odin's spear. Who would break such an oath?" he turned to Ragna."Who is this?"

"Fjorn, this is Wallace, a godi of the White God," said Ragna.

"Abselema has left Midgard," added Sigurlina.

Fjorn smiled at Wallace. "Thank you, he proved a good friend."

"Why are you here? What is going on?" asked Wallace.

"Nothing you need to know about." Fjorn looked serious.

"In three days we will let you go," said Ragna.

"Three days." Fjorn turned to her.

Ragna nodded. "It's done by then, or it won't matter."

"Then you can tell us on the *Apenhet*." Fjorn turned to five oarsmen standing by the fire. "Baylegr. You're in charge when I leave."

One of the men seemed to puff up.

"In three days, not before, release the prisoners. My father will give you your skatt in Orkney when you deliver my note. Use the coin I'm leaving with you to get there." Fjorn faced the smuggler captain. "If they do not come to Orkney, I will hunt you down and make you beg for the cold of Niflheim."

The prisoner bowed his head. "I have no doubt you would. You have taken my goods. My men have died at your hands. Other of my crew are taking ship with you. That is all business." The captain smiled a crooked smile. "Your men will need passage to Orkney."

"What would you want?"

"I'm no fool. A trifle over eager when it comes to skatt sometimes, but no fool. I've heard your men talk. I have no love of the crusaders. Bunch of hypocrites ask me. More blood on their hands than mine."

Fjorn moved closer to the other captain. "So?"

"I'm thinking this is an opportunity. I lived in Norveig before I was declared outlaw. My wife still lives there, as best I know, and my boy. Give me a letter for Jarl Erik saying I helped you and asking him to pardon me, my men and our families. My boy shouldn't be shamed because of what I done years ago. I figure you're in good with the jarl, or he wouldn't trust you to do whatever you're doing. Give me the letter before you go, and give me your word that you will speak for me and my men, if you live to see the jarl again. Do that and send a letter of credit to your people for let's say three thousand skatt for what you've eaten of my wears and all your ship will carry, and I'll take your men home for you. If the jarl pardons me, then I'm off to my wife and son. If he doesn't, you let me sail on from Orkney and I know you tried."

"I'll get some parchment." Fjorn shook the other captain's hand. "Baylegr, tie up Father Wallace, then get him something to eat and a cup of mead."

Father Wallace looked up from where he was standing in the corner. "What?"

"Don't worry. Baylegr knows better than to cross Fjorn. In three days, this will all be over. Here." Ragna pushed a bag of coins into the priest's hands. "It's worth more than I promised."

"I don't care about money," said the priest.

"Then use it to feed the poor." Ragna smiled at the priest.

Fjorn had moved to the men putting white cloth over the ring. He picked up their creation and inspected it. "Good. It looks like a shield, but when you get close you can see it isn't a shield. We'll hoist it on the mast and hope no one looks too close."

"A shield on the mast?" Wallace sounded completely confused.

"Don't you know anything?" Ragna walked Wallace to a place on the wall where Baylegr was laying out a blanket. "A white shield on the mast is a pledge of peace. But that isn't a shield, it just looks like one. If Hakon's warriors are too lazy or stupid to check, it is no stain to Fjorn's honour to break the laws of the guest."

"You Northerners have strange customs."

Ragna shrugged. "For what it's worth, a girl could do a lot worse than you. Goodbye Wallace." Ragna kissed the priest's cheek and fell in behind Audun, Vidurr and a pair of oarsmen who were carrying the cage pieces out of the warehouse.

Nearly an hour later the cage sat amidships on the *Apenhet*.

"I do not like this," snarled Vidurr.

"I will not repeat the mistakes of my gods. Vidurr, I swear to you there is no trickery here. And if you will take my word, when we meet on the Plain of Vigrid, I will not challenge you unless we are the only two left. You are my friend, son of Surt."

Vidurr nodded. "Then it is. Unless we are the only two, we will not challenge, child of degenerate gods." Vidurr smiled then howled, becoming the giant, red wolf. He entered the cage, lay down and looked mockingly at Fjorn. A latch that required hands to open was sealed locking the wolf in.

"You had to say it." Fjorn sighed and took his place in the bow.

Minutes later Audun guided the *Apenhet* into open water. The torches on other ships twinkled in the night, but the *Apenhet* was a dark ghost. Halla swam ahead piloting them as she had on the way in. Fjorn held the ropes on Audun's ankles. Once they were away from shore Fjorn tugged twice on the rope Halla was pulling. She released it. He pulled in the line and removed the guiding stick from the gunwale. Sigurlina and Kjorn lowered the platform into the water and brought Halla aboard.

"Light the torches and hoist the false shield," ordered Fjorn.

Sigurlina pulled a cover off a lantern. Lighting a spill from the wick she sparked the kindling set in the brazier. The dry wood flared up. Kjorn lit a torch and thrust it into a gunwale sconce. Oarsmen followed his example while Ragna lit and hung the fore and aft lanterns. Sigurlina added charcoal to the brazier before it burnt down and hung a cauldron of water over it to heat. Kjorn had the oarsmen hoist the false shield and sail. For all appearances they could have been sailing for days.

"Time to get dressed." Fjorn opened his sea chest taking out the clothes he's bought in Alvaldsnes.

"Finally," commented Ragna.

"You already got a new dress," remarked Sigurlina.

"And who crawled through a privy? I deserved it."

"Get dressed; we still need to talk before we get challenged."

Minutes later Fjorn, Sigurlina, Audun, Ragna, and Kjorn huddled around Vidurr's cage. All the humans were dressed in new, expensive clothing bedecked with braid and rich furs. Fjorn eyed Sigurlina and could barely believe she wasn't the highborn lady she was pretending to be.

Sigurlina stole glances of Fjorn. She'd known he was a karl's son but in the clothing, with a brass circulate on his brow, he truly looked the part. She remember when she'd been little and pretended with her friends that they were princesses and the jarls and karls were coming to play court to them. She smiled hoping she survived to experience the reality that had been a children's game.

"The horn is going out to sea in three days. It's definitely in the treasure hall. They also have foreign ships in the harbour that they're loading with oil and cloth. They had something that looked like a sideways bow on them. I couldn't get close enough to see more," said Ragna.

"We can use this against them. If we can get the fire skui Munin said they put in the treasure hall to cooperate. All the oil on those boats will burn nicely if we spark it," said Audun.

"How can we spark it though?" asked Fjorn.

"Get me some wood axes, a bit of oil and some rages and I'll give you a fire. The fire Skui will do the rest, if it is willing." A vicious smile filled Audun's face.

"Good. We have a plan. How much of a distraction can the town's people provide?" asked Fjorn.

"How much are you wiling to spend?" Ragna shrugged.

"The purse is getting light." Fjorn tilted his head in thought. "We are overstocked for food, and we'll want to be light and fast leaving. Trade for what we need as much as you can."

"People are desperate from the taxes and tithes." Ragna sighed. "Food will be more welcome than skatt. It's harder for the church to steal."

They had barely finished planning and dispersed to the various stations on the ship when a large vessel approached them.

"Drop sail and prepare to be boarded by order of Hakon, rightful king of Norveig, acting steward of Wessex." An officious voice called from the other vessel in Anglic. Silence followed.

"They want us to lower the sail and let them board." Ragna translated into Orse. She called back in Anglic. "Try some other tongues if you want to be understood. Fjorn, son of Karl Geldnir of Orkney has come to treat with King Hakon and learn of the White God's ways. He doesn't speak Anglic. You need to get someone who can manage some proper

Orse." Ragna rolled her eyes then added softly in Orse, "You wedge."

"Ship sail," ordered Fjorn.

Minutes passed as a large longship pulled alongside and ropes were thrown over. Oarsmen pulled the ropes until the hulls met. A plank was lowered between the vessels. A slender man with a large, hooked nose and a self-important air wearing in a monk's robes boarded the *Apenhet*.

"Welcome aboard. I am Fjorn, son of Karl Geldnir of Orkney come to treat with King Hakon and learn of the White God's ways." Fjorn approached the monk with his palms held open in front of him.

Vidurr growled from inside his cage making the man jump.

"What is that?" gasped the monk in heavily-accented Orse.

"A gift from the far north. A great, red wolf. I have heard that your pope is fond of collecting vicious creatures and there are none more vicious." Fjorn kept the scorn he felt at the monk's obvious fear out of his voice.

"I have never encountered this type of beast before."

"They are creatures of the far north. Maybe knowledge of them hasn't reached the lands of outer Midgard," remarked Sigurlina.

The monk looked down his nose at her. "A woman and she speaks." His voice dripped with displeasure. "I have studied in the libraries of great Rome itself. If it exists, there is record of it there. I was simply confused by your Orse name. Yes, Lupus Maximus. The Caesars encountered them on the northern extreme of the Gallic campaign. Noted for their voracious appetite. An interesting creature. This is a particularly large specimen. It will be a welcome addition to *His Holiness'* menagerie. Who is the woman?"

"My betrothed, the Lady Sigurlina. I have come with my household to treat for peace. May I know to whom I speak?"

"I am Aemilianus, adviser to Hakon King of Norveig." The monk eyed them with distain. "Give my captain a tow line and we will bring you to the harbour. Once we are ashore guards will escort your household to the royal compound. I will go ahead and speak to King Hakon regarding an audience for you."

"Accommodation must be made for my gift." Fjorn moved closer to the monk and spoke softly. "To be honest, it is making my crew frightful. It howls and growls constantly. None of us has had much sleep for the entire voyage."

"Yes. I can see how it might be unnerving to uneducated Northmen. I will have the crusaders take it to King Aethelstan's treasure hall with the other beasts." The monk crossed to his ship and the plank was drawn back. A tow line was attached to the *Apenhet's* bow and the larger ship deployed ores to enter the harbour.

"Just like we planed," Fjorn whispered to each of his crew in turn.

Sigurlina whispered to Munin who leapt into the air and flew towards Winchester.

The docks were a hive of activity as they were pulled in and tied to the end of a pier that thrust into the sea far enough that it accommodated six small longships to a side.

Ragna stood beside Audun and pointed at the end of the middle pier as they docked. "Those are the ships with the oil."

Audun scanned the harbour. "If we do this right, this whole harbour could burn."

"Then do it right." Ragna hopped up on a sea chest and kissed the big man on the cheek. "For luck."

Audun smiled. "It is you know."

"What is?" said Ragna.

"Proportionate."

The small woman blushed.

After they were tied off to the dock, a squad of crusaders came and took Vidurr, cage and all. Several of them eyed the huge wolf with trepidation as they carried him up the pier then along Tradesmen Street.

"I hope he's all right," remarked Sigurlina.

"He'll be safer than the rest of us soon enough," remarked Kjorn.

"Audun, stay with the ship. Have the crew get some sleep and a meal or two." Fjorn nervously scanned the harbour.

"Don't forget, we still have a debt to pay," whispered Sigurlina.

"You just want to go to those baths," joked Ragna, but it fell flat.

"Leave your staff and sword on the ship. We'll get them later if you need them. They aren't use to shield maids here. The fewer reminders of how dangerous you really are, the less guarded they will be to your attacks."

Sigurlina and Ragna smiled but there was something predatory in it.

Minutes passed in tense silence.

Aemilianus returned. "I have obtained an audience for you and your house with his Majesty. It was most difficult. We must go at once."

Fjorn nodded and stepped onto the pier. Sigurlina moved to his side and took his arm.

Kjorn fell in behind scowling at everything. Ragna moved beside him.

"Another woman?" the monk sniffed.

"Ragna is my translator. Kjorn is sworn to my protection. They are of my house." Fjorn spoke in a measured tone.

"I see. Very well. Come."

Fjorn noted the town as he walked. First came the great halls the crusaders were using as barracks. These were in good repair and each bore the symbol of the cross. He guessed that in total the barracks housed three hundred blades. Later came individual hovels lining the street, these were battered. Waste of all varieties stained the ice and snow. A pair of houses were burnt ruins. As he passed, a woman emptied a bucket of human waste into the street where it lay steaming.

At the end of Tradesmen Street the road circling the royal compound came into view. The palisade loomed up. They were led to a gate of logs lashed together. Guards stood by the entrance. Ragna kept her hood up and tried not to be noticed as she walked by Lister who was guarding the gate.

After the palisade, the compound spread out into a large yard. Four great halls made of wood stood side by side. Guards and monks made trails through the ice and snow between them. A fifth hall, made of cut stone, obviously salvaged from the Roman ruins, stood at the end of the row to the right. This hall's roof was terracotta tile and peaked, the walls were low, being little over a man's height. A guard stood at the heavy, iron-bound, wood door at its front while another guard patrolled around the outside. There were no windows. There was a long building, built on a raised platform against the palisade by the stone building. A long, narrow wagon was parked beneath the long building. The stench of a privy assailed Fjorn when the breeze blew from that direction. A set of stairs led up to the doors of the elevated structure.

Sigurlina scanned the compound searching for shadows from which the treasure hall's door was visible. The raised building was close enough to meet her needs and cast a shadow against the palisade from a torch positioned in its eaves.

Aemilianus guided them to the hall on the left end of the row. Guards eyed them with professional disinterest. Their chain coats were polished until they gleamed, and they all wore thick, grey cloaks.

Ragna examined the inside of the palisade. There was an archery platform about the height of an average man's chest down from the top of the fortification. Men with bows stood at intervals along the platform.

Aemilianus led them into the hall on the left and stopped just inside the door. "You must surrender your weapons."

Kjorn grit his teeth. "I am ordered to guard--."

Fjorn interrupted him. "If it is the king's law, I will obey." Drawing his long sword, dagger and boot knife he placed them on a blanket spread over some kind of crate.

"Is my eating knife too fearsome a blade?" asked Sigurlina.

"A woman is no threat, blade or no," snapped Aemilianus.

Kjorn added his blade to Fjorn's.

"We are unarmed," said Fjorn.

Aemilianus whispered into the ear of a loose-skinned man with a shaved head wearing a rich robe who stood by the hall's inner door.

"Announcing Fjorn, son of Karl Geldnir of Orkney," called the loose-skinned man.

Aemilianus led them past the entry area into the great hall.

The centre of the floor was filled with a blazing fire. A wooden platform surrounded the dirt floor around the fire trench, but instead of women weaving, grinding flower, sewing and men mending nets, armour or working leather, as in most great halls, the platform was filled with monks writing on scrolls and bustling to and fro in seemingly pointless effort. They all wore sombre, but rich, clothing.

Hakon sat on a thrown in front of a wall that cut the hall in half. Fjorn blessed his father for insisting he grow his beard. Hakon's jaw line was a twin to Fjorn's own, and Jarl Erik's. Hakon's complexion was pale and his eyes a deep brown. His golden hair was tied back while his lean, muscular body moved with economy, as if every shift of his weight was considered, vetted then acted on. He was clad in a blue robe with gold embroidery. At odds with the richness of everything else around him he wore a cowbone cross on a leather thong around his neck.

"Fjorn, son of Geldnir, heir to the seat of Orkney, do you come to kneel before the true king of the north?" Hakon's voice was clipped and precise as if each word was cut off with a knife.

Fjorn stepped forward and, swallowing his gall, knelt before Hakon's throne.

"You come with a petition." Hakon continued.

"Your Majesty, we have been at odds for too long. Blood has been spilt on both sides. I would treat with you for peace and learn the way of the White God so that we might be friends."

"Have you taken the wafer?" demanded Hakon.

"I wish to learn all that entails first, Your Majesty."

Hakon snorted. "There is naught to learn. There is only one path, but at least you see your heathen ways are in error. I will arrange with my monks to educate you. Look up all of you; I would see your faces."

Fjorn swallowed and raised his face.

A slow smile spread across Hakon's features. It was thin and brittle and conveyed all the warmth of a snake that had spotted a mouse. "Much becomes clear, brother Fjorn. The Lord surely has brought you to me so that you can save Orkney from heathen ways and my half-brother Erik. A man ruled by an evil woman is not fit to command the smallest of vessels; let alone a kingdome. Wouldn't you agree?"

"Yes, Your Majesty." Fjorn tried to ignore the similarities in the face he looked into, but couldn't. There was no denying that the man before him was his half-brother.

Hakon lifted his left forefinger and a boy walked up to the throne bearing a gold platter full of fruit. Hakon selected a pear then motioned for the boy to serve his guests.

"Please, I know that fruit is a rare pleasure in this time of cold and dark. Accept my hospitality."

Fjorn accepted an apple and the tray moved on. "Thank you, this is most generous."

"Not at all." Hakon watched the serving boy depart with a

predatory gleam in his eyes. "Such a pity he can't sing. Now, Fjorn. Why should I believe that Orkney, that has so long been a vassal to that heathen pretender to the throne, would suddenly speak peace with me?"

"Erik has only recently seen my face, which has given my father pause. As well, one does not fight the sea storm. Erik is afraid to set ships to sea. We are an island without a sea defence our towns could be easily burnt. All I wish is to follow my father and keep our holdings. I have no ambitions beyond that service to my people."

Hakon smiled and nodded. "Well said, and as it should be, but why do you fear your towns burning?"

"Sire, neither of us is a child. It is hard to hide a cog armed with ballista and stocked with oil. As you have your eyes and ears, so do the other houses and powers. Can we be honest with each other on this point?"

Hakon nodded. "You need say no more. If Erik was not too craven to challenge me on the waters, the cogs would be no threat to his holdings. I thought to mount the ballista on dragon ships, but the crusaders spoke against it. They claimed the longships were too unstable. Perhaps together we can put that to the test?"

"It would be an interesting endeavour, King Hakon."

Hakon smiled. "What a force that would be. Stand, all of you."

Fjorn and his house obeyed.

"Introduce me to your household." Hakon's eyes seemed to slide over Sigurlina leaving a trail of slime in their path.

"My betrothed, Lady Sigurlina of Finnmark." Fjorn fought to keep his ire in check.

Hakon stood and moved to kiss Sigurlina's hand. "A pleasure. You remind me of my mother, and she was a great beauty."

"Thank you, Your Majesty."

Fjorn continued. "My man at arms Kjorn."

Hakon barely acknowledged Kjorn.

"My translator, Ragna."

Hakon stared down the gap in the top of Ragna's dress. "You are of Pict lineage, are you not?"

"I am, Your Majesty. I was taken as a child in a raid, but earned my freedom." Ragna struck a pose bordering on the provocative.

"Interesting." Hakon's tone was dismissive. He returned to his throne. "I saw the beast you brought as tribute. Impressive. I'm sure *His Holiness* will be pleased. Were you with the party that captured it?"

"Yes, Your Majesty," Fjorn noticed the long sword that sat in easy reach of Hakon's hand. Small, gold crosses, too many to easily count, adorned the scabbard.

"We will have to go hunting. There is interesting prey in the highlands."

"I look forward to it."

A monk brought a scroll over and stood three paces from Hakon's thrown. Hakon gestured with his right hand and the monk approached. Hakon examined the scroll.

"Tell them that they suffer for their sins. If they would root out the heathens among them, they would be able to pay their tithes and taxes and have enough left to avoid starvation. The petition is denied."

The monk whispered something.

Hakon made a dismissive gesture. "If they are so devout then they won't mind joining god's army for our glorious campaign. That will be fewer mouths they have to feed. Tell them that I am their King, appointed by the White God. To deny me is to deny the White God and His Holy Church." Hakon turned to Fjorn. "There are always those who don't understand. Authority is like a river; it flows from god to the pope to the king, then through his nobles to the men of the family. All must bow to those closer to the source. This is the will of the White God. With the cold and dark it is difficult for us all, but that is no excuse for not seeing to our obligations. Wouldn't you agree?"

"Yes, Your Majesty."

"Exactly! I have affairs of state to attend to. I will have Aemilianus provide for your needs. I fear that we have no space in the royal compound, but there are fine inns in the town. Speak to my monks before you go to your rest, they will tell you of the one true faith."

Fjorn and the others bowed and backed away. When Sigurlina turned she could almost feel Hakon's eyes on her backside.

"Follow me," stated Aemilianus.

"Thank you," said Fjorn.

Sigurlina cleared her throat.

"Yes, my sweet. I will see." Fjorn faced Aemilianus. "My lady has heard that you have restored a roman bath. It is an ambition of hers to bathe in one. Could you oblige us?"

Aemilianus dipped his head. "I will have a guard escort her. The baths can be a wholesome pleasure, though there are temptations there to taint a man's soul. Still, a lady, even though they are innately corrupt, should be safe enough."

"See Sigurlina, easy as asking. We'll meet back at the *Apenhet* then find an inn."

Ragna cleared her throat. "My lord, I need to purchase supplies for our return voyage."

Fjorn smiled at Aemilianus. "We traveled light knowing we would dock here."

"You may wander the town but I cannot let you re-enter the royal enclosure without escort." Aemilianus looked at Ragna with distaste. He snapped his fingers and a guard returned Fjorn's party's weapons.

"I'll find lodging at an inn." Ragna tried to keep the distaste from her voice but failed.

"I'll do the same, if it please you, lord. It's been a time since I've slept ashore." Kjorn looked at Fjorn.

"With Aemilianus's permission. Leave a message with Audun at the ship about where you can be found." Fjorn shrugged. "It's been a trying trip with the wolf."

"Very well. Enjoy the pleasures Winchester offers." Aemilianus made a dismissive gesture.

#

Vidurr watched from his cage as he was carried into the treasure hall. Items in gold and silver glistened on one side. Beasts in cages lined the other. A spider, the size of a war horse, stared through its many faceted eyes as he passed.

"Let me out and I will lead you to a treasure," hissed a ten-stride long, snow serpent from another cage. Its white fur caught the light of the crusaders' torches like new-fallen snow.

A dreyri screeched from another cage. A polar bear occupied still another. Suspended over a large cauldron of water by a length of hemp rope, a metal cage contained a human looking creature about the size of a cat. It had red and orange wings with rust-coloured hair and golden eyes.

At the back of the treasure hall, Vidurr saw an oddly shaped object. It was a cone as tall as his shoulder and as large around as his head at one end, tapering to about the circumference of his little finger at the other. A pattern of what looked like tentacles was embossed over its surface. The cone sat upon a wooden stand supported on a low, marble platform. An iron cage had been constructed around it.

To one side of the cage containing the horn was a platform draped in linen, at its centre was a ring made up of coloured bands. On the horn's other side, a stand supported a mail coat bearing the royal crest of King Harald. A royal-blue bag with silver runes embroidered on it stood on a table to one side of the mail.

The crusaders pushed Vidurr's cage into position at the end of the row then left the treasure hall. There was the sound of a bolt being driven home then darkness. A red glow came form the cage over the cauldron of water. Vidurr howled taking on his human form then, sliding back the bolt on his cage, he stepped into the treasure hall.

"That was interesting. What other tricks can you do, you clever puppy," remarked the snow serpent in perfect Orse. The voice was cultured and the serpent tracked Vidurr with its eyes.

"I can survive, serpent. Listen all of you. In a few hours I will open this hall and my companions will attack. If we stand together, we can escape. At the least, we can make those who took you pay for the affront."

The polar bear stood on its hind legs and roared.

"What did he say?" demanded Vidurr.

"What did he say? And that you look delicious," replied the serpent in a mocking tone. "They don't feed us much here."

"You can speak polar bear?" queried Vidurr.

"Please, I can speak everything."

The spider made a chitering sound. The snake turned to the spider. "I agree, the puppy does seem a little slow."

Vidurr glared at the snake. "I'm not the one stuck in a cage about to be shipped off to fight to the death for some human's enjoyment."

The spider chittered.

The snake sighed. "You're right, he does have a point. Very well, puppy. Allow me to introduce myself. I am Hisstor. My leggy friend here is Kukkk." The name sounded like steel striking a flint stone. "Don't try to pronounce it, you'd likely hurt yourself. Spider will do."

"Vidurr."

"Very well, puppy. Tell me your plan. If I find it an improvement on waiting for the Pope's hospitality, I'll speak to the others for you. This should be interesting at the least. Unlock my cage and we can proceed."

Vidurr bared his teeth in a predatory smile. "You can listen in there until we reach a deal and oaths are sworn."

The snake laughed. "It would seem you're a little brighter then I thought. Pity, you do look delicious."

#

Sigurlina stepped through the door into the restored Roman bath with a royal guard on her heals.

"Quintinus, EGO edoctus vos pro vos prohibeo addo vestri own puella. Haud derideo carus," said Daldis.

"S est era Sigurlina a hospes of Rex rgis Hakon. Is vota facio thermae. Is fatur tantum gentilitas Orse." Quintinus looked disdainful.

Daldis bowed and switched to Orse. "I am sorry, my lady. If you will wait I will have one of the private tubs prepared for you. Please take no offence at my prior comment. When I saw you with Quintinus I assumed you could speak the church tongue."

"Think nothing of it. I would ask. Do you have a Daegal working at this bath?"

"Daegal, oh my yes, he's been with us for years. But how would a high-born lady know a bondi working the baths?"

"I know his son and have a message for him. Could you summon him while my bath is prepared, and give us a private place to speak?"

"A message from Daegal's son. I... I will find him myself. This. You may not know this, but Daegal has blamed himself for the boy running off all these years. It has been an open wound for the poor man." Daldis ushered Sigurlina into a seat in the alcove opposite the door. "If it please you, my lady, I'll find Daegal and bring him here."

"Thank you." Sigurlina smiled at the madam then turned her

attention to Quintinus. "You may depart. I will likely be some time."

Quintinus stood in the hall and stared at her.

"He can't speak Orse. I've seen him before. He's a regular here." The shade of Banning appeared beside Sigurlina.

Sigurlina pretended to inspect the candle sconce built into the wall on the back of the alcove and whispered, "I thought the crusaders believed in chastity."

"As long as they pay for the indulgence, they can do whatever they want. This one likes Mae. She has--."

"I don't need to know."

"My father is coming."

Sigurlina turned back to the hall to see an old, bald man dressed in worn and stained tunic and trews rush up the hallway.

"My lady," he came to a stop in front of the alcove and bowed his head.

"Daegal?" Sigurlina stood and motioned the old man into the alcove.

"Daldis said you had word from my boy. Has he forgiven me?" Daegal's face filled with pleading.

"Please tell my guard to go get a horn or something. I'm going to be a while, and I want to talk privately."

Daegal turned to Quintinus they had a brief conversation in Latin. After a moment Sigurlina reached into her pouch and pulled out several skatt that she held out to Quintinus. "Tell him I'm going to be a while with the bath, and he won't be following me into the tub."

Daegal relayed the message. Quintinus took the coins, replied and left.

"He's going to the inn across the street. He will be back soon to wait for you. Now what did my boy tell you? Please."

"Tell him I'm sorry I had no choice," Banning spoke beside Sigurlina.

"Banning wanted me to tell you that he loves you. He left because he overheard King Aethelstan ordering his priest to cut him. To make him a half man, so that he would keep his singing voice."

"My god, so it wasn't me. It wasn't because of the fight we had."

"It never was. He always loved you but he had to flee or be cut.

He only escaped because of what you taught him about the baths."

Tears welled up in the old man's eyes. "I... I always thought he'd follow me at the baths. He dreamed of traveling. Sometimes when I dreamt I thought I could hear his voice. Damn Aethelstan. We were loyal. I helped in the rebellion." Daegal clenched his fists. "If I were a younger man...Where is my boy now?"

"Tell him I took ship. Say I never came back because I was afraid that Aethelstan would be angry with me." Banning's voice held a note of relief.

"He's a traveler. He has gone places I've never been. He hasn't come back because he fears Aethelstan's wrath."

"He was always a smart boy. When you saw him did he look well? He'd be full grown now."

Sigurlina eyed Banning's shade. "He looked well, though you could still see the boy in the man. He was a good friend to me and my friends. He helped us when no one else could. I know he was friends with a godi of the White God."

Daegal sighed. "That is good. That would have made his mother happy, Marry keep her. You cannot know what this message means to me."

As Sigurlina watched a white light appeared. Banning's ghostly arms encircled his father in a hug. Abselema appeared in the light. "Time to go, Banning. Cloelia and my son are eager to meet you."

"I love you, papa," whispered Banning, then he, Abselema, and the light were gone.

"You're son loves you very much," said Sigurlina.

Daegal had tears in his eyes. "I know that now. If you see him, tell him I miss him."

Sigurlina nodded. Daldis came from around the corner, her eyes were red and her lip trembled. "Your bath is ready. I've put out the good oils." She paused to quickly hug Daegal. "You see. I knew the boy still loved you." She turned to Sigurlina. "I'll show you the way."

After a long, hot soak, Quintinus escorted Sigurlina back to the royal compound. Sigurlina felt like a weight had been lifted from her shoulders. Her debts were paid and now she could focus on what she needed to do.

CHAPTER 13

THE BEST LAID PLANS

Ragna and Kjorn left the royal compound and started down Tradesmen Street.

"They're on our stern," commented Kjorn.

"The two men dressed as thralls?" Ragna pretended to stop and examine the tradesmen's sign hanging on a smith's shop. Kjorn stopped beside her and the two thralls slipped behind a building.

"They don't move like thralls."

"Do you feel like a drink?" Ragna moved towards an inn across the street.

"I'm parched. Will they have the mead we want though?" Kjorn followed her into a great hall that displayed the sign for an inn. The sign had a gilt edging and when they entered the hall was clean with a rich smell of quality food filling the air.

Ragna giggled. "A rich man's inn in a village known for trade and politics? They'll have what we need."

"What can I do for you?" asked a broad, squat man in fine clothing.

"A way out unseen and no questions," said Kjorn as he passed over several coins.

"Go to the blonde by the entrance to the private rooms section, call her Edda. Same again and you were never here."

"Same again. I remember when half what I gave you would have done the deed," objected Kjorn.

The squat man shrugged.

"Come on." Ragna led the way towards the curtain that separated the private rooms at the back of the inn. A young, blonde woman sat by the curtain.

"Are you Edda?" asked Kjorn when he reached the curtain

The blonde smiled. "Nanna, actually." She held out her hand. "Room, door, or both?"

"Door, but if they ask room." Kjorn pressed coins into her hand.

A sound from the main entrance caught his attention. The two thralls were trying to enter the hall.

"Left hand door, end of the hall, just follow the passage. Pig wallow is frozen solid, gate is on the other side." Nanna smiled.

Ragna and Kjorn slipped past the curtain. They walked along a hall past several doors. At the last one on the left, they pulled it open. A blast of cold air enveloped them. They entered a short, dark hall that ended in another door that opened into an open space surrounded by a tall fence. There was a pig trough on the frozen ground at one end of the area and a gate to their right. They exited the gate and found themselves in a side street by the inn.

"We should be good for an hour before they even start to wonder," commented Ragna.

"An hour. I should be offended." Kjorn smiled at her.

"Oh listen to Bragie go on." They went their separate ways.

Kjorn slipped back onto Tradesmen Street and found a smithy. Minutes later he walked out with a pair of splitting axes. He then followed side streets to the docks.

Audun waited on the *Apenhet* while Kjorn boarded.

"Fjorn is still in the royal compound." Kjorn passed over the axes.

"I'd rather the sea air. We've supplies and mead enough," remarked Audun.

The church bell sounded eight times.

"I'm off to find the privy and a few hours sleep at the Karl's Rest. The fifth bell will tell the tale. See you before the sixth." Kjorn picked up a keg of mead and started along the dock.

"The fifth bell." Audun inspected the *Apenhet* once again. The crates of cargo were loosed, leaving only those needed for a quick trip to Orkney secured. The oarsmen feasted on pork and vegetable stew. The sail was ready to be raised at a moment's notice, and the oars were set for departure. Lights burnt on the other ships in the harbour and at the end of the dock as well as by the ships on frameworks. Men laboured on the landed ships, re-kinking planks and shaping wood to replace spars.

Taking a seat in the stern, Audun caressed one of the axes. Clearing his mind he started tracing a pattern of runes on it. When he was finished he gave the axe and a small bag of skatt to an oarsman who left the ship and went to an inn for the night.

Audun began enchanting the second axe.

#

Fjorn followed Aemilianus out of Hakon's great hall. "Is that your privy?" he asked pointing to the raised building with the wagon under it.

"Yes. A bondi comes with a horse after the fifth bell and changes the wagon. It's not like the plumbing in the holy city, but it's better than a ditch. I make it a point to go to the baths." Aemilianus looked at the structure disdainfully.

"Could I."

"But of course."

Fjorn mounted the steps to the raised building. The long structure was pierced by six doors. Fjorn opened one and entered a narrow room with a bench that had a hole cut into it at the back. He was disgusted to see that there was no cleansing spoon. He stood to relieve himself then rejoined Aemilianus. The monk led Fjorn to the hall in the centre of the compound. The peek of the roof of this hall was adorned with a large, wooden cross. Just in front of the hall stood a huge bell under a roof supported on pillars so the sides were open.

A monk sat by the bell watching an hour glass attached to the support pillar in such a way that it could be turned when the sands ran down. Fjorn entered to find that half of the hall was a single room. At its end was a raised platform with an altar set in its centre. The back wall supported a huge, gold cross. A pair of robed monks polished a silver cup and a gold plate beside the altar. The fire in the central pit gave off enough heat that Fjorn wanted to take off his cloak. Rich curtains covered doorways that led to the rest of the hall.

"Brother Aemilianus, weary of King Hakon's service so soon?" The monk polishing the gold plate put it on the altar and moved to face Aemilianus.

"I relish the king's favour, Brother Titus. Are the shepherds still giving you problems?"

"God's warriors are, robust. Why are you here?"

"I bring a supplicant. Fjorn is a heathen but he wishes to learn of the true path. Hakon wishes you to teach him."

"Very good, my son. Let us begin by baptising you." Titus took a step towards the altar.

Fjorn stared at the monk. "I wish to learn of your god. I will swear no oath in ignorance."

Titus sighed. "We are all in ignorance before we accept the one true path, my son."

"Still, I would see for myself." Fjorn stood his ground.

"Very well. What would you know of the one true faith?" Titus sounded paternal.

"Perhaps he could attend a service," suggested Aemilianus.

"You are welcome to the guard's mass. Come when you hear the fifth bell. The crusaders mass comes after six bells. They can be less than welcoming to strangers, king's sanction or no. You seem a man of good heart and mind, so I'm sure that seeing the glory of our Lord will open your eyes." Titus's voice was soothing. "I will do all I can do to save you from the torments of hell."

Fjorn nodded. "Thank you. May my betrothed attend as well? If we embrace your way, it is easer if we both do so."

Aemilianus smiled. "That is wise and I am sure it would please King Hakon."

"So long as she knows to be silent. Women are innately corrupt, and I would not see the service disrupted." Titus smiled and nodded as if granting Fjorn a boon.

Aemilianus smirked towards Titus as he spoke to Fjorn. "I should let you know what to expect. Brother could you fetch us some chairs?"

Titus gritted his teeth, scowled at Aemilianus, and then left the room.

"Let me begin by saying we are all born in sin. This is because..." Aemilianus began his lecture.

Hours later Fjorn returned to the *Apenhet* with a dull pounding behind his eyes. Sigurlina lay in the bow wrapped in blankets with Munin perched beside her. Audun sat in the stern tracing runes onto an axe.

"What is the word?" asked Audun when Fjorn approached.

"Just as we planned. When they sound the fifth bell, we begin."

"Best tell the messenger." Auden looked at Sigurlina who slept in the bow with Munin beside her.

"I wish I could just let her sleep."

"I know. And I wish the sun and moon had shone all my days. Trust in the Norns, I think they have bigger plans for us."

Fjorn nodded. "Do you know where everyone is?"

"Munin does."

"That will do." Fjorn moved to wake Sigurlina

#

Vidurr sighed. "If you fly off before the archers are dealt with, they will shoot you." He glared at the dreyi.

The snake made a series of screeching sounds. The dreyi screeched back.

"She says she can fly very fast." Hisstor slapped its tail against its forehead at the same time that Vidurr palmed his face and the spider tapped the claws on its front two-legs together.

"She's a fool, and she is going to get us all killed. But she won't listen," finished Hisstor.

"Then I won't open her cage until we're ready to go. She can draw the bowmen's fire at least."

"Good point, puppy." Hisstor nodded.

The polar bear made a series of gruffing sounds.

"He still wonders why we should trust you, human," relayed the snake.

"Don't call me human. I am Ulfhednar; I am the wolf that walks on two legs. Humans deceive, humans are cruel. We have all killed for food, fought for mates, defended our territories, but never have we killed for the joy of killing. That is a thing of man. Any or all of us may die as we leave this place, but I will not lead you to death because that is not a wolf's way. I will not pit you against each other and sit back to enjoy your suffering then leave your broken forms to rot as I slaughter sweeter meat. I am Ulfhednar. Are you with me in this or not?"

Hisstor made a series of grunting noises. The polar bear stood on its hind legs and roared.

Hisstor spoke in a series of hisses and crackles that sounded like a fire.

"I understand him, snake breath!"

"You speak Orse?" Hisstor sounded surprised.

"You pick things up. Wolf brain, I'm in. It sounds like fun. If I flame the harbour, it might just catch me up to my cousin Crakler. He played a prank in Rome a few years back and has been bragging about it ever since. Stupid humans gave the credit to one of their own. A guy named Nero." The fire skui's voice was thin and hissy, like gas escaping from a burning log, but clear.

The spider made a clicking sound.

"She is with us," remarked Hisstor.

"It still surprises me you understand Orse." Vidurr addressed the spider directly.

The spider clicked and clacked at him.

"She says she learned it from her meals while they were tenderising. She just doesn't have the mouth for speaking it. Just as well, humans rarely have anything worth saying."

A bell sounded eight times.

"Good, then--," began Vidurr. A clunk from the main door cut him off.

"Get in your cage. It's feeding time." Hisstor spat.

Vidurr dove into his cage, closed and locked the door, before howling to assume his wolf form. The treasure hall's door opened and a crusader, the cross embroidered on his cloak marking his position, strode in scowling. He moved to the bag sitting beside the cage and wrenched it open. Reaching into the bag, he pulled out a dead badger and tossed it to the dreyri. The dreyri screeched and started ripping into the meat. The crusader then poured water from a bucket he carried into troughs shoved up against the cages. And, with a final scowl at the animals, the crusader strode from the hall bolting the door behind him.

"They should leave us alone until after the bells have gone to twelve then eight again," remarked Hisstor.

Vidurr howled, returning to his human form and unlocked his cage. "Good. Can I count on you all?"

There was a chorus of strange noises. "I think that is your answer. Though, don't trust the dreyri. She still thinks she can out fly an arrow," advised Hisstor.

Vidurr moved to the blue bag the badger had come from and opened it. There was a dead badger inside. "What is this?"

"Our food. Whatever they put in it, there are two of them the next day. It is quite an interesting and useful trick. The cross types say it's the devil's food and won't touch it. That doesn't stop them from feeding it to us soulless beasts." Hisstor sounded sardonic.

Vidurr pulled out the badger. "We won't be here long enough for the magic to work again, so who wants the head?"

The spider clicked and clacked as she took down a bundle from the back of her cage.

"She says there wouldn't be time to properly tenderise it so none for her," translated Hisstor. "Our fiery friend doesn't care for badger," he added.

"That makes it simple." Using his sword Vidurr cut the badger in two giving half to the polar bear and half to Hisstor before folding the bag into his pack.

Taking the mail coat from the rack, he stripped out of his cloak and tunic then put the armour on. He wrapped the ring in his tunic and put it in a canvas bag he had stuffed in his pack along with some of the gold stacked at the side of the room.

"Aethelstan is going to be angry with you," smirked Hisstor.

"Good." Vidurr pried at the lock of the cage around the kraken horn. The metal gave way and the cage door opened. "We should get some sleep. Can you arrange a watch? We begin with the fifth bell."

\#

Ragna sat on the wooden platform in the Karl's Rest inn facing Tolan. Beyond him a man was having a bloody gash in his forehead stitched and bandaged by a woman in overly tight clothing. Past them a man and woman lay under a blanket acting as if they had the common room to themselves. All around men and woman hoisted horns of watery mead.

"Can't be done," remarked Tolan.

The bell sounded eight times in the distance.

Ragna played her finger over the back of his hand flirtatiously. "Just a little distraction at five bells, then a bigger one at six. For me?"

"You're a fine one, Ragna, but you're not worth dying for. If we attack the royal compound we'll be cut down like wheat."

"Attack?" Ragna looked shocked. "I said a distraction. I'm shy on skatt but my ship is well provisioned. Send some men round the docks to pick it up and you'll do well enough out of this."

"Still, not worth dying for." Tolan took a long draw from his mead horn and his voice dropped to a whisper. "'Tween you and me, the higher ups as I see it, aren't too fond of Hakon. Bit more clever than they like. Still and all, I won't die for them."

"There's no need to. You men, you always get above yourselves. I've some thoughts. If you hear me out, it could mean your drinking better mead than this troll's piss." Ragna quaffed from her horn. "Awful stuff."

"Costs me nothing to listen."

#

The bell sounded ten times.

Audun sighed as he watched the rough looking men with Ragna carry away the loose stores from the *Apenhet.*

"She is a looker but I'm thinking she stashes nuts for the winter," remarked Tolan to Audun as Ragna walked down the pier.

"You don't know the half of it," Audun shook his head then smiled. "Still and all, it makes for interesting times. You can't ask better than a good death after interesting times."

"With a bit of skatt in the purse to smooth the way."

The two men shook hands. "I'll get her back to you. I got me people spreading word about the race. It's gonna be a sight. Probably have the monks whipping themselves for a month."

#

The bell sounded four times.

Kjorn carried the keg of mead to a wagon that was submerged up to its pull pole in the harbour. A long, sloping ramp led up from the sea and a lane let onto the town streets. The wagon was long and narrow with solid sides along its cargo area. A slender man, with corded muscles, dressed in a filthy tunic, stood at the wagon's front beside an old-looking, plough horse. The horse munched on the contents of a feed bag. The air stank of human waste.

"Hello friend," Kjorn lurched up to the man by the wagon.

"What do you want?" The slender man pulled his thin cloak tight around himself.

"To share a horn or two. Tossed me out of the inn they did, just because I said the owner's wife looked like a wench I knew over Rahrike way. She were a sweet piece. Could get her ankles right up 'round her ears, and a screamer to boot." Kjorn set the keg on the ground, breached it, and dipped out a horn.

The slender man smacked his lips. "I'll drink your mead, friend. I've time 'fore I have to hitch up old Samson here for our run." He patted the horse affectionately.

Kjorn passed him the horn. "Who am I drinking with?"

"Ham."

"Kjorn. What's your trade that you're out soaking a wagon in the dark?"

Ham downed the horn. "I'm a scat man. I collect the scat from the royals and inns and dump it in the sea."

Kjorn refilled the horn and passed it to Ham. "How does a man come to be doing that, I wonder?"

"Had a farm once. Worked five years as an oarsman, saved me skatt and bought a place. It weren't much, but it were mine, and I got by. Then the sun went dark. Can't grow crops without sun. Me wife dragged me to Winchester to be close to her kin. I took what work I could get."

"At least you've got your wife." Kjorn refilled Ham's horn and dipped his own, half filling it. They both drank. Han wiped his lips on his sleeve.

"That's a good drop o' mead. Tell you true. Wife ain't half the blessing the priests said she'd be. 'Ham, you are useless. Ham, you smell like a privy. If only I'd listened to my mother. I could have married Bjorn the tanner. He keeps his wife proper.' She weren't bad when I was up. Now-a-days, I ain't done naught right in three years, hear her tell it."

"Poor bugger." Kjorn filled the horns again.

"You're a good fellow. She takes all me skatt, so I can barely afford a horn. What she spends it on, I don't know." Ham took the horn and drained it.

"She sounds like a right one."

"More 'en you know." Ham beckoned Kjorn closer then spoke in a drunken whisper. "Gots me a plan." He touched his nose. "Surprising what folk drop down a privy. Year back, give or take, I found a crusader's purse while I was dumping me load. Had near a thousand skatt in it. I made a mistake then. Told the wife. Was like old times for a week; 'till she spent it all, then I was the scat man, failure again."

"That is unfortunate." Kjorn refilled Ham's horn and sipped from his own.

"Never should o' told her." Ham slurred. He quaffed from his horn. "Got me to thinking; I got me a net. Keep it under that tree over there." He waved with his horn to a dead oak by the road. He then drained the horn. Kjorn refilled it. "Now when I dump me load I spread the net cross the back of the wagon. Most days nothing, but some times, some times." He drained the horn. "Just say, rich folk seem to think they're too good to pull anything out of a privy. I got almost enough, almost. Then it's the road for old Samson and me. Let her see what life's like without us."

Kjorn tipped the last of the keg into Ham's horn.

"Finish this up 'en hitch up old Samson." Ham drained the horn stumbled to his feet, teetered over and hugged the plough horse around the neck. "You still love me, right boy. Remember our farm. Green fields and you your own stable for when it were cold. Them were good times." Ham closed his eyes and smiled at the memory then tears trickled onto the horse's neck. "All gone now, and all we can do is haul other peoples..." Ham slid down the horse's side and lay on the ground. Samson nuzzled his owner's side affectionately.

The fifth bell rang.

Kjorn unclipped his cloak and wrapped Ham in it off to the side of the ramp. Taking Ham's filthy, worn and thin cloak he pulled it on, hitched Samson to the wagon and drew it out of the sea. Water spilled out of it. Removing the net across the back and closing the tail hatch took minutes, then he led the horse onto the town streets.

"Don't worry boy. I wrapped him up warm. I'll have you back to him before the ruckus starts. "Poor bugger. I'll leave him the cloak and some skatt. Figure the jarl can afford it."

Samson nickered.

CHAPTER 14

FIVE BELLS

Fjorn waited at the gate to the royal compound with Sigurlina on his arm. The guards regarded them with professional disinterest. Their job was to hold people at the gate beyond that they were dust to them.

"Fjorn, son of Geldnir Karl of Orkney, I hope the day finds you well." Aemilianus strode up to the gate. "I have them." He addressed the guards.

"I am well, though I fear that the king's largesse with giving my lady fruit has had unforeseen consequences," Fjorn looked pityingly at Sigurlina.

"What is the matter?" Aemilianus stared at Sigurlina.

"I..." Sigurlina stared at the frozen ground.

The fifth bell rang once.

Sigurlina looked up wide eyed. "Privy, please."

Aemilianus pointed to the raised building.

Sigurlina managed a very un-lady-like sprint onto the platform, opened the door of the end stall and vanished within.

"Women. Truly as weak as the teachings say," commented Aemilianus.

"She is likely to be some time. Perhaps you can tell me more of the White God." Fjorn casually moved so that to face him Aemilianus had to turn his back to the privy.

The bell sounded a fifth time.

"He is our saviour who suffers in our place saving us from the eternal torment of the Devil."

"But if your god is so powerful, why doesn't he just kill or imprison this devil?"

"Because he is merciful."

"But wouldn't the greater mercy be to stop this devil from torturing people? Odin chained Loki because he betrayed the Aesir."

"But the devil is bound in hell."

"Then, how can he tempt people and try to take over Midgard?"

"You ask too many questions. You must have faith. It is not the place of any but the priesthood to interpret scripture. You must accept the salvation of the White God unquestioningly."

"So, you're not supposed to think?"

As they talked, most of the men in the compound filed into the church leaving only the standing guard.

There was a crashing sound and the guards on the parapets raced towards the far side of the compound. The gate and treasure hall guards remained at their stations.

"What was that?" asked Fjorn.

"Young hoodlums. It happens every few months. We should work them all and make them attend mass when there is no honest labour they can perform. The guards will see to it. It is what they are paid for," Aemilianus sounded dismissive.

#

Vidurr opened Hisstor's cage and the fur snake slithered into the treasure vault. Next he unlocked the polar bear's cage. The bear plodded out and shot the dreyri what could only be a smug look. The dreyri screeched. Finally, Vidurr opened the spider's cage. The spider leapt out and stretched its legs.

"The dreyri isn't happy about staying locked up."

"Tell her that she will be freed the second time we open the door." Vidurr moved to the fire skui's cage, lifted it away from the cauldron of water and broke its lock. "Go to the docks and stay out of sight until my friends open the oil ships to you."

"I will do this. This will be fun," hissed the fire skui.

Vidurr pulled a candle lantern from his pack, lit it and moved to the treasure hall's door with his allies. He hung the lantern so it cast a shadow just inside the doorway. The double doors were bolted on the outside, but designed to keep intruders out not people in. Vidurr pushed up the wooden pegs that held the door hinges on one side.

The bell sounded five times.

Vidurr began counting aloud. "One longship, two longship, three longship."

Confused sounds came from beyond the door.

When Vidurr reached two hundred longship, he wrenched open

the door.

The spider shot out a web entangling the door guard and pulled him into the treasure hall. Hisstor struck, enveloping the guard before he could yell. The polar bear exhaled a cloud of cold and mist that formed a billowing fog a stride in front of the doorway, and the fire skui darted out into the darkness of fimbulwinter.

#

The bell sounded five times.

Sigurlina counted, her lips moving in silence. "One longship, two longship, three longship"

When she reached, "Two hundred longships," she opened the door of the privy stall and darted for a shadow cast by the palisade wall. She cast the spell, stepped into the shadow then stepped out from shadow into the treasure hall. Her head was swimming. Vidurr caught her, pushed the horn of the kraken and another bundle into her hands and turned her towards the shadow she'd come from. Bracing herself, Sigurlina stepped into the darkness emerging by the privy. She felt like vomiting and her legs were weak. Stumbling back into the privy stall, Sigurlina dropped the horn and bundle down the toilet hole. They fell onto the contents of the wagon below with a splat then sank out of sight. Staggering, Sigurlina left the stall, stumbled down the stairs and lurched towards Fjorn and Aemilianus, almost falling. She half fell into Aemilianus and let the weakness the spell had left her with flood into him.

"Are you able to stand, my love?" asked Fjorn.

Sigurlina straightened. "I'm feeling much better. Aemilianus, are you unwell? You look pale."

"I do feel unwell. I think I should lie down. Please, attend the mass. I'm sure the other monks will be happy to answer all of your questions."

Fjorn and Sigurlina proceeded to the church hall while Aemilianus staggered away.

#

Vidurr pulled the cloak and helm off the guard. The man's skin seemed to be on fire and he was swelling up from Hisstor's bite.

"After the sixth bell. We will escape." Vidurr donned the stolen clothes.

"We know. Now get out there, puppy, before they notice the missing guard."

Vidurr slipped out the door and the polar bear pushed it closed behind him. Vidurr arranged the cloak to cover the crest on the mail he wore and stood guard outside of the treasure hall. The few royal guards who were at their posts were too involved wondering what was happening on the other side of the compound to notice him.

#

Ragna smiled as Tolan and his men turned the wagon of fire wood so it faced the landward gate then unhitched the horse. They left the torch by the driver's seat burning and walked away. The bell tolled five times. At the first toll a boy of maybe twelve raced up to the wagon and threw the lever that released the friction break. The wheel creaked on the slope. The wagon crept forward. As the bell tolled, the creep became a roll.

Ragna started to count with the fifth ring of the bell. "One longship, two longship, three longship."

The wagon picked up speed until it careened down the sloping street. Ragna had reached 'one hundred longship' when the wagon slammed into the royal palisade. Fire wood went everywhere and the torch fell back into the pile. A fire caught. The archers on the palisade clustered to see the wagon. Moments later, buckets of water were being thrown down onto the flames. The landward side of the palisade was lined with guards and monks, some passing buckets, others gawking at the accident.

"Haven't done naught like that since I was a boy." Tolan wore a broad smile.

"Some things you never outgrow." Ragna laughed.

"I'll make it right with Gar. A barrel of salt fish and a keg of mead should do it. They got the fire out and his wagon don't look to be more than singed. Kids have been pulling this one two; three times a year since the compound got built. It's almost a tradition."

"Good. We should get ready for the race."

#

Kjorn led the horse pulling the empty privy wagon to the royal compound's gate. He paused as the guards looked him over.

"Where's Ham?" demanded one of the guards.

"Sleeping it off. I made port a couple nights ago and saw him. We were oarsmen together, back in the day, so we split a keg."

"And you took his wagon?" remarked the other guard.

"Owe the man. Was a time he'd of put me on the floor with drink, but I'm guessing that wife of his got him pretty tame nowadays. Figure since I was the one brought the keg it was only fair I saw he didn't catch it in the teeth for not doing his run."

"Good to know old Ham has some friends left. That Daldis is a mean one. Poor old Ham catches more than his share of nasty. Full cart's over there." The guard gestured towards the privy. "Ham usually parks the empty on the far side as the ground slopes down a bit. When you pull the full out, you can man haul the empty into place. Saves having to hitch and re-hitch the horse. Give it a bit. First guard's mass just let out, so it's a busy time. Set up and you'll be out before six bells. Trust me friend, you want to be out before six bells."

"Why the rush?" asked Kjorn.

"The crusaders' mass. God's gift to us all, the way they go on. You seem a decent chap, so take the hint and keep your distance from those holy types, or they'll tie you to a post and whip you for the good of your soul," remarked the second gate guard.

"How is Dagmar?" asked the first gate guard.

"He wore a tunic yesterday."

"Poor bugger. It wasn't even that funny a joke."

Kjorn looked uncomfortable. "I better get set up."

"Move along," spoke the first guard.

Kjorn pulled the wagon over by the privy, which had a lineup waiting for it, and unhitched Samson, re-hitching the old horse to the full wagon. Fjorn and Sigurlina stood in front of the church and watched him. Sigurlina looked a little pale in the torchlight.

Climbing onto the driver's bench of the full scat-wagon, Kjorn moved it forwards. Frozen liquids that had seeped out of the cart and frozen on the wheels, but after a jerk the wagon moved ahead. Stopping in front of the gate, Kjorn set the friction break before moving back to the empty scat wagon.

As he passed the full wagon he glanced in. The top was

mounded with fresh deposits from the church goers, leaving nothing suspicious to view. Gripping the empty wagon's draw pole, Kjorn hauled it under the privy building then set the friction break. A short line had reformed at the privy stairs by the time he was done. The men vanished into the privy as Kjorn mounted the full wagon and pulled it through the gate. The two guards barely glanced at the wagon's contents before they motioned Kjorn into the town proper.

#

Vidurr watched Kjorn guide the wagon out of the gate. It was nearly time for blood. His hand rested lightly on his sword handle.

A guard with a line of gold braid on the collar of his cloak walked towards Vidurr. "Where's Ebbe? This is supposed to be his duty," demanded the guard when he got close enough to see Vidurr's face.

"He..." Vidurr looked towards the privy not wanting to look the guard in the eyes.

"Well, where is he?" demanded the guard.

"He needed to go."

"Oh. You're new."

"Yes," agreed Vidurr.

"In early for the six bell call?"

"Yes."

The guard nodded. "Ebbe knows better than this. This is the royal guard, not some raiding boat. If a man has a shift he works it. Is that clear?"

"Yes," answered Vidurr.

"Ebbe had no business calling you over, and you had no business spelling him out of turn. Is that clear?"

"Yes."

"Good. You will report for discipline after your duty shift. Tell Ebbe when he comes back that if I don't see his sorry face when the seventh bell stops ringing, I'll report him to the crusader captain." The guard strode away muttering.

Vidurr took a deep breath and silently thanked Surt that the cloak hid the crest on the armour he was wearing.

#

Ragna stood on a crate in the cargo space of a wagon. The

palisade of the royal compound was opposite her and the street was crowded with women of all ages. Lines of men were stretched out along the street making bets and jeering. The palisade was crowded with guards and monks looking down at the spectacle.

Tolan mounted the wagon beside her and remarked. "If this doesn't drive up the sales, naught will."

"You better get started then." Ragna watched as a line of men wearing cloaks marked with the crusader's red cross filed into the royal compound. They seemed to be trying to ignore the women on the street.

"Right you are." Tolan stared out over the crowd. "Listen up. The Karl's Rest has in mind to offer you all a bit of entertainment. This is the Winchester Women's Foot Race. Here's the rules. You start at the line me assistant is lying down on the street right now."

Ragna hopped off the wagon and unrolled a long strip of material on the ground. Pushing and shoving the women on the street all took places in a jumble behind it.

Tolan's voice continued. "Rules are simple. First to run around the royal compound three times and cross this line is the winner. Winner gets an entire salt pig. Second prize, gets a barrel of salt cod, and third, a keg of mead. Rest, well the rest of yous is too slow, for running at any rate." Tolan leered as several men in the audience made rude comments. "Race starts with the sixth ring of the sixth bell. Them's the rules. After the race, you's all welcomed to the Karl's Rest for a horn. First horn for all runners that finish the race is free. So men come on to the Karl's Rest to support our lovely runners."

The bell tolled once.

The women on the street all pulled off their cloaks and threw them to people waiting in the crowd. Most wore little or nothing underneath the cloak save sandals.

Ragna watched as the crowd on the palisade seemed to double.

The bell tolled again.

CHAPTER 15

SIX BELLS

Fjorn stood by the gate and watched as the crusaders filed into the royal compound. They moved directly to the church and entered barely bothering to acknowledge the royal guards. Some of the crusaders scowled up at the men crowding the palisade's walkway.

The processional of crusaders cleared the gate. The two gate guards pulled the gate closed and sealed it.

The bell tolled once. A moment passed. The bell tolled again and the few guards in the compound rushed to the parapet to watch the race. The eyes of the archers, that normally scanned both the compound and the street around it, were focused on the street.

Fjorn looked around the compound. Aside from Vidurr, at the door of the treasure hall, and a guard that patrolled its walls, there were the two gate-guards and a guard at the door of each of the great halls and the church.

The bell tolled a sixth time. The monk manning the bell station flipped the hour glass then bolted to the palisade.

Fjorn sang softly to himself,

"As great Odin in combat his foes set to flight,

"Grant this one for battle great Odin's might."

A huge shout went up from the crowd watching the race.

Sigurlina touched the ground muttering, her voice lost in the crowd's roar.

A black skeleton clawed its way out of the ground. "Keep him from warning those inside," she commanded into where its ear would have been pointing to the crusader at the door of the church hall.

Fjorn threw himself at the guards on the gate. He felled the first one before they could react and turned his blade to the second.

Vidurr drove his shoulder against the treasure hall's door. It opened a crack then jerked open so fast he stumbled into the hall. He let his momentum carry him to the dreyri's cage and he threw open the locks. The dreyri exploded into the hall and raced for the open door. The spider, Hisstor, and the polar bear were already in the compound. Vidurr ran after them as the treasure hall's wall guard appeared in the doorway.

Vidurr charged letting his rage envelop him. The figure in the door stepped back, leaving itself open to a savage thrust. The mail turned the cutting edge while the force of the blow drove into the guard's abdomen, causing him to buckle at the waist. Vidurr stepped to the side and brought his sword down onto the guard's neck. The guard's head rolled into the treasure hall while his body fell to the frozen ground. A strangely clear part of Vidurr's mind noticed that there was no sign of the door guard they'd taken earlier. Turning he could see Hisstor battling another guard. The snow snake seemed to be wider at the middle than Vidurr remembered. Howling, he becoming the wolf and bounded towards a door guard who was turning to enter the second great hall.

#

Sigurlina watched as her skeleton fell on the crusader guard by the church's door. The roaring of the crowd covered the sounds of battle. The crusader threw off the skeleton and with a savage blow took off its arm at the shoulder. A spider as big as a warhorse leapt in front of the church hall and plastered the door shut with webbing.

A snow snake sped across her vision and slammed into the crusader, who was fighting the skeleton, from the rear. The snake bit then entwined the crusader as the skeleton used its remaining arm to tear the sword out of its enemies' hand.

Sigurlina ran to her skeleton's side and shouted where its ear would have been. "Block the far hall's door. Don't let anyone out."

She could faintly hear a strange sound and glanced up to see the serpent singing as it squeezed the life out of the crusader guard.

Vidurr passed her in a blur of speed.

"Munin," she called in her mind.

'*Here.*' The raven landed on her mistress's shoulder.

"Tell Ragna we'll need the wagon. Then go check on Kjorn and Audun. Help with the distraction at the docks, if you can."

Munin leapt into the air and flew away.

#

Fjorn battled the remaining guard at the gate. Without surprise to aid him, he was finding the man's skill with a blade a match to his own.

"The Shields of Asgard are shields of might.

"Turn the wrath of giants to flight.

"Shields to hold a warrior's might.

"The Shields of Asgard are shields of might."

As he sang the roar of the crowd stole the sound, still the sparkling half-sphere of light shielded him, allowing him to divert attention from his defence to attack. He made a telling blow against his foe's leg.

The guard fell back favouring the wound in his thigh and aimed a blow at Fjorn's head.

Fjorn parried the blow and pressed his opponent, forcing the guard to put weight on his wounded leg. Fjorn leapt back.

The guard fell forward into the snow and felt a cold blade press into the back of his neck.

#

Vadurr knew that fast as his wolf form was he wasn't going to reach the guard before the door was opened and the alarm raised then it was like his feet had wings. He ran faster than ever before and pounced on the guard just as he opened the door driving him to the ground. Sharp teeth tore into the back of the man's thighs, hamstringing him and leaving the blood to stain the filthy snow and ice.

#

The Polar Bear surged out of the treasure room ignoring the first two halls in its race to reach the third. The guard at the door was staring up at the palisade and was taken by surprise as the bear bowled into him. A massive paw tore into a mail-clad side, shattering the ribs beneath the armour. From the corner of its eye the bear noticed the door creeping open. The bear turned using its weight to crush the man beneath it and exhaled on the door. A blast of freezing cold enveloped the fingers on the door's edge and they snapped off. A mighty paw slammed the door closed and the bear rushed to put its shoulder against it.

#

The spider leapt to the second hall and sealed the door. It then leapt to the third and tapped the back of the polar bear with an extended leg. The bear glanced at the spider then shifted so the spider could seal the door.

#

The dreyri flew out of the treasure hall and straight for the town wall. The archers on the royal palisade were all busy watching the race. The dreyri was nearing the town wall when a deadly hail of arrows came at it. She flew faster but the feathered shafts from the town wall were faster still, and she tumbled from the sky. The master of the wall guards sent a runner to the royal compound to report.

#

Fjorn considered for less then a second, took the point of his blade back and slammed his fist into the back of the guard's neck. The guard went limp in the snow. The other guard still bled. If he received help, he would probably live. Turning to the gate, Fjorn lifted the beam that held it closed out of its brackets and tossed it aside.

#

The door to the final great hall opened and Hakon stepped out sword in hand. The skeleton lunged using the crusader's blade. Hakon blocked the blow, driving the blade into the door jam, then in a masterful stroke, used his recovery to decapitate the skeleton. It took less than a second. That was long enough for Vidurr to charge, ramming Hakon, throwing him into the opposite door jam. Hakon recovered with a savage, back-handed slash that Vidurr escaped with a minor scratch. Hakon turned his attention to his attacker as a band of webbing struck his arm tying him to the building. The bear raced up and landed a thundering blow against the building's door, slamming it into Hakon's face, driving him into the hall. The spider sealed the door and they all raced to the compound's exit.

#

Munin landed on Ragna's head. "Yura bitch." The raven's voice was lost in the roar of the crowd.

Ragna shooed the bird away in annoyance. Sighing Ragna left the race and hurried to the top of Tradesmen Street where a wagon with a horse already hitched waited. She took the driver's seat and reviewed the route in her mind.

#

Kjorn hauled the cart to the ramp leading into the sea. Leaping to the ground, he tugged on Samson's reins. The old horse knew its routine and carefully backed up. Kjorn stopped the horse when the back of the wagon was just over the water. Opening the wagon's gate allowed a small avalanche of waste to tumble into the sea. He clipped the net into place then let the horse back up the rest of the way. Kjorn spent anxious minutes unhitching Samson and leaving what skatt he had beside the sleeping Ham. When he returned to the wagon two objects could be seen lying in a bed of human waste. Grimacing with the cold, and the thought of the filth he was pawing through, Kjorn pulled out the horn and the bag that Vidurr had thrust into Sigurlina's hands. Moving away from the scat wagon he rinsed them and himself off in the sea, despite the frigid water, before racing towards the pier where the *Apenhet* was docked, as the bell began to toll.

#

Audun sat on the *Apenhet*, which rode light and high in the water, ready to flee. The oarsmen were all well rested and fed.

"Now? I'm bored," complained the fire skui that stood on the ship's brazier.

"He may have a point. We don't want to leave it too late," observed Halla, who stood beside Audun wrapped in a cloak.

"When the sixth bell starts to toll. Not before." Audun looked inland.

"They'll be all right. Fjorn has a good plan."

"He's good at plans but there's always risk. And for this there is too much risk."

Halla nodded.

The bell tolled.

"Remember, wait for the second boom." Audun addressed the fire skui.

"I get it. Wait, wait, wait all you humans ever do. Of course you scream too. I like screaming, it's fun. I like to have fun."

"And so you shall. Now we begin. Take down the false shield." Audun checked that he had his battle axe in its shoulder sheath then hoisted a keg under his arm.

Halla threw off her cloak, slipped into her seal skin and took something in her mouth before entering the water. Two oarsmen lowered the false shield from the mast and left it on the pier. Audun led several oarsmen off the *Apenhet*. The guard at the end of their pier barely acknowledged them as they walked past. Two of the oarsmen started arguing about a gambling debt and the guard focused on them. The man didn't know he was dead until the keen edge of a dagger slid across his throat. He tried to shout through a ruined neck but no sound came out.

The sixth toll of the bell sounded.

Audun pushed the body into the sea. The sound of the workmen repairing the grounded vessels continued uninterrupted.

Audun hoisted the keg to his shoulder and started towards the pier where the cogs were docked. Two of the oarsmen raced back to the *Apenhet* where they threw off their cloaks and donned two of the crusader's cloaks Audun had acquired.

#

Fjorn beckoned from the gate. Sigurlina was the first to join him then Vidurr in his wolf from bounded to his side. The polar bear and spider joined them next then Hisstor.

The spider made a clicking noise.

"Good luck," said Hisstor. "She says she is going to try for the side wall. She can scale it easily. The more we divide their attention the better all of our chances are. I'm out too. I can hide and slip out later. Sorry puppy, I don't like your odds from this point on."

The polar bear looked at Vidurr and made a gruffing sound.

"He's with you to the docks," translated Hisstor.

"Thank you all." Fjorn threw open the gate and they all sprinted into the town.

Fjorn led the charge across the royal compound's ring road to Tradesmen Street, cutting off a pair of naked women who were fighting to finish their final lap.

Ragna sat in the wagon her eyes going wide when she saw the giant spider and snow snake burst from the gate and move in opposite directions. Fjorn, Sigurlina, Vidurr and a polar bear charged towards her. They leapt into the back of the wagon and she snapped the reigns.

The sound of screams followed them down Tradesmen Street to the first cross street where they turned right. They took the next left, heading to the harbour.

#

A scream went up from several runners as a giant spider leapt past them, landed on a roof top, and leapt again, moving towards the edge of town.

The men on the parapet around the royal compound who were watching the race turned to look inward and paused. A guard raced to a horn by an archer's station and sounded it three times.

People flooded off the parapet into the courtyard. A young monk, still blushing from what he had just witnessed, hurried to the gate and started treating the wounds of the fallen guards. Other guards and monks started tearing at the webbing sealing the great halls' doors. Still others moved to the treasure hall. Using the confusion as cover they slipped in, grabbed what they could and slipped out once more.

#

Kjorn had reached the end of the pier where the *Apenhet* was docked when he heard the three horn blasts. A dark figure dropped to his shoulder. He jumped and the raven squawked.

"Freya's tits! You scared me, bird. Is all well?"

"Good bird. Good bird."

"I'd best get aboard." As Kjorn spoke crusaders poured out of their hall and raced up Tradesmen Street towards the royal compound.

"Go see what you can do for Sigurlina and Fjorn." Kjorn hurried to the *Apenhet*, boarded and secured his packages.

#

Audun watched as crusaders raced up Tradesmen Street. He strode up to the guards at the end of the pier where the cogs were docked . "What's that all about?" he asked with a smile on his face.

The two crusaders glared at him with dower expressions. "None of your concern, Northman." The crusader's tone made the word Northman sound like an insult.

"Just curious. I hear tell you warriors of the cross are some of the best swords men in all of Midgard. Makes you wonder what could get you so riled up. Would you care for a horn? Makes a cold watch pass faster."

"Leave us, Northman," snapped the larger of the crusader guards.

"Right enough. Will you look at that?" Audun pointed down the pier.

The crusaders looked to see Halla standing naked on the pier lit by the torches beside the cogs.

"You there." Both crusaders charged the naked beauty.

Audun set down his keg and followed them several paces up the pier. He then loosed his battle axe from its sheath and swung, catching one crusader in the side. There was a blasting sound and the crusader was thrown into the water where the weight of his mail dragged him under. The second crusader turned to Audun, blade drawn and made to raise the alarm only to find a garrotte line thrown across his throat. Halla leapt up like she was riding the big crusader piggyback and pulled on the thin line of wire with all her might. The crusader stumbled backwards trying to bash her off against one of the pier's support posts.

Audun whipped off his cloak and threw it over the torch that lit the area. The world went dark casting everything into silhouettes. He then swung his axe into the crusader's abdomen. The mail turned the blade but the force of the blow doubled the man over. With a savage kick, Audun sent the crusader into the sea with Halla still on his back. Halla surfaced and Audun pulled her shivering onto the dock.

"It's not as cold when I'm a seal," she commented.

"Then get your skin on. You did good work here."

Halla raced to the end of the pier. She picked something up. A moment later, a seal slipped into the sea.

Audun pulled his cloak off the torch and left it on the pier. Retrieving the keg he'd been carrying he pulled one of the crusader's cloaks he'd appropriated out of the barrel and put it on. Taking the snuffed torch he lit it from the next one down the pier and replaced it.

"Quis es vos effectus?" demanded a voice from one of the cogs.

Audun held up the torch and spoke in Anglic. "It went out. I'm relighting it."

"Spurcus Insula. Tabellae lemma suo Deus's exercitus. Operor non vel narro verus Latin. Operor ignoro quis orbis terrarum est oportet," grumbled the voice.

Audun looked down the pier to where two of the oarsmen stood at the watch station draped in crusader's cloaks. Audun sheathed his battle axe and casually moved to the side of one of the cogs.

#

Ragna slowed the wagon. The polar bear and Vidurr lay in the back making themselves inconspicuous. Fjorn took a seat on the driver's bench.

"You made me miss the race," observed Ragna.

"If it helps, we missed it too," commented Sigurlina from where she lay nestled between two furry beasts, one hand gently petting each. Munin landed on the wagon's side railing.

"Munin says that Kjorn is at the ship with the cargo and that Audun will be ready by the time we get there."

Fjorn looked at Sigurlina and shook his head. "What am I getting myself into?"

Ragna glanced back at her friend. "At least she won't mind the weasel you're growing on your face."

When they reached the docks, the bear lumbered out of the wagon, gruffed at them, then slipped into the water and swam out to sea.

Fjorn led the way to the *Apenhet* where Kjorn awaited them, ready to cast off.

"Munin, check on Audun and tell me what you see," ordered Sigurlina.

"Good bird. Good bird," said Munin.

#

Audun gestured and one of the figures in a crusader's robe raced up from the end of the pier and passed him one of the splitting axes. Winding up, Audun swung the axe with all his might into the side of the cog. The unreinforced wood planks of the southern ship imploded. Reaching into the barrel he pulled out a pile of rags soaked in oil, pushed them through the hole, then tossed one of the pier torches in after them. The oily rags caught. A small, red and orange body flew by. "Finally," it hissed and vanished into the hole in the cog.

The other oarsman in a crusader's cloak raced up and handed Audun the second splitting axe. Audun blasted a hole in the other cog, tossed in rags from the barrel and another of the pier torches.

By this time dark figures, with drawn blades that glinted red in the torch light, were coming up the pier and down the gang planks from the cogs.

Audun raced to the very end of the pier with the oarsmen and turned at bay.

A raven called from above.

#

Munin landed beside Sigurlina. "They're trapped at the end of the pier with the cogs." Sigurlina's voice was near panic.

Vidurr howled, taking on his human form. "We can't leave them."

Fjorn nodded. "Cast off. Where in Svartalfheim is Halla?"

A seal barked from in front of the ship.

"Good. We have to pick up our crewmen then to sea." Fjorn put the spike of the navigation rope home in the bow. "Halla be ready. We're going to run dark as soon as we pick up Audun. Cast off. Full oars. Kjorn, Vidurr, man the boarding plank. Sigurlina, I need a skeleton to cover their backs," ordered Fjorn.

"I need to go ashore to make it," said Sigurlina.

Fjorn nodded once. "Hurry. Vidurr watch her. Delay cast off. Be ready."

Sigurlina practically flew down the pier with Vidurr on her heals.

#

Audun swung with his battle axe keeping the crusaders at bay. His advantage was the width of the pier only allowed three of his attackers to come at him at once. His disadvantage was that he had no place to go. The raven cried again.

"Be ready," he ordered. Crusaders pressed forward and he blocked blows. The oarsman to his right took a spear to the belly and toppled into the sea. There was a roaring sound and things grew brighter as the flames in one of the cogs breached its deck. A small, orange being darted across Audun's vision, laughing as it went, and entered the other cog.

"I know you," snapped a crusader who pushed up from the rear. It was the small, dark-haired shepherd from the iceberg.

Audun gripped his axe tighter. "Want to try again?"

"You choice. Surrender." The crusader spoke in broken Orse.

"To Odin's halls I go." Audun lifted his axe as the flames roared through the deck of the cog to his left. Inside the cog clay vessels heated and shattered spilling oil that fed the flames. Oil spilled out into the harbour.

In that moment of distraction the *Apenhet* appeared at the end of the pier. There was a thump as the boarding plank landed behind Audun. A black skeleton, armed with a staff, charged across and attacked the crusaders with an insane furry. Audun and the oarsman raced to the *Apenhet*.

"Full oars. Starboard full rudder," commanded Fjorn's voice.

Audun scrambled to the tiller station, slipping the rope loops around his ankles. Fjorn tossed the steering line to Halla who took it and swam out to sea.

Kjorn and Vidurr raced around dousing each of their ship's torches.

Looking back, Sigurlina watched as her skeleton was cut down. They were close enough that she could still see the crusaders eyes. Both cogs were engulfed in flame. Oil spread, burning across the icy harbour towards the other piers.

Horns sounded on the shore and the floating dots of light on the sea that were Hakon's fleet converged.

"There's too many of them. We'll never get by," commented Kjorn.

"We--," began Fjorn.

A shadow moved in the darkness to the side of the ship.

"What are you--?" Fjorn was cut off by a muted horn blast.

Vidurr released a gasp of pain and the Horn of the Kraken fell from his fingers into the sea as he toppled onto the deck.

"Odin's teeth!" swore Fjorn.

Sigurlina reached her fallen comrade first, and woozy as she was from calling the skeleton, she focused. A light dew formed over Vidurr and his breathing deepened. Audun traced runes on the Ulfhednar.

Fjorn knelt beside his unlikely friend and sang.

"Youth to the gods, golden apples of grace.

"Idun's power, heal mortals of faith."

Vidurr opened unfocused eyes.

"Why?" demanded Fjorn."

"Learned from you. Give them something else to think about." Vidurr settled into an exhausted sleep.

Fjorn moved to his station in the bow and relayed the directions form Halla. Time passed in the muffled creak of silenced oars, and the cold bite of a wind changing to seaward. A large longship drew near. Another blocked their way ahead. Halla swam back and forth as if unsure of the way. Behind them fires burnt in the harbour back lighting a longship coming up on their stern.

Fjorn felt Sigurlina move to his side and take his hand. She kissed his cheek. "We got the horn and burnt the ships. We mattered," she whispered.

Fjorn squeezed her hand. "In Valhalla."

"In Valhalla."

The night filled with screams. Back lit by the flames, tentacles were coming up around the ship following them. Men were hacking at the kraken, which seemed to be as big as Jormungand itself.

Sigurlina recognised the scene from her vision. The wind fully turned to seaward. Fjorn released her hand and picked up the steering ropes. "Hoist sail," he risked shouting the command.

The sail raised and Halla pulled them into a gap that opened between two longships. On one side Fjorn could see that one of the blockading ships was being attacked by a kraken.

"Ship oars," Fjorn whispered the order and all became silent and dark.

EPILOGUE

For two days they traveled in darkness. Only then the torches and brazier were lit. The blue bag was brought out, adding to their stores. Sigurlina examined the ring that Vidurr had retrieved.

"Orkney will be good to see." Fjorn sat beside Sigurlina at the bow as the Alba coast sped past.

"I'm looking forward to it. Can I show you something?" Sigurlina reached into her pouch and pulled out two purple stones.

"Those are the magic stones your grandmother gave you. I've seen them before."

"There use to be three."

"You lost one?"

Sigurlina smiled. "I don't think so. Grandmother always use to say that I needed to slow down, practice what I'd learned instead of trying to learn more so quickly. With all we've done, I think I finally did that. I feel, I don't know, stronger. I think the stone went away because I don't need it anymore."

"You're the Seithkona, not me, but it makes sense. I feel that way myself. Not that I'm done learning things. There's too much to see and do."

"I know. That's why I want you to teach me how to read." She sat up with a bright innocent smile, so at odds with the powerful Seithkona he knew her to be that he almost laughed. He smiled instead. "I'd like that."

She kissed him. "So would I."

"Get back here you black chicken, so I can stuff you proper!" Ragna raced the length of the ship chasing frantically-flapping, black wings.

"That was my leg, wench," growled Vidurr from his oar station when she stepped on him.

"Ragna, birds just do that sometimes," soothed Audun's voice from the tiller oar.

"Not on my best cloak they don't," countered Ragna.

"Children," Kjorn's voice was strained.

Sigurlina and Fjorn both chuckled then kissed again.

Soon afterwards, they reached Orkney and received a hero's welcome.

FATE OF THE NORNS

ANDREW
VALKAUSKAS

PRESENTS

SEITH AND SWORD
CHRIS CHALLICE

Fate of the Norns: Ragnarok
SAGA - FAFNIR'S TREASURE

Fate of the Norns: Ragnarok
CORE RULEBOOK

FATE OF THE NORNS

Fate of the Norns: Ragnarok
LORDS OF THE ASH

PENDELHAVEN PUBLISHING